P9-DCY-803

The INCREMENTALISTS

Books by Steven Brust

The Dragaeran Novels

Brokedown Palace

THE KHAAVREN ROMANCES

The Phoenix Guards

Five Hundred Years After

The Viscount of Adrilankha, which comprises *The Paths of the Dead, The Lord of Castle Black,* and *Sethra Lavode*

THE VLAD TALTOS NOVELS

Jhereg
Yendi
Teckla
Taltos
Phoenix
Athyra
Orca
Dragon
Issola
Dzur
Jhegaala
Iorich

Other Novels

To Reign in Hell

The Sun, the Moon, and the Stars

Agyar

Cowboy Feng's Space Bar and Grille

The Gypsy (with Megan Lindholm)

Freedom and Necessity (with Emma Bull)

Books by Skyler White

and Falling, Fly

In Dreams Begin

The INCREMENTALISTS

Steven Brust
and
Skyler White

A Tom Doherty Associates Book
NEW YORK

This is a work of fiction. All of the characters, organizations, and events portrayed in this novel are either products of the authors' imaginations or are used fictitiously.

THE INCREMENTALISTS

Edited by Patrick and Teresa Nielsen Hayden

A Tor Book
Published by Tom Doherty Associates, LLC
175 Fifth Avenue
New York, NY 10010

www.tor-forge.com

Tor® is a registered trademark of Tom Doherty Associates, LLC.

The Library of Congress Cataloging-in-Publication Data
is available upon request

ISBN 978-0-7653-3422-0 (hardcover)
ISBN 978-1-4668-0931-4 (e-book)

Tor books may be purchased for educational, business, or promotional use. For information on bulk purchases, please contact Macmillan Corporate and Premium Sales Department at 1-800-221-7945, extension 5442, or write specialmarkets@macmillan.com.

First Edition: September 2013

Printed in the United States of America

0 9 8 7 6 5 4 3 2 1

For Tappan King

Who Took the First Incremental Step

and

For Scott

Who Keeps Making Things

A Little Better

ACKNOWLEDGMENTS

The authors would like to thank our families for putting up with us while things went onto the page and not so much with the real world. Thanks to Dr. Flash Gordon for medical advice, Steve Dutton for the hospitality, Sarah at The Palms, and to Emma Bull, Tim Cooper, Pamela Dean (who went above and beyond with translations to the Jacobin), Marissa Lingen, Bruce Schneier, Adam Stemple, Will Shetterly, and Pat Wrede for many helpful comments. Mark A. Mandel helped with some linguistic questions. Nancy Hanger did a wonderful job copyediting the manuscript, for which we are grateful. Thanks to Jennifer Melchert for additional proofreading. Thank you also to Patrick and Teresa Nielsen Hayden for the amazing fourteen-hour editing marathon and the stew. Several Incrementalists were sufficiently cooperative to make up for those who weren't. Without your help, this wouldn't have gotten off the ground.

The INCREMENTALISTS

ONE

You Entering Anything?

Phil

> **From:** Phil@Incrementalists.org
> **To:** Incrementalists@Incrementalists.org
> **Subject:** Celeste
> Tuesday, June 28, 2011 10:03 am GMT - 7
>
> You've all been very patient since Celeste died. Thanks. Since no one responded on the forum, I'm asking here before I go ahead: I think I've finally settled on a recruit for her stub. If some of you want to look it over, the basic info is the hemp rope coiled on the bottom branch of the oak just west of my back gate.

There. That finished what I had to do; now I could be about earning my living. I put the laptop in its case, left my house, and drove to The Palms. Just like anyone else going to work. Ha.

Greg, the poker room manager, said, "You're here early, Phil. No two-five, just one-three."

"That's fine," I said. "Put me down for when it starts."

Greg nodded. He always nodded a little slowly, I think so as not to risk dislodging his hairpiece. "We have an open seat in the one-three if you want it," he added.

"I'll wait, thanks. How's the boat?"

"It's still being a hole to sink money into. But I should have it working again by August. Going to take the kids out and teach them to run it."

"Why, so they can burn out the engine again?"

"Don't even joke about it. But if I ever hope to water-ski, I'm going to have to. . . ."

Five minutes later I disengaged and went to 24/7, the hotel café, to relax until the game started.

While I waited, I drank coffee and checked my email.

> **From:** Jimmy@Incrementalists.org
> **To:** Phil@Incrementalists.org
> **Subject:** Re: Celeste
> Tuesday, June 28, 2011 6:23 pm GMT
>
> Looks good to me, Phil. I have no problem with you going to Arizona to do the interview.

I hit Reply.

> **From:** Phil@Incrementalists.org
> **To:** Jimmy@Incrementalists.org
> **Subject:** Re: Celeste
> Tuesday, June 28, 2011 11:26 am GMT - 7
>
> The World Series of Poker is going, so this is a good time for my sugar spoon and a bad time for me to go to Phoenix. Feel like crossing the pond? Or finding someone else to do the 1st interview? I'll still titan. Or we can put it off a week; there's no hurry, I suppose.

I hit Send and closed my laptop as I felt someone looming over me.

"Hey, Phil."

"Hey, Captain."

Richard Sanderson, all 350 pounds of him, slid into the booth. We'd exchanged a lot of money over the years, but I was glad to see him. He said, "Phil is here before noon. Must be WSOP week."

"Uh-huh. Which now lasts a month and a half. You entering anything?"

"I tried the fifteen hundred buy-in seven stud and got my ass kicked. That's all for me. You?"

"No. The side-games are so full of guys steaming from the event, why bother?"

"No shit. I played the fifteen-thirty limit at the Ballaj last night, had three guys who were on tilt before they sat down."

"Good game?"

"Hell of a good game."

"How much did you lose?"

"Ha-ha. Took about twelve hundred home."

"Nice work. Next time that happens, call your buddy."

"If I ever meet one, I will."

We bantered a little more until they called him for the one-three no limit game. I opened my laptop again, and Jimmy had already replied, saying that he didn't feel like going to Phoenix (made sense, seeing as he lives in Paris), but he'd be willing to nudge the recruit to Las Vegas for me. I wrote back saying that'd be great, and asking him to get her to 24/7 at The Palms on Thursday afternoon.

Then I took out my copy of *No Limits* by Wallace and Stemple and reviewed the section on hand reading until they called my name for the two-five. I bought in for $500 and took seat three. I knew two of the other players but not the rest, because I didn't usually play this early in the day and because there were a lot of people in town for the WSOP.

I settled in to play, which mostly meant looking at my hand and tossing it away.

I have a house not far from The Palms. I have stayed in many houses, apartments, condos, hotels, boarding rooms, sublets. I've lived in many places. But nowhere feels like home quite as much as a poker table. I watched the other players, making mental notes on how they played. I picked up a small pot on an unimproved ace-king, and wondered if the finger-tap from the Asian woman in seat one meant she'd missed the flop.

Sometime in the next couple of days, I was going to see whether Celeste's stub would work with Renee, and if it did, whether we might have a chance to not tear each other apart and maybe even do a bit of good. That was important; but it wasn't right now. Right now, it was only odds and cards. And right now is always important.

A couple of hours later, I was all in with two kings against ace-queen. The flop came ace-high, and I was already reaching in my pocket for another buy-in when I spiked a king on fourth street and doubled up. I'd have taken it as an omen, but I'm not superstitious.

Ren

From: Liam@GlyphxDesign.com
To: Renee@GlyphxDesign.com
Subject: Meeting with Jorge at RMMD in NYC
Tuesday, June 28, 2011 1:06 pm GMT - 7

Ren, I hate to spring this on you, and I know I said I wouldn't ask you to travel anymore, but we need you in New York on Friday. The PowerPoint deck looks great, but Jorge has concerns about the audio component of the user interface. I'd like to have you there to field his questions. Get flight details etc from Cindi.

I chose Twix for anger control and Mountain Dew for guts, but nothing in the rows of vending machines between my cubicle and my boss's office looked like lucky, or even wheedle. I bought Snickers as a bribe, and ate the first Twix bar on the way upstairs.

I poked my head around Liam's office door, decorated since Memorial Day for the Fourth of July in silver tinsel and tiny plastic flags. He waved me in, tipped so far back in his ergonomic chair that a dentist could have worked comfortably. Liam laughed and said, "I understand," and "She's not going to like that," into his phone headset, and winked at me.

I ate the other Twix bar.

"Okay, let me know. Thanks." Liam pulled off his headset and waggled his eyebrows in the direction of the Snickers. "Is that for me?"

"Maybe."

"Because you love me?"

"That depends," I said, but it didn't really, and Liam knew it. I slid the candy bar across his empty desk. "Working in a paperless office is different from not working, you know," I told him.

He grinned and ate half the Snickers in one bite. "I hate to do this to you, I really do."

"Then don't. You don't need me in New York."

"I'm guessing you have a date for Friday."

"I'm guessing you're worried about the cost estimates."

"It's an awful lot to propose spending on a feature they didn't request."

"They would have written it into the requirements if they bothered to read their own research. I did. They need this. Jesus. Is the air at the top of the corporate ladder so thin it's killing off brain cells? Don't either of you remember what happened last time?"

Liam opened the bottom drawer of his desk and produced a giant peanut butter jar full of darts. I scooted my chair out of firing range and shut the door to reveal the big-eyed baby chick in an Easter bonnet Liam had snagged from Cindi's previous decorating campaign.

"Who's the guy?" Liam lofted a dart at the pastel grotesque.

"Someone new. He's making me dinner."

"I'll buy you dinner. After the meeting—Eden Sushi, very posh."

"I've had sushi with Jorge before." I held up my hands like a scale. "Cold fish in bad company. Homemade gnocchi with a hot guy. Gosh, Liam, how's a girl to choose?"

Easter Chicken suffered a direct hit to her pert tail feathers.

"Move your date to Saturday."

"Can't," I mumbled. "He's in a band."

The dart fell onto the carpet as Liam let out a wheezy whoop. "Is the air in your blues clubs so smoky it's killing off brain cells?" He leaned back in his chair far enough and laughed long enough for a molar extraction. Which I considered providing. "Don't you remember what happened last time?"

"One bad guitarist boyfriend isn't a pattern of poor dating choices, but half a million dollars in post-prototype changes should have turned Jorge into a research fetishist. Have you tried just reminding him?"

"He specifically asked me to bring you."

"Oh, come on."

"Sorry. But I can't really say no, can I?"

"What, to your boss? Who would do such a thing?"

From: Cindi@GlyphxDesign.com
To: Renee@GlyphxDesign.com
Subject: Your Flight Info
Tuesday, June 28, 2011 5:46 pm GMT - 7

Hi Ren! Jorge's PA just called me, and he's going to Vegas for some poker festival. So guess what?!? So are you! All the Friday AM flights are full, so I bought your ticket for Thursday. You're staying at The Palms.

Have fun!

There's just no vending machine voodoo for this sort of day. I went home for ice cream.

Phil

From: Jimmy@Incrementalists.org
To: Phil@Incrementalists.org
Subject: Renee
Wednesday, June 29, 2011 12:49 am GMT

Her flight arrives Thursday early afternoon. She's got a gift coupon for 24/7 Café bigger than her per diem, but no telling when she'll use it.

I cashed out around nine, posting a decent win, and went home to log it, check my email, and seed the Will Benson meddlework. I could imagine Oskar being all sarcastic about it: "Great work, Phil. Six dozen signs that won't use quotation marks for emphasis. That makes the world tons better." Fuck him. I hate quotation marks used for emphasis.

When I'd finished seeding, I checked our forum and added some noise to an argument that was in danger of acquiring too much signal. Then I watched some TV because I was too brain-dead to read, and much too brain-dead to graze. The Greek unions were striking, Correia beat the Blue Jays in spite of Encarnación's two homers. I hadn't recorded the game because no one cares about interleague play except the owners. When I felt like I was going to fall asleep in front of the TV, I turned it off and went to bed.

Wednesday was a good day: poker treated me well, and after a pro forma hour hunting for switches for Acosta, I just relaxed. The most exciting thing on TV was *Jeopardy!*, so I reread Kerouac's *On the Road.* I wish I'd met him. I wish I'd met Neal Cassady. I almost did, once, in San Francisco, but I got into a fender bender at Scott and Lombard and never made it to the party.

From: Jimmy@Incrementalists.org
To: Phil@Incrementalists.org

Subject: Renee!
Thursday, June 30, 2011 3:55 am GMT

Phil, I just happened to come across some of Renee's background.

What are you trying to pull?

Funny. Jimmy "just happened" to come across some of Renee's background, like I "just happened" to raise with two aces. And what was he doing up at that hour?

Well, I'd meet her sometime tomorrow, and decide then. When dealing with the group, especially Salt (myself included), it's easier to get forgiveness than permission. Tomorrow would be a busy day: I needed to talk to Jeff the cook and Kendra the waitress, and I had to prep the café before Renee got in.

I went to bed and dreamed of high seas.

Ren

I couldn't get the wi-fi in my room to work, but I had a nice apology gift certificate from Liam for the hotel café, so I went downstairs with my netbook and nooked into one of the high-backed booths. I ordered matzo ball soup because I thought it was funny to find it on a casino menu, but I worried about it as soon as the waitress left. Theirs might be good. Maybe even as good as my nana's, but it didn't stand a chance against my memory of hers. I flagged the waitress down and changed my order to a veggie burger, which would have offended my grandmother to her beef-loving soul. Then I opened Google Reader.

It was late for lunch and early for dinner, so I had the place mostly to myself when he walked in looking like all the reasons I've never wanted to go to Vegas. He wore a ball cap pulled down over predator's eyes in an innocent face, and I couldn't tell whether the hunt or the hunted was real. Still, there's no conversation you want to have with a tall, dark and handsome man who sidles up to your table in the café of a Vegas hotel. I knew better. I put my earbuds in, and I didn't look up.

"Hi," he said, like he just thought of it.

I unplugged only my left ear, and slowly, like it hurt me. "Sorry?"

"Hi," he said again with one of those smiles that means "I play golf!"

"Um, hi." I touched the molded plastic of the earpiece to my cheek, but he kept a hand on the backrest of the chair beside me. He squatted next to it, graceful on his back foot, bringing us eye-level, and I stowed every detail to bludgeon Liam with.

"I know you're not looking for company, but when I travel I'm always curious where the locals eat. Just wanted to let you know you've found it. There's no better bowl of soup in town."

"Good to know," I said. Liam would actually feel guilty about this.

"But if you want a drinkable cup of coffee, you have to get out of the hotels."

"I don't drink coffee."

"You'll be okay then, as long as you're only here a day or two."

"Because you drive tea-drinkers out of Vegas with pitchforks?"

"Oh, no. We just leave them to starve."

The serious nod that accompanied his starvation of the caffeine-adverse made me laugh. Maybe all the earnest was a game. I was pretty sure I could see a dimple twitching under the edge of his mustache.

"I will leave you alone if you want," he said. "I'm just talking to you on a theory."

"What theory is that?"

"That you have absolutely no trouble fending off sleazy pickup attempts, and you like talking to interesting strangers, and you can tell the difference pretty quickly."

I hesitated. "Okay," I said. "Any insider tips beyond coffee?"

"Do you gamble?"

"No."

"Then no."

"And if I did?"

"I could tell you where not to."

"And why would you do that? I'm guessing you're not universally generous with your insights."

"You might be surprised," he said, and I caught a whiff of sincerity through a crack in the banter. "But I'd offer you all my secrets, if I thought you'd invite me to sit down. My knees are locking up."

"Here's your tea." The waitress put it down just out of my reach and turned to him. "Get you anything, Phil?"

He glanced at me. Then she did. And whatever anonymous pleasure I'd been getting from a stranger's privacy in public places seemed like less fun. I shrugged. "Have a seat."

"Coffee would be great, Kendra." He stood just slowly enough to make me think his knees ached, and slid into the booth. He told me secrets for eating cheaply and well in Vegas, until the waitress came back with a bowl of matzo ball soup. It wasn't the sandwich I had ordered, but with its two delicate dumplings floating in a broth that smelled like sick days when Mom had to work and took me to her mother's, I decided to risk it.

"Shall I let you eat in peace?" he asked, with enough Yiddish inflection to make me check his eyes for a joke.

He smiled at me and, maybe feeling daring because my matzo ball gamble had paid out so tasty, I smiled back. "No, stay," I said, "and tell me what the locals do here besides eat."

Phil

I decided that that part had been harder than it should have been. "I'd love to say something clever, like, laugh at tourists. But the fact is, get away from the Strip and locals do the same things they do anywhere else."

"And in your case, what does that involve?"

"Poker."

"Just like everywhere else," she said.

I felt a shrug asking to be let out, but suppressed it. "It sounds more glamorous than user interface design, but when you're running bad, you miss the steady income."

There wasn't even a delay and a double take; she got it instantly. She nailed me in place with her eyes and said, "If you claim that was a lucky guess—"

"Not at all, Ren. Usually, I'd call you Renee until you okayed the nickname, but I know how you hate your dad's French aspirations."

She sat back. "Who the hell are you?"

"My name is Phil, and I'm here to recruit you to a very select and special group. The work is almost never dangerous, and best of all we don't pay anything."

Her eyes narrowed.

"Yes?" I asked.

"What I'm trying to figure out," she said slowly, "is why I'm not calling security."

"I can answer that," I told her. "Mostly, it's the soup. It tastes like your grandmother's. Also, if you listen closely, you can hear Pete Seeger and Ronnie Gilbert singing 'The Keeper Did A-Hunting Go.' And if you look behind me—"

"Oxytocin," she said, staring at me.

I was impressed, and I didn't mind letting her see it. "Good work. That saves a lot of explanation."

"You're triggering memories to make me feel trusting."

I nodded again. "Just enough to get the explanation in before you have me thrown out. And so you'll believe the impossible parts at least enough to listen to them."

"This is crazy."

"It gets crazier."

"I can hardly wait. What are the impossible parts?"

"We'll get there. Let's start with the merely improbable. Do you like the MP3 format?"

"Huh?" Her brows came together.

"A functional sound format introduced and standardized. Do you think that's a good thing?"

"Sure."

"You're welcome."

She stared, waiting for me to say more.

"It almost didn't happen that way. That's the sort of thing you can do with oxytocin and dopamine and a few words in the right ears."

She was silent for a little longer, probably trying to decide if she only believed me because I was meddling with her head. Then she said, "Why me?"

"Because you almost got fired for telling truth to power in a particularly insulting way, and you did it for the benefit of a bunch of users you'd never met, and you expected it to cost you a job you liked. That's the kind of thing we notice. On good days."

Kendra came by and refilled my coffee, which gave Ren time to decide which of the ten million questions she wanted to ask next. I waited. Her fingernails—short and neatly trimmed—tapped against the teacup in front of her, not in time to the music. Her eyes were deep set and her face narrow, with prominent cheekbones that made me think American Indian somewhere in her background. Her brows formed a dark tilde, her nose was small and straight, and her lips were kissably inviting and led to creases at the corners of her mouth that acted as counterpoints to the laugh lines around her eyes. I wondered what a full-on smile would look like.

"Jesus Christ," she said.

"He wasn't one of us," I told her. "I'd remember."

Ren

Somehow, to my list of bad habits, I had recently added the practice of tapping my eyebrow with my index finger like an overgrown Pooh Bear with his absurd *think, think, think*. I caught myself at it and balled my fingers into a fist. Phil had his long body draped casually in his seat, but it stayed taut somehow anyway. He reminded me of a juggler, with his large hands and concentration. "Are you hitting on me?" I asked.

He laughed and relaxed. "No," he said, and I trusted him.

"Just checking." I sliced into a matzo ball with the edge of my spoon. "Because guys who ask to join me in restaurants, and make small talk, and recommend soups, and invite me into secret societies are usually after something."

"I didn't say I wasn't."

That shut me up. I ate some soup and pretended to be thinking. But mostly I was just drifting on chicken fat and memories. Eating hot soup in a cold café in the desert felt a long way from my grandmother's house. "My, what big eyes you have," I muttered.

Phil frowned.

"Little Red Riding Hood," I explained, but it didn't help. "I'm feeling like I've strayed from the path in the woods."

"Been led astray?" he asked.

"Maybe just led. How did you know to find me in Vegas?"

"We arranged for you to be here. Sorry about your date with Brian. But if he has any sense, he'll be waiting for you."

"Is my boss one of your guys, or Jorge?"

"No. But one of us helped one of Jorge's daughters a few years back, so it wasn't hard to arrange."

"So you have people in Vegas and New York. Where else?"

"Everywhere. Worldwide."

"Phoenix?"

"Not yet." His cheesy wink reminded me of the parrot in *Treasure Island,* the way source material seems clichéd when you don't encounter it first.

"Why Vegas? Is the organization headquartered here?"

His laugh startled me, and made me smile, which startled me more. "No," he said. "There are only around two hundred of us. I'm the only one out here."

"So they brought me to you, specifically."

"Right." There was not a whisper left of his smile.

"You couldn't have come to me?"

"The World Series of Poker makes this a bad time for me to leave Las Vegas."

"So you wanted me enough to screw up my life in a couple of directions, but not enough to miss any poker?"

"Well, it's not just 'any poker.' It's the WSOP, but I would have come to Phoenix for you if I'd needed to."

"Why?"

"I already told you."

"No, you told me why me. Now I'm asking why you."

Phil put down his coffee cup. It made no sound when it touched the table. "I can't tell you that."

"You arranged for me to be where I am. You planned how you would approach me, what I'd eat—no matter what I ordered—and what music would be playing in the background."

"Yes."

I listened again. Sam Cooke. Family washing-up after dinner music—energetic, but safe. "And you've been manipulating me ever since."

"That's right."

"Manipulating me really, really well."

He inclined his head in something between a polite nod and a wary bow.

"I want to know how you do that."

His smile came slowly, but he meant every fraction of it. "That's what I'm offering," he said.

"You and this small but influential, international, nonpaying, not-dangerous secret society of yours?"

"Right."

"Like the mafia, only with all the cannoli and none of the crime."

"Well, we're much older."

"An older, slower mafia."

He looked a little disconcerted.

"And you fight evil? Control the government? Are our secret alien overlords?"

"Try to make the world a little better."

"Seriously?"

"Just a little better."

"An older, slower, *nicer* mafia?"

He stood up. "There's substantially more to us than that. For example, most people can't get Internet in the café. I've gotten about half the shockers out of the way, and next time we talk I won't be meddling with your head. Sleep on it." He took a small plastic dragon from his pocket and put it by my plate.

"I used to collect these things!" I said. "But you knew that, didn't you?"

Kendra the waitress stopped him on the way out, said something to him, kissed his cheek, and came to clear our table with her face still pink. I put my earphones back in and logged into Gmail using the wi-fi you can't get in the 24/7 Café to find two messages waiting for me.

From: Liam@GlyphxDesign.com
To: Renee@GlyphxDesign.com
Subject: Tomorrow's Meeting Rescheduled
Thursday, June 30, 2011 5:46 pm GMT - 7

Hi Ren,

Hope you're enjoying Vegas. Jorge has pushed our meeting back. Something came up for him at home, so you have an extra day of fun in the sun on our nickel. Take yourself to a show or something. My flight is the same time, but on Saturday now instead of tomorrow. Sorry, but I know you can entertain yourself.

L.

and

> **From:** Phil@Incrementalists.org
> **To:** Renee@GlyphxDesign.com
> **Subject:** Breakfast?
> Thursday, June 30, 2011 5:01 pm GMT - 7
>
> Assuming you're free.

And somehow, as trapped and arranged and manipulated as it all felt, I knew I was.

TWO

You Can Do That?

Phil

Usually, the first interview without switches is the tricky one, so after yesterday, I was wary. I got to the café first, on the theory that her walking up to me would be less threatening than the reverse. Ren normally woke up at eight and spent forty-five minutes getting ready, subtract fifteen minutes for her being out of town, giving us 8:30; I arrived at 8:20. Katy was hostessing, and she had a dramatic fake coronary, while making comments about seeing me before noon.

"I'm meeting someone," I said. "So two, please."

She led the way, remarking, "It can't be business, so it must be personal. A girl?"

"She is certainly female, and this has nothing to do with poker."

"Well, my my."

"Tell me how your heart is now broken."

"Not mine, but I can think of a couple of waitresses who will be disappointed."

"Katy, why don't you tell me this stuff when it will do me some good?"

"Looking out for my staff," she said.

"I think I won't ask what you mean by that. Here she is. Katy, this is Ren."

"You know everyone here, don't you?" she said, sliding into a chair. "Hello, Katy." Ren was wearing pants and a sleeveless green sweater that would have looked purely professional if they hadn't been tight.

"Enjoy your breakfast," said Katy and went back to her post.

"She thinks we're involved, doesn't she?"

"She's a doll, but she has a limited imagination. And you are every bit as observant as I'd been led to believe."

A waiter named Sam came up, looking like the dancer he probably was. I ordered a Santa Fe Breakfast Wrap and coffee. Ren looked at me. I said, "It's all you, this time." She nodded and ordered Frosted Flakes and tea.

The instant Sam walked away, she said, "What qualifies as better?"

"We argue about that a lot."

"What are your criteria?"

"That's part of the same argument."

"Okay, who gives the green lights?"

"For meddlework? Usually—"

"Metal-work?"

"Meddlework. Two d's. Our term for it. Like what I did to you yesterday. Meddling with someone's head so you can change his actions. Usually no one has to approve, you just do it. If it's something big, you're expected to run it past the group first, and people usually do. When they don't we scream at them a lot. There's a group called Salt that sort of oversees the discussions but has no real power."

Her stare was intense. Her mouth was set in a firm line, and her hands weren't moving at all.

"What if you're wrong," she said. "What if you do something big, and it makes things worse?"

There is a curving boulevard that leads to a half-moon–shaped park. Buddha watches over the street at various points. The park is dominated by a curved colonnade that looks more Greek than Asian. Along the boulevard, in the park, on the shiny, glittering street, bodies of men and women, boys and girls, old people and infants, wait to be buried. They've all been murdered, but not here; there is no blood in the street; everything is neat and clean, except for the bullet holes. There are thousands upon thousands of dead, and they are all looking at me.

"That can happen," I finally said. "It really, really sucks. We try not to do that."

Ren

Trouble moved over his face, lining the edge of his brow and cheekbone like a felt-tip pen. It aged him and put depth under the handsome. It made me want to touch him, but of course he would know the sexy of vulnerable, and I wasn't falling for that. I had questions.

"How long can you keep me here?"

"Do you want to go?"

"I mean how long can you keep me in Vegas, Liam in Phoenix, Jorge in New York, and RMMD paying for it all?"

"We have time."

"How do you know? And how can you possibly track all the implications of what you do? You make it so I'm here because this is where you need me, but maybe Brian is my soul mate, and while I'm gone, he meets some other girl and they fall in love."

"He's not your soul mate." Something fierce in Phil's calm voice made me wonder whether it was soul mates or Brians he was so certain of.

"I meant as an example," I said. "Maybe Jorge goes ahead and commits to a design without hearing from us first, and we lose the auditory prompts his own research demonstrates his users need, and a bunch of old people don't get reminders to take their medicine?"

"Or maybe you join us and I show you how to get even more effective alarms written into the requirements, plus maybe shift Jorge's priorities a little."

"You can do that?"

"*You* can do that. You're designing a monitoring and assistance device for Alzheimer's patients. Maybe Jorge's mom would be interested in joining the beta test pool."

"That's what you do? You get nonhuman corporate entities to make decisions on a human level?"

One of Phil's eyebrows contracted in a way that, if both had done it, it would have been a grimace. Somehow it conveyed interest. "That's one thing we can do. Sometimes."

"Sometimes? What determines whether you can do it?"

"Lots of things. How drastic the change is, how well we know the Focus—the person we're trying to meddle with, how good we are at meddling. No one is going to turn Rupert Murdoch into a liberal, but a few nudges might convince some British investigators to follow up on what he's doing, if they're inclined in that direction anyway."

"That was you?"

"Someday I'll tell you what we *didn't* do. It would have been big. And ugly."

"So if I want in, what do I do? Confirmation class? Dunk in the river? Prick my finger?"

"You come home with me."

"And?"

"You come home with me and find out."

Phil

Something closed up behind her face. It was as if she suspected the process would be unpleasant, and I didn't want to tell her about it. Or maybe I just imagined that because it was and I didn't. On the other hand, maybe she just thought I was hitting on her, and really, I wouldn't blame me if I did. In an attempt to undo the damage, I said, "Not right now. You can take as much time as you want to think about it. And I'm not meddling with you."

"I know you're not," she said. Then, "But I don't know who you are."

"Me, or the group?"

"You. Who are you?"

"That's a hard question to answer. For anyone. How would you answer it?"

She nodded slowly. The food arrived, and Sam asked something about it, and I answered. We ate for a little while, and I drank coffee. Then she said, "What's the most important thing you aren't telling me?"

"Good question, but an easy one," I said. "Because it's the next thing we get to. The big one. The one you need to know before decid—"

"Just say it," she said. "I hate prologues."

I knew that. "The process involves giving you the memories of one of us—of someone who died. No, don't ask how that's done. Later. The point is, you'll be getting the memories of a woman named Celeste. You'll be what we call her Second, with all of her memories, in addition to all of your own. Which brings up the question of—"

"Who will I be?"

"Exactly."

"What's the answer?"

"There's no way to know."

She put her teacup down and looked at me. "Oh, well, that's just peachy. It isn't dangerous, but for all intents and purposes, I could just disappear?"

"Your memories won't."

"But I might."

I nodded.

"And I should even consider this—why?"

"That whole thing about making a difference. Don't tell me that isn't important to you; I know better."

She said slowly and distinctly, "Shit," pronouncing it very carefully as if to make sure there would be no confusion.

I ate some more wrap and drank some coffee.

"Who was Celeste?"

I felt my face do something, and it was like I'd just let my eyes widen after flopping quads. Crap. The chances she'd missed it were zero, so I said, "She was someone who was very important to me."

"You were lovers?"

"Only briefly in this lifetime."

"Jesus Christ," she said. "This lifetime? How many lifetimes have you had?"

"I do not," I said, "wish to answer that question at this time."

"I kind of think you should," she said.

"You are risking what is left of this lifetime. You may, as you, gain others. You may not. There's—"

"How old are you?"

I shook my head. "That's an impossible question. This thing I'm asking you to do, where you get someone's memories. I've done that before. So, do you mean the age of this body? The age of my personality? How long the original—"

"Stop it. How long have you been you?"

I inhaled and let my breath out slowly. And I wondered why I was getting upset. This was predictable; part of the normal process. Why was it getting to me this time? One plus zero is one. One plus one is two. Two plus one is three. Three plus two is five. Five plus three is eight. I got up to 610 and said, "I've been around for about two thousand years. What else would you like to know?"

"Two thousand years?"

"Me, as me, yes."

"Do you have memories from before that?"

"Yes, all the way back to the beginning. But—"

"The beginning of what?"

No way around it. "The human race," I said.

She stared at me.

I continued as if it were no big deal. "But the ones way back are, well, hazy. I can refresh any of them I want to."

This was where part of her would be saying, *All right, just pretend you believe it, and go from there; worry about reality later.* "But you've been Phil for two thousand years."

"Two thousand and six, yes."

"Same personality?"

"Same basic personality. It alters some with the body you're put in. My personality in a woman's body is subtly different, and things like sexual orientation are, in part, wired into the brain, so that changes. But I've thought of myself as Phil for, yeah, about two thousand years."

"You've been a woman?"

"Several times."

"Why did you pick a man this time?"

"We don't get to pick. The others pick for you. That's why it's me talking to you instead of Celeste."

She sat there for a long time, first looking at me, then through me. Then she said, "Is it worth it?"

I discarded half a dozen glib answers, then realized that without them I didn't know what to say. "That's sort of an impossible question," I said. "For me, it's worth it, yeah. Even with—even with the times we blew it. Was it worth it for you to tell your boss he made Bill Gates look like Richard Stallman?"

Her face twisted up as she tried not to laugh. "You know about that, huh?"

I grinned at her, and she let herself smile. I was right about wanting to see it.

Then she said, "Meddlework. That's what you call it?"

"Yes. What about it?"

"You do that to people, and change them, to make things better."

"Yes."

"I want to watch you do one," she said.

Ren

"Look how stupid this is." I held the passenger door open while Phil moved bags of clothes and boxes of paper from the front seat of his Prius. "Car manufacturers know even married people drive alone more frequently than with a passenger, but we still have cars with five seats and no storage. If this seat simply folded flat easily, think how much better it'd be for you."

"But not for you," he said with a flourish indicating the cleared seat.

"But you almost never have anyone else in here, so most of the time, it'd be better."

Phil turned his oddly twisted eyebrows to me and I felt stupid. He'd rather have a regular passenger. Obviously.

"It's just bad design," I said.

He pointed his eyebrows at the windshield and pulled into traffic.

"The car, I mean," I said. "How long were you and Celeste together?"

"A while."

I stopped talking. It seemed prudent. We drove in the quiet through the visual noise of Las Vegas. It faded quickly into a suburban west that could have been Phoenix or Houston or here.

"I can show you the file I'm building for a guy named Acosta, but I'm still gathering switches, so there's not much to watch yet."

"Switches?"

"Information I can use to get past his defenses. Like your matzo ball soup. I'm still collecting them."

"But you can show me one?"

His mouth smiled, but not his eyebrows. "Switches aren't something you can see. They're not actual toggles or whips. They're metaphorical."

"So you just remember them?"

"Sorta. We store them in the Garden."

I just waited.

"The Garden is . . . um. We have forty thousand years of individual memories times two-hundred-odd minds, plus switches and other information. We have to keep it somewhere. The Garden is what we call that somewhere."

"Somewhere outside yourself?" I asked. "You can store your memories remotely?"

"Sorta," he said. "It's hard to explain. But in effect, yeah. You'll either understand when you need to, or you won't need to."

His house was small, but bigger than a man living alone needs, with a rock yard he didn't care about and room for two cars. Inside, the emptiness felt more Zen than lonely, and comfortable.

"I know you don't drink coffee, but I haven't bought tea for you yet. Can I get you anything else?"

"You weren't expecting me to come home with you today?"

"No. Most people need to think it over."

"That's what I'm doing."

"No, you're experimenting with it."

"I'd take a beer."

Not just the one, but both eyebrows spun out. "Now you're just fucking with me," he said.

"Yeah," I agreed, and made myself cozy on his sofa. "Tell me about Acosta."

"One of our pattern shamans tipped us off to him." Phil stayed in the kitchen, making coffee, getting me a glass of water, talking while he worked. "He's sales manager at a midsize manufacturing company here in town, but moving up the ranks. He started on the line. Couple of months back, he hired a new sales guy, but he's not working out. Acosta's given him every chance. He's loaned him money, covered for him. They're friends. But now he has to fire him." Phil hesitated with his hand on the fridge door, his back to me, looking for words. "What Acosta ends up telling himself about this—that he can't be a boss and be a friend, that his buddy's been trying to play him, or was never really his friend—will make a difference in how he manages everyone else for as long as he works—and we think that's likely to be a lot of folks. He's teaching himself a basic rule here, and I want to help it be a good one."

"How can you know it's that pivotal?" I took the water from him and he sat down with his coffee cup beside me on the sofa.

"We've learned to spot that in people," he said. "When lives are at a turning point."

"By comparing your collective experience of people over so much time?"

"Right," he said.

"Shared in the Garden?"

"Yeah. Shoulders and backs show you what they're going through is big; their hands tell you it's urgent; and the jawline lets you know if it's temporary and immediate or a true pivot point."

"Do you see that in me?"

He looked at me. "No."

"You said you're responsible for the MP3 format."

"We helped."

"What else?"

"Excuse me?"

"What else have you done?"

He opened his mouth, then closed it again. "Are you asking for an example, or an exhaustive list? If you want the list, I have to decline; I have plans for next February."

"An example would be nice. Something like the MP3 thing, where you did something that had a broad effect."

He was quiet for a few minutes, then he nodded.

Phil

"All right," I said. "Ever heard of John Rawlins?"

She shook her head, her eyes narrowed and focused on me the way a snake focuses on a bird.

"He was Grant's chief of staff."

"Grant? General Grant?"

"Right. The one buried in Grant's Tomb. What do you know about him?"

"Um. Lee surrendered to him?"

"Right. What else?"

"He was a butcher, a bad president, and a drunk."

"Yeah, that's the guy. Except none of that is true."

She started to speak, and I held my hand up. "The drinking thing. I don't know, maybe. But he probably never got drunk during the war, and certainly never when it mattered."

"Then how did he get the reputation?"

"Short version: jealousy in the officer corps, and the fact that he did have a drinking problem when he was in the army after the Mexican War."

"He beat it?"

"With help from John Rawlins, who took it upon himself to make sure Grant stayed sober."

She nodded. "And?"

I remembered the flag of the 46th Ohio, tattered and shredded. I remembered myself, after Shiloh, retching from the smell of bodies and saying over and over to myself, *You didn't run, you didn't run.* I remembered huddling on the ground after the second assault on Vicksburg, thinking about the last screaming fight with Celeste and half hoping I'd get a wound so brutal it'd force some sympathy out of her. I remembered the long, ugly march to Tennessee, trying to get a song started and failing as the cold and wet and the mountain paths almost did what even Johnston couldn't.

"Yeah," I said. "We saw how important Grant was after Donnelson. We didn't know if he'd start drinking, but we couldn't be sure he wouldn't."

"So you meddled with him?"

"No," I said. "With Rawlins. You could say Rawlins meddled with Grant, though he wasn't one of us."

"I'm not sure what you're saying."

"I found Rawlins's switches—oysters, saddle-leather, I don't remember what else. I meddled with him to make sure he took it upon himself to keep Grant from drinking."

"And if you hadn't done that?"

"Who knows. Maybe nothing. Or maybe Grant would have been drunk at Shiloh. One thing I know for sure: if the Union had lost at Shiloh, things would have been even worse."

"So you made him better."

"I think so, yes."

She frowned. "But everyone remembers him worse. Why don't you set the record straight?"

"How would we do that? We meddle a bit with biographers and historians and archaeologists, and point them towards evidence, but other than that, what can we do? Who'd believe us? If someone announced, without evidence, that half the books destroyed in the library at Alexandria were works of erotica, would you believe him?"

"Were they?"

"Not half."

"So there's nothing you can do?"

That stopped me. The question was either too big or too small. After some thought, I said, "You know what we call people who aren't one of us?"

"I didn't know there was a term for them."

"Of course there's a term for them. Every group has a term for outsiders. We call them, 'those who forget.' "

"What's your point?"

"That we remember."

She was quiet for a couple of minutes. Her shoulders shifted back a little, and she rolled her head as if her neck was stiff.

"That's it," I said.

Ren

"In my jaw and shoulders?"

He nodded. "And your hands." And he was right.

"Can you guys find a nice girl for Brian? Maybe someone a little more rock-n-roll than me?"

"We could, but so could you."

"Oh, right. I can't tell anyone, can I? I can't call my mom and say good-bye?"

"No." He held my eyes the way you'd take a sick man's hand. "But you won't just vanish. Even if your personality doesn't stay on top of Celeste's—the other, older personality—it'll be a meld more than a swallow. And gradual."

"But I will always be there in the external Garden? Just packed away, stored remotely?"

"Your memories will be."

"Okay," I said.

"Okay what?"

"Okay I want in. Whatever it is you have to do to make me one of you. I'm ready."

"Okay," he said, and put his coffee down.

THREE

That's Backwards Too

Phil

Ritual and memory; pain and understanding.

Ritual has a mass, a weight, a gravity. It pulls you into itself, and as you use it, it uses you. It takes power and it gives power. Ritual is the same every time, otherwise it isn't ritual. It is different every time, otherwise it has no power. No matter how many times we experience the same ritual, it transpires differently than it lives in our memories.

That's especially true of the ritual I performed on and with Ren, because we never remember any of the details between reaching into the Garden to shape the stub, and using the stub in its new shape. Here, of all places, as part of the ritual, our memory fails.

What is memory? Some say our memories are ourselves, which is oversimplified, but not wrong. But if there were a symbol of memory, what would it be? Would it be wood that came from a living thing as our memories continue to grow and change after the events that created them have passed? Would it be shaped by a human hand as our personalities are shaped by our experiences? Would the shape be pointed, to represent that we are always moving forward? Would it be on fire to represent the memories of passion without which we aren't human, and leaving behind ash to represent the memories of regret, without which we shouldn't be?

That's just rationalization, though. I don't know why memory is symbolized as a burning wooden spike. But it is, and it always has been, for any useful definition of always.

I finished around nine in the evening, Ren sleeping comfortably on my bed. I pulled a chair up next to her, exhausted by the ritual as always, unable to sleep afterward as always. See previous remark about "always." I waited, rested, read some Ashbless poems, and wished I could sleep. The Pirates were playing Toronto again, but I couldn't summon up the energy to check the score.

About three hours later she woke as we always do, a scream starting on her lips continuing the one that almost passed before; then she realized that the only pain was a dull headache, and so the scream never emerged. Then she brought a hand to her forehead, touching it to see if there was a wound. It was a gesture I'd seen thousands of times, and made hundreds.

Eventually, her eyes focused on me: fear, anger, wonderment, confusion. What had I just done to her? How much of it was real? Did it matter if it was real? Why hadn't I told her what I was going to do?

And then, as I watched her eyes, I could see the first taste of Celeste reaching her. I knew that the strongest, sharpest, clearest of Celeste's memories would first seep into Ren's head like floodwater under the door. She'd remember when Celeste went through the same ritual, and perhaps she'd remember when Celeste did the same thing to me. Maybe. I can't reach Celeste's memory, except through Celeste. We can't reach anyone's memory, except through what they tell us. We trust our memories even though they lie, and we cherish our memories, even though there are some we wish we could scrub like burned egg off a frying pan.

The memory of pain would be present, clear, sharp, but behind it would be understanding. Pain and understanding are always at war with each other. We are fighters for understanding, but we can only get there through pain. We are keepers of memory, but we can only get there through ritual.

Her eyes focused a little more. I got up, sat down on the edge of the bed, and held a glass of water to her lips. She drank a sip.

"Hello, Ren," I said. "Welcome back. How's the head?"

Ren

"You asshole," I said, which tightened the tenderness I'd seen softening the edges of his eyes enough to keep me from crying. "You shoved a burning stake between my eyes, how the hell do you think my head is?"

"I'm sorry," he said. "It's the only way."

"Jesus Christ. In how many thousand years of evolution, that's the best you can manage? Talk about a terrible user interface."

"Something for you to work on, then." But the tiny lines beside his eyes had gone from care to patience, and now cracked into smile. "But you should eat something first," he said. "Are you hungry?"

I had to think about it. My body, arranged politely in the dead center of his bed seemed farther away than the Renaissance. "Yeah," I said. "I think so. Got any lark's tongue in aspic?"

He grinned. "I'll go check." He stood up, and I panicked. Without his weight on the mattress, I felt like I might float off the bed. "I know I've got peanut butter and jelly," he said.

My field of vision opened to include both of us, him standing, me on the bed lying rigid, the Ikea furniture and the clean tile floor. "And frozen pizza," he said. But I was falling out of a well backwards, away from the confines and claustrophobia, and into something much worse. He put a receipt in the open page of the book and closed it.

"Or we could order in," he said. "You can get almost anything delivered." He turned back to me, and both of us were small and distant. "Really. Almost anything. Except, for some reason, pizza. You can't get pizza late at night in Las Vegas. Is that weird, or what?" I could see his living room too, and the kitchen, the little yard in back with a palm tree. "Are you okay?"

If I blinked I would lose sight of us altogether in the weave of bungalows and sidewalks.

"Ren?" He touched my arm.

"Ren?" His fingers closed over my shoulder and trapped the whole suburban block between his palm and my skin. He was sitting, leaning over me, trying to see into my eyes. I let his eyes come into focus. Brown with flecks of something lighter—yellow, or gold maybe, almost amber, and concern. No, worry.

"Peanut butter and jelly, dear chef?" my voice said. "Do not a gas-flame stove and electrical refrigeration and every modern contraption invented to make the preservation and preparation of food into a trivial act or an outrageous hobby now attend your pleasure, where once the collection and preparation of food occupied you so utterly that you scarcely netted even the calories it cost to fell and section meat and wood? Where even the simplest grains and meanest, hard apples were once daily defended from spoilage and rot, frost-burn and rodents. Do not now apples from Oregon, oranges from Florida, and bananas from Mexico all await you at the minimart you pass before you reach the grocery store in whose vast and air-cooled domain everything from pork loin to fish eggs now stands packed in glass or wrapped in cellophane to be eaten by its expiration date or thrown away? Yet with all of this—all this splendor, all this wanton excess, you offer me either pizza, knowing I abhor it, or crushed peanuts and squashed strawberries mashed between two slabs of something that bears no more resemblance to bread than this flat futon does to a feather mattress. Having, only hours hence, seared me, cursed me yet again, and impaled me upon the tip of your flaming stake, you now offer to feed me on children's food?"

"Oh, hello Celeste," Phil said. "I have good bread. From a bakery."

"Fuck off."

Phil's mouth twisted into a screamlike shape. With a snarl of warning or rage or despair, his hand spanned the back of my head nearly ear to ear. He kissed me. And when he took his mouth from mine, he held my head still, our temples pressed together. I felt his shoulders shake. "I loved you," he said, choked.

"You should quit smoking." My voice was tart.

"I did."

"Not this lifetime."

"I never started this lifetime. Celeste—"

"I loved you too," she said, but I didn't believe her.

Phil was quiet a long time. I watched the hairless little hollow where his collarbones met and tried to remember what the big deal was about peanut butter.

"I'm sorry you had to see that, Ren." Phil stood up and walked to the bedroom's little window. He shoved the curtains back and looked into the yard like it'd better not have anything to say about it.

"Maybe we should go with pizza," I said.

He looked back suddenly and caught me testing the skin of my lips for razor burn.

"I'm sorry about that too," he said, very quietly.

I shrugged and swung my legs over the side of the bed. "Will Celeste keep doing that?" I asked him. "Just talking out of my mouth that way? She's kind of long-winded."

Phil's face ran through a range of emotions. "I don't know," he said. "Do you want her to?"

He held his hands out and I took them. I stood up slowly, but it still ground the headache tighter.

"Pepperoni or Deluxe?" he said.

Phil

You're always sleepy and hungry as a new Second; you're always sleepy and jumpy as a new titan. Ren managed some pizza and then fell asleep. I opened my laptop, disposed of email, and seeded the ritual, leaving it as a bright blue flower in a vase just inside the front gate. I looked around while I was there; a knee-high statue of Iupiter stood next to a full-size brick oven, and on top of the oven was a basket holding six loaves of bread; and just past that were three coils of hemp, followed by nine or ten candles. I didn't bother looking in the other direction; I was going to need to clean the place up or I'd be unable to graze my own Garden.

Not now, though. Now I had to deal with a new Second, and, dammit, I was missing all the WSOP side action. I'd expected to do the interview, then leave Ren to think about it for a week or two.

I leaned against the wall that existed in my mind and rubbed a virtual hand over a symbolic cheek. Why hadn't she had to think about it? I walked over to the oven and grabbed the second loaf, ripped off a hunk, and started eating it. The loaf remained in the basket because that's how things work. I swallowed, and the memory became part of me and I examined it.

She'd been one of those precocious children who pronounce words wrong because she'd read them before hearing them, but it had bothered her more than most, and as a teenager she'd taken to reading with an online dictionary open so she could hear the pronunciation of words she didn't know. Interesting, but so?

I bit into the next loaf of bread and recalled how she'd gotten into user interface, and how angry she got over poor design, and realized that she took bad design as a personal insult directed at everyone who used it. Again, interesting, but so?

I continued, and got nothing; but, as so often happens, the accumulation of little things built up an obvious answer so gradually that it had been sitting in front of me for some time before I realized it: She hadn't hesitated, because there was something she wanted to do. She had an agenda I hadn't seen.

And I was her titan—responsible for her and it, whatever it was.

Crap.

I let the Garden dissolve around me and there I was, shaking and in desperate need of the pizza that was all the way across the room.

According to the clock on my laptop, I'd spent more than two hours grazing.

I ate cold pizza, then threw myself onto the couch.

I was going to have a lot to talk to Ren about when she woke up.

Ren

I woke up happy, with the heavy-boned tired you get from swimming all afternoon in a summer lake. Easy, and not wanting to hurry back to the real world—whatever that means when half my work and all my correspondence exist only electronically. After pizza, I'd stripped down to my skivvies and crawled into Phil's bed. Now I dove back out of it and dug through the pile of my clothes for my phone, but a short message from Cindi settled me down. Phil—or someone in the Big Power Tiny Action organization I'd just joined—had jiggered things overnight to keep me in Vegas and Liam in Phoenix through the rest of the weekend at least. A longer note from Liam apologized a lot and promised to make it up to me. I sat back down on Phil's bed and pondered whether I could fit out his window. Head first or feet? Shoulders stuck in the opening or ass wedged in the wall?

Not like he—they—couldn't find me, even if I managed to squeeze through. Where would I go? And it wasn't really Phil I wanted to flee, just everything I'd seen while I slept, and what it all meant.

I stood up and stretched. Celeste had been right about the futon mattress—it was unforgivingly firm. I wanted a shower and clean clothes and decent food and time to think it all over. I settled for Phil's vintage bathrobe of white-and-blue, striped cotton, soft enough to make me wonder if Celeste had a stash of favorite clothes hidden for me, and if they'd fit, and whether she would have been prettier in them.

I tiptoed past Phil, sprawled on his sofa, looking more poleaxed than asleep, one arm thrown over his eyes, the other fallen off his chest. He was still wearing all his clothes. I could have walked right out the front door and slammed it and gotten away, but I guess I didn't want to. I rubbed my lips, remembering his rough mouth.

His narrow galley kitchen was separated from the living room by a Formica bar. The fridge, pantry and stove all stood on the opposite wall in a line with the sink. A very squashy work triangle, but useable enough until you opened the fridge.

"What are you doing?" Phil sank onto one of the barstools.

"Good morning!" I said. "Wow. That's backwards too."

"What?"

"The morning. We shouldn't be seeing each other with morning hair and the sleep stupids before we've had sex. We should be all after-glowed and satisfied before we have to look at each other in this condition."

Phil scrubbed at his face. "Why is the refrigerator door in the hall?"

"It was backwards. I noticed it yesterday. The handle and hinges were on the wrong sides."

"So you're switching them? Before breakfast? God, before coffee?"

I surveyed Phil's kitchen, then his face. They were both a bit of a wreck, honestly. Both probably my fault. "I don't drink coffee," I reminded him.

"But I do," he said and stalked into his bedroom.

Fifteen minutes later he had showered and dressed, and I had reassembled his kitchen and done my best with his coffeepot. Five minutes after that, he suggested we go out for coffee.

"Ask a carpenter to dress you and you'll wear wooden clothes," I snapped, then tried to figure out what the hell I meant. Phil waited. I said, "You didn't ask for any of this, did you?"

He shook his head and looked tired. "It's okay," he said. "I did know you do that—order your physical environment when you feel frightened."

"I do that, or Celeste did?"

His rogue eyebrow twitched upward, but his voice stayed calm. "She did too, actually, but I wasn't thinking about her."

Nothing in his face moved. He sat impassively on the barstool, swiveling gently, looking out through the sliding glass doors into the yard.

"Bullshit," I said.

He swiveled back to scan my face.

"No, not Celeste," I said. "It's all me."

The eyebrow quirked a question mark my direction.

"You've been thinking about Celeste since we met," I said. "She's been a shadow under everything you've said. So either you're so repressed you don't know you have feelings at all, or you're lying to me."

"I have not lied to you."

I mirrored his total lack of movement.

"But I haven't told you everything," he said.

I stayed quiet; it was working for me.

"Let's go get some decent food," he said. "I think we'd both be better for it." He stood up and walked into his bedroom.

I got as far as the barstool side of the kitchen before I realized the bias-cut green dress and difficult stockings I was planning to put on belonged to a woman seventy years ago. I had darned the silk where it wore thin at the toes and could feel, on the backs of my knees, how they bagged before synthetics. I don't wear nylons often. It's too hot, and my legs are dark enough. But they've always been nylon. Celeste was mixing into me.

I faced Phil's icebox. No, his fridge, hinged properly now. But the sharp edge of the counter bit into the palms of my hands, and my fingertips went cold with the effort of not trailing after him. I wanted him here to hold me, lock me down, grip my wavering reality in his big hands and bend it into sense.

Phil hit the light switch on the way out of his bedroom and started reeling the blinds over the glass patio doors. "Saves on the A/C," he explained.

"I gotta go," I said. "Make whoever do whatever and get me back to Phoenix. I need to stop and think this through."

"It's a little late for that."

"What do you mean 'a little late'?"

"The memories are going to keep coming back, Ren. You can't stop them. The best you can do is let me show you how to organize the lifetimes of personal information you'll be getting. And how to graze the shared memory you have access to now. And how to put the two together and start your own meddlework."

"Until I fade away altogether under Celeste?"

"Until it all settles out."

There were no lines in the skin above his eyebrows, no sign of worry or concern, just information, but he came to stand where I was milking the Formica.

"You're not an impulsive person," he said. "You knew you could take your time to think this over. You wanted to experiment with it—watch me meddle, learn more about us." A strange tenderness turned his voice liquid. "But you took the spike last night without waiting for any of that." His words slipped over my shoulders like bathwater. "You already had some meddlework in mind, didn't you?"

I turned to look at him. "Did you know you can drown someone in two inches of water?"

The one wild eyebrow shot up, then dove. Surprised, then angry. "You've never drowned anyone."

"No, I haven't. But how do you know that? How could you know what I am? Can you even see me through all the Celeste hanging over me?"

"I'm not the only one looking." There was no morning softness, no sluggishness left to his face. My bathtub iced over.

But I didn't care. Whatever else he was going to tell me I was or wasn't, I knew for plain fact I wasn't needy. I wasn't helpless or pathetic or wanting protection and a big strong man to save me. I might be in over my head, but I wasn't wasting air shouting for the lifeguard. And I wasn't giving up my secrets. "You told me you see patterns," I said. "That your whole niceness mafia is based on changing people by knowing what triggers them and orchestrating those triggers, by manipulating them to be better, right?"

"To do better; being better sort of comes along naturally."

"How?"

"I explained that, Ren. We each draw from lifetimes of wisdom and have access to a collective memory that houses almost every fact about anyone. We know how to make someone trust us, we know how to find a memory that will cause gratification. We manipulate and suggest."

"Then nothing can surprise you? Ever?"

"You have."

I leaned against the corridor wall. Phil dropped back onto a barstool, one wary eyebrow watching me.

"Then we're even," I said. "We should eat something."

Phil nodded.

"I want the full Vegas experience, lavish buffet, dancing girls," I said. "I want you to show it all to me, and I want my boss to pay for it."

"With all of human history available to you if you close your eyes, you want to see Las Vegas?"

"Yup," I said. "Didn't see that coming either, did you?"

His wariness doubled in eyebrow. "Are you just trying to be unpredictable?"

"Would that be out of character for me?" I asked.

"Yes."

"Then no, I'm not," I said, like it was innocence and not exhaustion that kept me leaning against the wall. "But I'm not going to stay inside with the animatronics this time."

Phil waited.

"For my seventh birthday, my parents took me to Disney World. Mom was pregnant; I didn't know it yet, but I guess that was part of why we went: a last hurrah for the three of us, with the next two years going to be all diapers and learning to walk. The first morning, I had my first-ever room service meal and opened presents. I got a pair of plastic sparkle princess shoes from my nana's sister, tore them out of their plastic bubble-pack, and wore them for breakfast in bed with my Tinker Bell nightie and the room service tray. Do you know this story?"

He shook his head. "What happened?"

I pushed my back into the wall. "We got dressed for our big day at the park. Mom wanted me to put my Keds on, but I was the birthday princess, and either I convinced her that princesses do not wear sneakers, or she needed to throw up and just gave in. She packed the Keds in my new Belle backpack and sent Dad and me down to the lobby where I took them out and hid them in a potted tree.

"We took the monorail, stood in the entrance line, and half an hour into our day with only 'Dumbo the Flying Elephant' and 'Main Street USA' checked off on my pages-long list, my feet started hurting. 'It's a Small World' and 'Cinderella's Golden Carousel' later, I'd chewed a bloody place on the inside of my lip."

Phil chuckled, warm and easy, and I liked the sound and the way his shoulders sat down away from his ears now without the tension that always rode them. "What did you do?" he asked.

"What could I? Fess up and wait with Mom while Dad went back to the hotel to root through the lobby plants? Accept his offer of a most un-princessly piggyback? Keep walking till my awful, plastic torture shoes left trails of blood through the Magic Kingdom?"

"No?"

"Never!"

"What then?"

"Develop a sudden and unnatural love for the 'Hall of Presidents.' No lines. All sitting."

"Very clever," Phil said.

I sat down on the stool next to him, but couldn't quite meet his eyes. "I need help," I said. "And I'm not willing to miss out on seven-eighths of the fun because I'm too proud to ask for it. But I'm scared and overwhelmed and have a lot to learn and I can't learn it all right now. After the dreams I had all night, I need a change of scenery.

I want to look away from all this and come back with clean eyes. I want to throw myself into an experience that isn't mine, a movie or not-a-memory, something I can't possibly be responsible for."

"Let me show you Las Vegas," he said. His eyes were the brown of bearskin.

"I'll get my walking shoes," I said.

Phil

Sinatra sang "Fly Me to the Moon" as the fountains at the Bellagio went through their paces. I watched her, pleased she was enjoying it, and wondering how the hell I was going to get her to tell me what she had planned. It was wall-to-wall people, as always, but she didn't seem to mind.

"I'm going to need a primer on the jargon," she said.

"It'll come back to you."

"No, not Incrementalist jargon; poker jargon."

"What brought that up?"

"You didn't hear the conversation behind us?"

"I wasn't paying attention, sorry."

"I think I can quote it. 'I had the nuts on the flop. He called my push with fuck-all, and hit runner-runner straight.' "

I nodded.

"What does it mean?" she said.

"That he's a whiner."

"No, the terms."

"The nuts is the best possible hand for a given board. A push means betting all of your chips. Fuck-all means—"

"I got that one. And I know what a straight is. What's runner-runner?"

I did my best to explain, which required explaining the basics of hold 'em, which took most of the cab ride to Treasure Island. We watched the pirate fight, which had been better before it was just another skin show. A short walk brought us to the Venetian, where we wandered around the fake canals and got Italian ice and Godiva chocolate and admired the lighting job and, again, fought our way through the stifling, dense Las Vegas crowds.

After a cab ride to and from the Luxor we were at the Mirage, where I'd parked. We had the buffet, and I explained that the volcano didn't start until night, and that we needed to wait for the Fremont Street Experience.

"There is," she said, "a roller coaster."

"Three of them, in fact, on the Strip."

"Incredible."

"If you consider America a large amusement park, Las Vegas is the Midway."

"That is an interesting way to consider America."

"It explains Las Vegas."

She was done eating her samples of this and that; I finished my shrimp creole and stood up. "Want to gamble?" I said.

"No. What would you do if someone was about to shoot me?"

"What?" I stopped in midstride and stared at her. A middle-aged couple in matching Hawaiian shirts stepped around us. "No one is going to shoot you."

"I know. But what would you do?"

"Convince the person not to. What are you getting at?"

"Convince the person how? Magic, or threats?"

"It's not magic."

"You know what I mean."

"All right. Magic, I suppose, if I thought it might work. I'm not very intimidating. Why are you asking about this?"

"You study people pretty thoroughly, don't you? If you're planning to meddle with them, I mean."

"Even more thoroughly if we're trying to recruit them. What of it?"

We fought more crowds, and eventually made our way out into the Las Vegas heat that always hits like a tangible object, no matter how used to it you are. She ignored it, but she was from Phoenix, where it's even hotter.

I handed the valet my ticket.

"Do you always do valet parking?"

"Habit," I said. "Three buy-ins for a two-five no-limit game is about fifteen hundred dollars. If you're walking around with that much cash in your pocket at two in the morning, a dark parking garage isn't your favorite place to be. Now, you've been getting at something for the last hour. Ren, would you please have pity on me and tell me what it is?"

"Not yet," she said.

"Are you enjoying this?"

"I'm not being coy. This is research. What did you and Celeste fight about?"

"God! What didn't we fight about? Religion, politics, morality, food—"

"Ever since you've been Phil and she's been Celeste?"

"She's only been Celeste a few hundred years. But yes."

"Meddlework. You were on opposite sides of a lot of them?"

"If it had been up to her, Antietam wouldn't have been fought."

"She thought it was too big."

"If it had been up to Oskar, the entire Southern aristocracy would have been dispossessed after the war."

The car arrived. I held the door open for her; I guess because she'd gotten my mind-set into an earlier age. She accepted it without question, maybe for the same reason.

"The big fight with Celeste," she said, like she was prompting me.

"The big one? This lifetime? The 2000 election. Florida. I still think she was wrong."

"Then why didn't you do something?"

"It was already done."

"I mean, afterward. You could have exposed it."

"It was pretty well exposed."

"Not completely. Why didn't you?"

"That would have been . . . I don't know. Oskar wanted to. No one else did."

"Why didn't you?"

"Christ, Ren. It would have been huge. I don't know. Because . . ."

I stopped talking and thought about it, trying to remember. I was in the Bellagio lounge when the election results were coming in. I was drinking Macallan 25. I was angry, disgusted. I picked up my cell phone to check flights to Florida. Celeste called right then, and said—

And said—

"Fuck. She meddled. With me. Long distance, for chrissakes."

"I just thought you should know," said Ren.

I turned onto the Strip from Spring Mountain, going through the red light. Of course, there was a cop there.

Fifteen minutes later, citation in hand, I pulled us out into traffic; extra careful the way you always are with those flashing lights right behind you.

"Will the car drive better if you pull the steering wheel off?"

I didn't answer, but relaxed my grip.

"You've been wondering," said Ren, "what piece of meddlework got me so excited I just went and jumped into this thing."

"Uh, sorry," I said. "Yeah, but this thing with Celeste caught me off guard."

"Right," she said. "The thing I want; I think Celeste started it."

FOUR

Young Blood Is So Important

Ren

Phil tucked the traffic ticket between the driver's seat and center console in a way that I knew he'd have no memory of tomorrow when he went to pay it. He drove on autopilot, navigating what I'd said about Celeste. But he didn't ask for specifics about what she had started, so I stayed quiet. It would have embarrassed me to say I coveted the connection she had had to him, and it would have hurt him to learn her interest was strictly in his unique relationship to the Garden. Sitting next to him felt like standing on a rotted pier over a winter lake. By the next block, we were speeding. "Where are you taking me now?" I asked, hoping to sound like the tourist I knew I wasn't anymore.

"Nowhere," he said. "Home."

"I do have a hotel room, you know."

He turned to me, then back to the windshield.

"I'll take you back to The Palms, if you want, but most Seconds like to stay near their titans for the first couple of days."

"So that's why you have a stash of new toothbrushes and baby toothpastes and travel-size shampoos and little wrapped soaps in your bathroom?"

"Yeah," he said. "No. You're the first person I've been titan to in this lifetime. Do you want me to turn around?"

"No, but I wish I'd thought to grab my bag when I went up this morning to change. I should charge my phone, and I'd like to have my own shampoo, and my makeup."

Phil took a corner so hard we both leaned into the curve like cyclists.

"But I look fine without it," I prompted.

He stopped at the red light. A full stop. Then he turned right and accelerated hard enough to invalidate his momentary lawfulness.

"You said earlier you could teach me how to manage the dreams," I said. "Can I get a first lesson before bedtime?"

"Sure."

We pulled up in front of his little house, which looked much more inviting now, in the early evening gloom with light pouring from all its windows, than it had when I'd first arrived yesterday morning. "I can't believe it's been just twenty-four hours since—"

"Shhh!" Phil stood by his car, shoulders taut, with one hand raised behind him as though to hold me back.

His front door was open. And I'd watched him turn out all the lights when we left.

We crept closer. The dark, and the stealth of our feet, the wordless communication of care and caution, and the leashed rage of hunters hurt my chest with its familiarity and danger. Orchestral music came from the house. I knew this man, this hunt, this opera. I straightened up by his badly trimmed hedge. "*Gilbert and Sullivan*?" I said.

The screen door banged open. "Hello, darling!" cried the tiny winged silhouette in the porch light.

"Irina?" Phil asked, none of the tension lost from his voice or body.

"My precious boy, come give us a hug! And this must be our new Ren! Come in, come in!"

Phil's restrained little living room and kitchen were gaudy with flowers. Great masses of hydrangea and tiger lilies, towering spikes of gladiola and fronds of fern shrouded the furniture and breakfast bar. The sparkly little woman disappeared behind them on her way to the fridge. Phil and I wandered in her wake like stoned ducklings.

Phil turned off the stereo, silencing the very model of a modern major general. "What the fuck are you doing in my house?"

Irina held the now-fully stocked fridge door open in one hand while hoisting two bottles in the other. "Campari? Prosecco? Alone or together? No? Come. We sit down."

Still clutching both bottles in one boney hand, Irina swooped three chilled champagne flutes from the freezer with the other. No way she could have done that if the doors still swung towards the back wall. She swept into the living room and enthroned herself, her bottles and her glasses in the center of Phil's small sofa. She looked like a paper doll cut from beef jerky, brown-red and sinewy, swathed in gauze.

"Jimmy called you," said Phil.

"Of course he did, darling."

"And you've come to pry."

"No, no! I've come to welcome our newest Second. Young blood is so important."

I resisted the urge to protect my neck with my hands. If Irina was a vampire, she was badly past feeding time.

"Ren, correct?"

"Yeah," I said.

"Still Ren?"

"Yes, still Ren."

"Cut it out, Irina," Phil snapped.

"Ren, be a love and fetch me the oranges I sliced in the fridge." She frowned. "The oranges in the fridge that I sliced. No. First I'm in the fridge, now I slice it. Phil, darling, what shall I say?"

I held up the bowl of fruit I'd been to the kitchen to get, gotten, and carried back.

"Ah, she is so clever this one!"

I wondered if wrinkles that deep hurt when you smiled.

"Drop the bullshit, Irina."

"I am holding no dung of—"

"I mean it!"

Irina dropped it. I would have too, seeing Phil's face.

She concentrated on pouring and garnishing, her words just as measured. "Phil, Jimmy said he asked you point-blank what you were playing at with this new recruit, and you didn't answer him. Now she's Celeste's new Second and I've seen everything you seeded about her, too."

"So?"

I looked from Phil to Irina feeling like a kid whose parents fight. Phil was pale around the eyes. Irina was shriveled—well, pretty much everywhere. Now I knew what Phil looked like afraid. I didn't like it.

"You volunteered to recruit for Celeste's Second. That took balls. We all respected it, and we mostly left you alone as you searched and selected. But you took it too far, Phil. You doubled the genome. That's risky for her. And for you. You had no right to meddle in that kind of work."

I knew what Phil looked like afraid, and what Irina looked like undead. Although from what I'd seen today, the sun-baked and starved-dry were hardly an oddity in Vegas. I thought this would be a terrible city for zombies. I wouldn't want to have to gnaw through Irina with a mouthful of loose teeth, no matter how tasty the brains.

"She's not listening." Phil's voice was low and dangerous. Somewhere between Irina handing out the aperitifs and my imagination, he'd gone from frightened to deeply pissed off.

"Well, poor love, who can blame her?" Irina had dropped all affectations from her voice. It wasn't young, but it was warm and strong. "All the memories would be just starting to come back to her now. There might still be breakthrough personalities. Christ, Phil, we can't know if she'll settle as Ren or Celeste, and she probably still has a monstrous headache."

"I want you to go," Phil said.

"But I have a tuna casserole in the oven."

"Leave."

"No chance in hell. Ren needs someone looking out for her."

"What do you think I'm doing, Irina?"

"I think you're looking out for Celeste. Or maybe just looking for her. To tell the truth I don't know what you're doing. But I know it's dangerous and stupid."

"What does that mean, 'doubled the genome'?" I asked.

Phil and Irina pulled their focus off each other and pointed it at me.

"Sounds sci-fi," I suggested.

Irina looked genuinely perplexed. Phil shrugged. "It's figurative," he said.

"Doctor, all the mutants have doubled genomes! They may never die!"

Irina scowled. "It means Phil put Celeste's stub into you because you are biologically linked to her previous body. In addition to being a good character match and a physical fit."

I looked for a good B-movie line, but came up empty, not even a pod people reference.

"That wasn't why," Phil said, but he wouldn't look up from his drink.

"Phil created a double link to Celeste in you, and probably a memory loop or two in the process. I'm guessing he hid all this from you? That you went into your Second blind?"

Phil was looking at me, but now I was the one eyeing my own feet. I nodded. "Did you ever wonder why zombies never have shoes?" I asked. "You'd think that's the one thing you'd want to keep track of, if your skin wasn't so much staying attached."

Irina rotated her head toward Phil. "Is she insane?" she whispered. "Already?"

"She's stressed."

"I'm right here," I said.

"It's a coping thing she does," Phil said. "She'll be okay."

"Hello?" I said again.

"Hello Ren, dear. Try to calm down," Irina soothed. "We're going to help you get through this. The first few days can be quite intense, but there are tricks, ways of thinking about what is happening, analogies and meditations that can ease the integration."

"Okay," I said.

"Why don't I take you back to your hotel?" Irina stood up and put a comforting hand on my shoulder. "I've arranged for us to have adjoining rooms, and I brought something special for your headaches." She smiled at me, her blue eyes a kind oasis in her parched face. "We'll have breakfast in bed on room service trays."

I stood up and leaned into Irina's embrace.

Phil shrugged. "Go if you want to," he said.

"I don't want to," I said.

Irina put a Slim Jim finger under my chin. "You understand Phil hid important things from you," she said. "He pried more than he needed to and discovered some very personal things about you, Ren, and he hid them in the Garden."

Phil made an odd noise, and Irina's eyes shot in his direction, but she didn't release my face. "Yes, you hid them ingeniously, but I'm very good with patterns."

I nodded. "Me too," I said. "I'm gonna stay."

"Very well. You know where to find me." Irina took car keys and an expensive leather bag from a barstool. "Don't forget the casserole. It won't be good if it's overcooked."

"Will she ride her broomstick to The Palms?" I asked Phil as she left. "Can you valet that?"

"Nah, she'll have a car hidden around the block."

"Wow," I said, maybe just a little acidly. "You guys sure think of everything."

Phil

I knew that whatever I did or said next was important. It's often the first, initial reaction after you've been busted that determines how things will go down. So I chose my next action carefully. I went to the cabinet, got the bag of powdered sugar that I keep for the one time a year I bake, and opened it. I got a spoon, stuck it into the bag, and then, very carefully, I tapped the sugar onto the sliced oranges. Then I put the powdered sugar back, got a couple of paper towels, and set one in front of her.

She was still standing, watching me like I was an exotic snake that might suddenly bite. I put the bowl of oranges between us. "Have a matzo ball," I said.

She picked one up carefully, and bit into it in slow motion, then chewed and swallowed. "It's good," she said.

"The mother of someone I was eighty years ago used to do that as a treat."

"You must pick up a lot of recipes."

"You learn what you like. Then you get a new Second, and you don't like the same things anymore. It's annoying sometimes."

She ate another one and wiped her fingers on the paper towel. "So, you had an agenda, and it didn't occur to you that I might have one too?"

"Something like that, yes."

"And it didn't occur to either of us that Celeste had one. Does Irina know that, too?"

"I haven't gotten around to seeding that part yet."

"Seeding?"

"It's how we put memories in the Garden for each other to see. We graze for them when we need to retrieve information."

"Do you water and weed them too?"

"Look, our words for things evolved, okay? It's not like we all sat down and made it up in accordance with a style sheet somewhere. You can make a project of that, if you need one."

"I'm plenty busy, thanks. Is Celeste going to be pissed I outed her meddling with you in the 2000 election?"

"It doesn't work like that. Either you'll become Celeste, and maybe wish you hadn't, or you'll stay Ren and live with your decision." A shudder went through her. I recognized it. I knew what she was going to ask next, so I answered it. "I was Chuck Purcell. Born in January of 1972, in Pittsburgh. In '94, I was driving home from work, and there was a fire, and I stopped, and I helped. Celeste recruited me. It took me a long time to decide."

"Is Chuck sorry you did?"

"Chuck is me, and I'm not sorry."

"But Chuck is gone."

"His memories aren't."

"Is there anything left?"

"I'm a Pirates fan. I never used to follow baseball."

"What about his family?"

"Mother and a sister."

"Do you keep in touch?"

"Christmas and birthday cards. That part is hard, when you change. That's the worst part."

"You could have told me."

"There was a lot I could have told you. But you said yes before I finished asking. I wasn't about to talk you out of it. Why did you say yes, by the way?"

She ate another slice of orange, then wiped her fingers. "Are you going to have one?"

I did. It brought back memories. The sugary, smooth, melting orange tasted like—

"What's funny?" she asked.

I held up the bit of peel left in my hand. "This is one of the things Celeste used as a switch on me. I didn't eat it, but something around me had a hint of the flavor, or the smell. She's very good. Why did you say yes?"

She stared out the window over my shoulder. I have a date palm back there. I never eat the dates. She said, "A couple of reasons."

"And one is?"

"At my work, we're trying to build a device that does what the Garden can: store memories remotely. It's kind of a passion project for me."

Out my front window there isn't much to see except a stone lawn and a dog fence. I haven't had a dog in years.

"And?" I said.

"And someone told me once that if I ever met a guy who shared my hidden dream, to jump at any chance he offered me."

Maybe I should get a dog. Times like this, I could use a dog to lick the juice off my fingers. And to nuzzle me and look up at me like I couldn't possibly have fucked up.

"Well?" she said.

"But they're a pain in the ass to take care of."

"What?"

"Nothing." I sighed. "Well, isn't this just grand?"

Ren

Phil had powdered sugar on his face, but I wasn't going to tell him. "I'm tired," I said.

He nodded.

"I want to go to sleep, but . . ."

"But I haven't taught you any of the tricks yet for managing your dreams."

I picked up another orange slice and put it down again.

"And the dreams are usually pretty intense the first couple of nights," he said.

"Yeah." I didn't want to relive last night if there was a way to funnel the torrent into something I could drink from rather than drown in. He was studying my face. I held his eyes.

We'd cleared a space in the flowers for the bowl of oranges, but he was framed on either side by the extravagant color and smell of bloom, stamen and leaf. His face could have been veiled too, for all I could read in it. "Can you trust me?" he said at last.

"Probably not."

He nodded.

"I have to touch you." It wasn't desire in his voice. Almost regret. "It's the only way I know how to get into your experience enough to shape it for you. It's not something I can do with language."

"Oh," I said.

"It's—" I could see, in the tiny muscle tic over his left eyebrow, what it was costing him not to drop my eyes. "It's intimate," he said.

"I'll close my eyes and think of England."

His smile only reached half his mouth. "Not like that."

"Okay."

"More."

"Stop it!" I snapped. "I said okay."

He walked into the living room like a man on the way to his own embalming. I followed too quickly and had to wait on the rug like an idiot while he found a CD and put it on. It was something low and wordless, all cello, or at least all strings. I've never been good with picking out instruments, Mom's efforts and Prokofiev's aside. But I thought it was odd, with everything he must know about me, that he wouldn't pick a music matzo ball. But maybe this was one of his.

He held his hands out in the universal symbol for "dance?" And I stepped into the hole his arms made, my right palm in his left, my left on his shoulder. He closed long, cool fingers over mine and rested his right hand lightly on my waist. Our feet made a slow, shuffling orbit around the empty space between our bodies, and for a long time, we just danced. My mind spun down, stopped grappling with what I'd heard and said, and finally quit listening to my thoughts. He brought the crown of his head to mine and rested it there, but none of the tension left the shoulder under my hand. He turned his head, and pressed his temple against mine, the way he'd done after he'd kissed Celeste on my mouth.

Wanting to articulate the magic of what I felt, and to share its power with the man who held me, I said, "Oh."

He pulled me against him.

"Close your eyes," he whispered.

The music held my feet and kept their little steps stepping, but everything that wasn't my body was soaring. My knees wove between Phil's. Our bellies, and his hips and mine floated over our feet and knees like boats in deep currents. My breasts against him made two polestars of white light. Our temples touched; we danced. And our dancing didn't matter. Our bodies were extraneous. Symbolic.

"Oh," I said again.

"Get to this place first, and the dreams slide through you," he said.

"Oh," I said.

"Can you tell me what you see?"

"Zombies," I said.

"No, love. That was just a game you were playing. Look."

I wanted him to call me "love," again, but there were definitely zombies lurching my way. They shambled and shed bits of themselves in obliging conformity to type, with one flagrant violation. "They've got guns," I mumbled.

"Ren," Phil's voice was calm, but louder. "Keep dancing with me."

"They're going to shoot me," I said.

"No one is going to shoot you."

But all I could feel of my body against Phil's was my heart banging its way toward my teeth. "She's going to shoot me, and you can't reason with her because she thinks brains are food."

"You're sticking bits of different memories together, Ren. None of this is real."

But it was real and what was stuck together were bits of rotting flesh. Celeste's body decomposing.

Phil's hands were hard on my back and my fingers. "Ren!"

The zombie raised its rifle to its shoulder and sighted down the barrel at me. It closed one eye, cocked the hammer and its eyebrow—Phil's one emotional eyebrow. I stepped back from his arms into the blank white of someplace inside my head.

"You wanted Celeste back," I said. I couldn't see Phil, but I could feel him there, and all the emptiness touching me without him. "You doubled up on Celeste to make sure I'd step aside for her. With her genes and all the other stuff you matched, you knew her personality could take over mine."

"I warned you that could happen," he said.

"Not could," I said. "Would. You knew it would. And you were okay with that. You wanted that."

"Ren."

"Ren knows you wanted her to die."

"Celeste. I warned her, Celeste. You didn't tell Chuck much more. I had no way of knowing she'd agree so quickly."

"She's not me."

"Not yet."

"She won't be. Here's a riddle for you, dear Mendel. Without generations to study or pea pods to plant, how can you still know a trait's not heritable?"

"Celeste—"

"When that trait itself would prevent genetic transmission, that's how. Renee didn't inherit martyrdom from me."

The whiteness went from rage-hot to bitter. I was shivering too hard to dance.

I opened my eyes. "Celeste killed herself," I said, and all I could feel were Phil's arms, like the metal hoops around a barrel.

"Will I remember this?" I asked him. "Can you make it so I won't remember?"

"I can't."

"What I do next, who I am next depends on what I remember."

"Always. But who I am also depends on what you remember."

"Everything you remembered about Celeste wasn't enough to change who she was."

"No."

"Phil?"

"Yeah?"

"Does hurting this much feel just like having her here?"

"I can barely tell the difference," he said, but his hands were lighter, and our feet were moving again. "Can you sleep now?"

"I think I already am."

FIVE

What Else Can I Get You?

Phil

Just like when I've spiked someone, I don't know if I literally or figuratively carried her to the bed, but when I left her there, my arms were shaking. That isn't conclusive, because the rest of me was shaking too. I was tired, and I was hungry, and I ached in places that weren't even metaphorical. But I wasn't going to rest. Not yet. There were used glasses and an empty beer bottle on the side table, and some dirty dishes next to the sink; I'd have liked a chance to redd up the place, flowers aside. But I wasn't going to do that either.

I sat down in my chair, closed my eyes, and smelled cherry blossoms and tasted chive. I opened my virtual eyes and I was in my villa, kicking aside dusty old memories in the shape of fruit and urns, candlesticks and furniture. I went out back, following a well-worn path. I'd once asked Ray why it is that paths showed up in our imaginations, and he suggested something about neural pathways in our brains that didn't sound very convincing. It didn't matter; I went past the orchard and out the broken wooden gate, leaving it swinging loudly behind me.

Jesus Christ, Celeste.

Four steps along the path brought me to the western orchard of my neighbor. There was a hole in the ground where once there'd been a bust of Juno until I'd pulled it up, fashioned it into a spike, set it on fire, and stuck it into Ren's head. What I was looking for should be right next to it, because time flows linearly.

Here's the thing: Anything in the Garden can be found by locating it along three of four axis lines. Ray calls them X, Y, Z and alpha. Most of the rest of us call them by more useful names: Who, Where, When and Why. Any three will do, in theory. In practice, that means knowing who seeded it, where the person who seeded it was, and when it was seeded, leaving Why undefined.

One axis must always be undefined, like a sort of psychic Heisenberg uncertainty principle, and that one is always Why. Why?

Because Why skips around a lot, and we pretty much ignore it. I mean, who knows why something happened? We either impose meaning on an event, or just shrug our shoulders. Why was the Civil War fought? To break the power of the Southern slaveholders so Eastern manufacturers could prosper? To preserve the Union? To defend the Southern homeland against invaders? To free slaves? To create a strong central government? Because a lot of pretty girls batted their eyelashes and convinced a lot of boys to go be heroes? To make a lot of national parks? When you get to a Why you don't have an objective answer, so the Why, what Ray calls the alpha axis, floats around and you locate a memory using the other three.

In practice, if you're Ray, you interpret these as numbers along the various axes and you simply concentrate on the place those numbers identify. For most of us, they're locations, and we follow paths in the imaginary world we've created to interpret the Garden until the object appears. When I seed a memory, perhaps it's a marble bust of Cicero on a pedestal in my atrium; but when Jimmy wants to graze it, he'll climb stairs to the turret of a medieval castle and find a bottle of wine sitting on a table, which he'll drink; to Irina it's an actual garden, and maybe she'll see a bright red rose which she'll sniff, whereas perhaps Matt sees a multicolored stone in a rock garden and he'll study its colors. It's all the same memory, but how we reach it depends on us. And, however you say it, the memory is found by locating the Who, the Where, and the When, leaving the Why undefined and variable.

Once a memory has been seeded, except for stubs, it's there forever. You can change the shape so it's less obtrusive or your memory would get so cluttered you couldn't find anything, but you can't get rid of it, and you can't move it without a deliberate act of will.

With me so far?

Next to where the bust of Juno had been was a ripe, red pomegranate. I knew that pomegranate; it contained Celeste's penultimate memory, in which she reported on a just-completed piece of insignificant meddlework and spoke of going to see the "grandbratties."

Between the pomegranate and the hole was nothing.

Celeste's last memory was gone.

I stood there looking at where her last memory should have been, appearing to me as a *kithara,* and I knew what had happened. You can't get rid of a memory once it's been seeded. And there's only one way it can move.

Who, Where, When and Why.

If the Why becomes known, one of the others becomes undefined.

I returned to the real world, turned off my cell phone, opened my laptop, and addressed an email to the group.

Ren

Phil was sleeping in his chair, the computer on his lap still open, mirroring his mouth in silent duet. For almost a day, I'd been certain Celeste was trying to assert her personality over mine, to swallow me up, or kill me, but it'd turned out to be Phil who was gunning for me. I considered hating him, but I went to the bathroom instead.

I turned the shower on and studied his shelf of tiny toiletries, letting the anger climb up my legs. I wanted my own goddamn shampoo. My hair is thin, and "rich conditioning formula" and "extra moisturizing" and "volumizing" all translate to limp and droopy on me. I wanted my shampoo and my spiky gel and my makeup and my fucking phone charger. I slammed the shower dial off, ran my fingers through my sad hair and crept back past Phil, still pinned to his chair like a butterfly.

I got my shoes and found his car keys, and went back to look at him again, a little embarrassed I wasn't handling this better. Still, if he knew me so well, he should have known that running away isn't out of my idiom. Broken mantel clocks stay broken, after all, no matter how much you didn't mean to drop them, and your rage at that injustice does nothing for your terror of the holy hell you know you're going to catch.

It wasn't a long-term plan, but a room in a hotel that wasn't The Palms under a name that wasn't Renee Mathers felt closer to the back of Nana's closet than anything else and would give me time to think. But not without my own damn shampoo.

I watched Phil a minute to make sure he was breathing. We both had reasons we'd rather not confess for why we had needed to pick up a clock and shake it. He'd risked maybe more than I had to bring Celeste back. He'd risked me, and yeah, I was still angry about it. But not so angry that I didn't want to know why. Was it possible his reason and my most secret one were the same? Did he just want her love? I closed his laptop and brought a cotton blanket in from the bed to cover him. I touched one finger to his wild eyebrow, and it twitched. I brought my lips to the naked space between it and his hair, and kissed him, lightly, on the temple. But I didn't leave a note.

Then again, neither had Celeste.

Phil

There are things about spending too much time in the Garden. One is that the real world takes a bit to adjust to, what with the sensory impressions being less vivid and not as compelling. Another is that it can be frustrating when the world doesn't behave the way you want it to, and you can't just make things appear, or change their shape, or move miles with a single step; you have to watch yourself, or you'll be spending all of your time grinding your teeth, scowling at strangers, and imagining satisfying but nonproductive meddlework. Still another is that you eat too much and sleep too much.

It took a few minutes after I woke up to realize that Ren had bolted, and another few to realize she'd done so in my car. I made coffee and ate a bagel. Then I drank coffee and ate another bagel, this one toasted; I put cream cheese on it.

It was five in the afternoon, and I'd slept about twenty hours in the last day and a half. Not so good. I took a shower, standing under it for a lot longer than you're supposed to when you live in the desert. I had some more coffee when I got out, after which I took a deep breath and checked the forums.

It was what I'd expected: panic in the ranks. People who hadn't said a word in ten years were suddenly chiming in, scared and disoriented. The most useful post was from Ray. He said he'd done a graze on a few random memories, and so far as he could tell, the Garden was intact. He pointed out that this had happened a few times before, and we'd dealt with it; he'd be pulling in those memories to figure out the next step. Meantime, he doubted panic would be all that helpful and suggested that perhaps Salt could meet in person after we knew more.

However much Ray and I have irritated each other—and we've done so a lot—at times like this there is no comfort like having a scientific mind at work on the problem.

I poured another cup of coffee, then turned on my cell phone and checked my voice mail. I had fourteen messages, which was fewer than I'd been afraid of. I listened to them all. One was from the dentist's office reminding me that I was due for a checkup. Twelve were from members of the group, either panicking or telling me I shouldn't. The last was from Irina, and it just said, "Call me."

I was deciding whether to do so when she walked through the door. She stared at me and said, "I didn't think you were home."

"I assumed that when you barged in."

"Nice bathrobe. Where's your car?"

"Ren has it."

"Where is Ren?"

"Either back in Phoenix, or in a hotel room in town under an assumed name."

"She bolted?"

I nodded.

"Any more coffee?"

I nodded again.

Irina helped herself, sat down on the stool next to me, and said, "You should have seen this coming."

"Good to see you, too, Irina. How's the sugar spoon?"

"Don't be glib. We have a problem here."

"Weren't you seeing someone last year? How did that work out?"

"Stop it, Phil. We need to decide what to do."

"I love your hair this way."

"Cartophilus!"

I put my coffee cup down. "What the fuck do you want from me, Iri?"

"Christ Jesus, Phil. Ren's walking around with the brand-new memories of a suicide, and she bolted. You don't think we need to find her?"

"No."

"Why?"

"Because she's doing what she needs to do. And I'm not going to get in her way. I owe her that much at least."

"I do not," said Irina carefully, "give a good goddamn what you owe her. I'm worried about what it is she thinks she needs to do. Have you any clue what that might be?"

"Nope," I said, and drank more coffee.

"So you're just going to sit here?"

"Actually," I said, "I was thinking about playing some poker."

Irina used several expressions I hadn't heard in years, not all of them in English. I waited it out. When she'd run down, I said, "You don't think Ren can take care of herself?"

"Right now? With all this going on? I don't think any of us can take care of ourselves. This is not the time to let a new Second go off on her own."

I shrugged. "I think it's exactly the time. Let her settle, let her deal with some of—"

"Have you spoken with Ramon?"

"No. Why?"

"Do you know what it means that we can't find Celeste's last memory?"

"In general, it means—"

"Specifically. The ramifications. For Ren and for all of us."

"Not entirely," I said. "So?"

"So what is happening in Ren's head, Phil?"

"I imagine it's the usual integration—"

"No. It's not usual when you've just gotten the memories of a suicide. Eleanor and Gaston aside, we don't do that often. And to have Celeste's last memory go missing in the Garden—what's it doing to her?"

I exhaled. "Okay. Point. I'll call her."

She nodded. I pushed Ren's number and it went right to voice mail. I should have stopped to figure out what sort of message to leave, but I never think of that. I said, "It's Phil. Celeste's last memory has gone missing in the Garden. We're a bit worried about what her memories will be doing to your head. I understand your desire to have some time to think this through, but I'd appreciate a call, just for reassurance."

I disconnected. "Satisfied?"

"Not remotely. But it's a start."

"What do you want to do?"

"Give her twelve hours. If we don't hear from her, we find her."

"All right," I said. "But I'm sure she's fine."

Ren

I left the valet tag for Phil at the hostess stand of the 24/7 Café at The Palms. She understood completely. So easy to leave with your boyfriend's ticket in your bag by mistake. If he came by, she'd be sure to explain for me. I crept like a spy down the hall to my own room, rifled through it for the essentials, and left again without letting the door make a noise and without turning on the lights. If Irina was listening at our shared door, she wouldn't have heard a thing. The doorman just nodded when I asked for "the hotel with the roller coaster" and told the cabbie to drive me to New York, New York, Las Vegas without a hint of irony. I guess he's had stranger instructions.

In an authentic New York touch, the guy behind the front desk was cute enough to be an out-of-work actor. I gave him an extra fifteen bucks for a room with a carefully enunciated "beautiful city view," and didn't ask which city. I told him my husband would be arriving soon with our bags, and he acted like he believed me. Someone should cast that guy.

Although all I wanted was to get to my room, close the curtains, and give some serious thought to my ridiculous situation, I was too hungry to concentrate on anything else. But the groutless cobblestones and indoor sidewalk seating were more compressed and wrong in time and locale than I could handle. I walked into the hotel shop and picked up a Twix and Mountain Dew, but I put them back; calm costs more than courage, and you can't buy a can of perspective anywhere.

"Welcome to Nine Fine Irishmen. Will you be dining alone this evening?" Phil owed me more than Liam, but Liam was buying.

I nodded and the hostess led me upstairs, deposited me with a menu, a wine list and the information that the bartender, Elise, would take care of me. I knew she couldn't, but I said, "Thanks," and climbed onto a barstool.

"What can I get you?" Elise was almost my height, but slimmer.

Younger too, with sweet, black bangs that almost covered her darkly lined eyebrows.

"I'm starving and exhausted," I told her. "I want whatever you can bring me quickly that isn't deep fried or made out of lettuce."

"Salmon all right?"

"Perfect."

"You got it," she said, and disappeared around the side of the bar. I'd never been particularly attracted to women before, but there was something in her shoulders and back that felt important, an urgency in her hands, even just pouring my water, and something in the set of her jaw that added a new twist of nervous excitement to my strange stew of exhaustion and anxiety.

Elise pushed the water across the muted wood bar to me. "Want anything else to drink?" she asked.

"I'd take a glass of wine, if you'll have one with me," I said.

"I don't do chicks."

"Neither do I."

She crossed her arms over her chest, and I couldn't help noticing what it did for her figure, but I also knew that wasn't the point. Everything about her—her purple-white skin and the cherry bomb lipstick that didn't match it, her small, natural breasts and the bra doing unnatural things to them—every detail of her was brilliant and real, held in a hyperfocus that extended just past her body, but no farther.

"You just looked like you could use one was all," I explained.

We can see when people's lives are at a pivot; Phil had told me: shoulders, hands and jaw. He hadn't said it was so exciting.

"Hey, Elise!" A tiny blonde waitress stood on tiptoe at the server's end of the bar. "Can I get a little dish of cherries for this kid at table nine?"

Elise turned away from me without a word.

"Hiya!" the waitress chirruped. "My name's Candy."

I could have guessed that.

"I'm Ren," I said trying not to watch Elise get the garnish. The focus wasn't physical, but it wasn't only mental either. I pointed my eyes at Candy.

"You look bored," she said, with an overplayed moue on her bubble-pink lips. Elise would do better with that shade of lipstick.

"Just tired," I said. "Business travel sucks."

"But you get all your food for free, don't you?" she said. "We just get sodas."

Elise put a little glass bowl of the lurid cherries on Candy's tray. Candy blew her a kiss and trotted off into the warren of snugs and cubbies. Elise rolled her eyes and got down two wineglasses.

"You here on business?" she asked as she poured.

"Yeah, but I'm thinking about moving here," I lied.

"God." She pushed a glass towards me and drank from her own. "Man or gig?"

"What?"

"Two reasons women move to Vegas: they're following a man, or they're chasing the showbiz dream."

"Which brought you?"

"Both," she said with a snort. "I was a ballet dancer in love with a drummer. We figured if I could just lower myself to showgirl, he'd join the band and we could work together all night." She drained her glass and repoured.

"What happened?"

"We couldn't get work."

"Either of you?"

"He's on the light crew for *Zumanity*."

Candy bounced back into the bar carrying a plate almost wider than her shoulders. She delivered it to me at the tall bar, still managing to lean over it enough to serve up two eyefuls of double Ds that looked younger than my salmon. "What are you girls getting all serious about?"

I looked at her with my mouth full of fish and widened my eyes in the classic "who me?" face. She giggled and marched back to the dining room.

A drink order came in on Elise's machine, and I watched her make the cocktails. "Ballet doesn't translate out here?" I asked.

"God," she said. "It's not just that. There are so many girls at every audition that they hire by how the costumes fit. Tailor the dancer to the outfits, not the other way around. Makes you pretty damn interchangeable. I walked away from a *corps de ballet* position with San Francisco Ballet. Now I'd kill for a spot on the back line. But I'm all wrong. Nobody wants a dark-haired girl who isn't ethnic, and I don't have the tits."

"But you're thinking about getting them?"

"I don't know." Her hands cupped her breasts, squeezed them together, something between disgust and despair on her face.

"Oh yikes! Sorry!" Candy made a production of stealth-loading the drinks Elise had made onto her tray. "Looks like you ladies are doing a fine job entertaining yourselves!"

Elise watched Candy bop back out with the loaded tray. "I kinda hate her," she said.

"She's damn perky," I agreed.

"I think she's fucking my boyfriend."

"Oh, hell," I said. "That slut."

Elise grinned and put her elbows on the bar. "Oh my God, you have no idea. The other night we had this eight-top in here, and the one guy kept dropping his bread roll. He'd drop it and she'd get down on her hands and knees and crawl after it."

"No," I said. "I meant your boyfriend. What a slut."

Elise stood up and stepped back. Her drink order machine spit out another piece of paper, and I went back to my salmon.

If I had time to gather the switches, if I had known any of the words or smells, or even her boyfriend's name, I could have done more. I could have taken the words she was trying on like costumes, words like "dancer" and "failure" and "fidelity" and meddled with what they meant. But everything I remembered about Celeste's early days as Nelle's Second, and Nelle's as Rita's, and Rita's as Fred's, all the way back to Betsy reminded me of how much I didn't know yet. I hadn't even been to the Garden.

I barely noticed Elise carrying the new drinks by. "What the fuck?" she said.

"I'm sorry."

She repeated the trip with two more filled glasses.

"Okay, seriously. What the fuck?"

I met her eyes. I shouldn't have touched this. I wasn't ready. I was exhausted, and I missed Phil more than I should, but all I could hear was Celeste.

"Someone called me that," I said. "Once."

"Were you fucking her guy?"

"No," I said. "I haven't."

"Well?"

"But I have still done things I'm not proud of."

"Yeah, me too," Elise said, the fight ebbing out of her.

"I've been things I only thought I wanted to be."

Elise looked at me. She nodded.

"I don't want to be a waitress," Candy whispered.

Elise held my eyes for a single second before we both turned to stare at the weeping waitress. "This isn't what I want to be at all," she said. "I want to be a singer. Or a dancer. I want to go on auditions. And have secret dreams like you."

"Candy?" Elise said.

"And I want to have a boyfriend who loves me and hangs out where I work just to get to see me an extra bit and never even notices other girls."

Elise stopped trying to talk.

"What were you doing when you were Candy's age?" I asked her.

"How old are you?" Elise asked.

"Seventeen," Candy said.

"Living with my mom and taking ballet."

"Okay." Candy sniffed back the tears and shook her ponytail. "Daddy said he'd buy me a ticket from anywhere, whenever I wanted. I'm going to call them and ask to come home."

"You're not from here?" Elise put her wineglass down.

"Your parents let you move to Vegas alone?" I asked.

Candy sniffled. "They don't know where I am. I ran away."

Elise gave a low whistle. "I never would have come out here on my own."

"Okay. I won't ever come to Vegas alone."

"And I finished high school," Elise said.

"I'll finish high school."

"And I always practiced safe sex."

"I'll always do safe sex."

"And I never fu—" I shook my head at Elise and she cut herself off. "Good luck, sweetheart," she said.

"I love you," Candy said. Then she blew her nose on a cocktail napkin and went back to work.

"Well, there are roles and models, and role models, I guess," Elise said with a shrug.

"Guess so," I said.

"I feel like I just made an audition. Role of a lifetime."

"Congratulations," I said, and gave her my corporate MasterCard.

Elise didn't charge me for the wine, and when she brought the ticket back, she'd added her phone number to it. "Just in case you do move out here," she said. "I owe you."

I told her she didn't, but I pocketed her number. I took the elevator to my room missing Phil like he'd been stolen from me. I showered with my own shampoo, but it wasn't the miracle I remembered, and wrapped myself—hair and body—in fluffy hotel towels. Sitting, still damp on the edge of the big, empty bed, I changed the outgoing message on my cell phone. "Hi," I said into the little microphone. "This is Ren. Leave a message." Then, choosing my words carefully I added, "Bonus memo to that special guy in my life, I'll plan to meet you at the 24/7 Café in The Palms tomorrow at eleven unless I hear otherwise from you."

Both Liam and Phil would think I was talking to them. I wondered which one I'd see.

Phil

Some memories you don't have to graze for, they're just there. It was, I don't know, about 1956 I think. Celeste and I were living in Chicago, where I'd tapped into a lot of private games. We had an apartment the size of a very small apartment. We took turns cooking, and she complained when I used olive oil instead of butter.

I was stretched out on the couch, feet up, the *Chicago Sun-Times* over my face.

"With all the advances in photography and film, with air travel now commonplace and telephone service for even the hillbillies of West Virginia, could not Irina have chosen an even moderately attractive girl to spike me into? I hate this hair more than I have words for. Twenty years ago, we were bobbing our hair and pinning it with papers. Now it's tongs or permanent waves. And mine simply will not take a curl. Are you even listening?"

I removed the paper, sat up, and looked at her.

"And glasses! Look at me! I'm hideous."

Bréch, our three-year-old Samoyed, lifted his head, thumped his tail once, and put his head back down. I'd have liked to do the same.

"Let me," I said, "take this in reverse order. In the second place, you are not hideous. You are delightfully attractive. Witness the, ah, ardor of, well, pretty much every night. But in the first place, is that really what you think Irina should have looked for in a recruit? No, no; can't have *that* genius with the heart of gold, her hair is too straight."

"Your ardor has nothing to do with me, Don Juan. And yes, I think Irina could have looked harder for my recruit. She's always been selfish, and I don't think she's ever liked me. I know coeds aren't plentiful, and yes, an Incrementalist must be intelligent before all else, but Pretty has a power Smart does not. Could I not gather switches more quickly by batting my lashes than grubbing through microfilm? I can't very well do the kind of work I need to for the organization if I'm only hireable at the back of the bank. I'm not even pretty enough to be a teller!"

I made myself stop grinding my teeth, because Celeste always noticed that. I said, "My ardor has everything to do with you. And—" I stopped. "You know what, Celeste? You've hit on something. Why is it so bloody important to be pretty, with such a narrow definition of pretty? That's something we could work on. Plant a few ideas here and there. Meddle with some fashion magazine editors. Hollywood. Pretty is nothing, and needing pretty is shallow. We could work with that. And quit glaring, you are pretty. Very."

"You're talking out both sides of your mouth, dear Janus. You offer your ardor as proof of my beauty, then argue beauty doesn't matter to you. But I watch you, and your eyes don't follow the ugly girls at the club."

"No argument. That's exactly my point. Yes, beauty matters to me. And, what's more, what I find beautiful changes each time I get a new Second. How much it matters changes, and exactly what appeals to me. But why should it matter so much? Sure, some of it is biology. But not all of it. Some of it is social. We should find out how much is which, and see what we can do about it. I'll write to Ray."

"He can do nothing for my flat, Irish hair."

"Your hair is adorable. So are your eyes. And I like your chin. Also, a particularly graceful neck. Shall I keep moving down?"

"You just like women. And I'm the only one you can screw."

I nodded, finally realizing that I was never winning this one. "That," I said, "is something else we should work on."

She shook her head, and gave me one of those smiles of hers—not dazzling, not even necessarily expressing happiness—a quirk of her mouth and glint of her eye that went right through me. Whatever Second she inhabits, Celeste has that same smile. When she was Fred, she, or rather, he, still had it, and that made me crazy. What is it in our coding that makes certain smiles hit us like that? Anyway, she didn't say anything, but a little later we went to bed, still annoyed with each other, and had crazy mad sex.

I've been Phil for about two thousand years. Celeste has been Celeste for about four hundred. You get to know someone pretty well in that time. I wanted to talk to her.

I stared at the phone and hoped Ren would call me back.

Ren

I brushed my teeth and climbed into bed. Phil had left a voice mail, but I was falling asleep as I listened. It was important. But I'd never heard of anyone named Celeste, so I turned off the ringer, plugged my phone in to charge and let sleep swallow me whole.

SIX

You've Been Meddled With

Phil

Irina filled me in on her latest romantic meltdown, which could be distilled to the usual: Either we date someone who isn't in the group, which is impossible, or we date someone who is, which is catastrophic. Irina goes for the former, I go for the latter. She politely asked about poker, to which I politely answered in generalities; I politely asked about her sugar spoon, clerking in Dade County, to which she also politely answered in generalities.

We continued being polite for a couple of hours, then Irina said she was going to graze for a while. I was just as glad. I turned on the TV and managed to catch forty-five minutes of the Fourth of July *Shadow Unit* marathon. After that, I was watching the news when Irina said, "Phil."

I clicked off the television. She was looking pale and tired. "Welcome back," I said. "Learn anything?"

"How long was I gone?"

"An hour or so."

"Have you heard from Ren?"

"No."

"Call her again," was the answer.

"Why? She either got my message, or she—"

"Call her every two hours until it's time to find her. Or I will."

It was easier to make the call than to argue, so I did, and got her new message. I hung up.

"What is it?" said Irina.

"She didn't answer. I got her voice mail."

"What about it?"

"Give me a minute to decide if I want to lie to you, and come up with a good one if I do."

"Jesus Christ, Phil. I can just call her myself."

"She left a message saying she'd meet me at breakfast."

"So? Why would you not want to tell me?"

"I don't know. I suppose wanting you the hell out of my life right now is part of it."

"Yeah, I'm meddling. Like we do."

"Not, usually, with each other."

"I know," she said, giving me a slow nod. "We're exempt."

"Generally."

"But you've been meddled with, and you don't like it."

"Am I supposed to? When we meddle, we're trying to do good, and it's usually the only way to accomplish it. Can you convince me that applies in this case?"

"No, Phil. I can't, Phil. I'm pretty goddamned sure it doesn't, Phil."

"So, why are you doing it?"

"Oh, sorry. I wasn't talking about me being here. I'm talking about what Celeste did."

I stared at her. "You know about that? I haven't seeded it yet."

"Wait. You know about it? Then why—" She broke off. She looked at me for a moment, then stood up and walked over to the refrigerator. She opened it, and a tiny part of me was surprised that it was opening the wrong way, or the right way. She pulled out a bottle of Big Sky IPA. She opened it with the magnetized opener on the door of the refrigerator. She carefully threw away the cap, came back, sat down, and drank some.

"Help yourself to a beer," I said.

"Phil, we may have . . . okay. What meddlework are you talking about that Celeste did?"

"Aftermath of the 2000 elections. I was with Oskar on that. I was ready to go to Florida, get some people to come clean, and blow the whole thing open. She stopped me. I just found out about it yesterday; she meddled."

"I see," said Irina quietly. "I hadn't known about that."

Irina had been a *maroon* in Haiti in 1754 and been stubbed by having her head crushed during a slave revolt. She had thought the revolt was a mistake, and her last seed, at that time, had been about loyalty, and the need to be with those you loved even when they were doing the wrong thing. The look on her face while she seeded that must have been much like the look on her face now.

"That isn't what I'm talking about, Phil."

"Irina," I said, "you have my complete and undivided attention."

She took another sip of beer. "This is good," she remarked. "Microbrew?"

"From Montana," I said.

She nodded and cleared her throat.

"I'll tell you what set off the alarms in my head," she said. "How long have we known each other?"

"About seven hundred years, give or take."

"What you did to that girl, to Ren—"

"What did I do to her?"

"For Chrissakes, Phil! You put Celeste into someone with close genetic ties to herself, and you let Ren take Celeste's stub without a full explanation, and you, shit, you did everything it's possible to do to arrange things so Ren would be wiped out and replaced, and you concealed what you were doing."

"I—"

"Shut up. That's what you did. The point is, it isn't like you."

"I—"

"However," she said, staring hard at me, "it is very, very much like Celeste."

I stared back at her.

It sank in. And sank. And kept sinking. Ramifications, implications, consequences. They all just tumbled home. I finally got it.

For the first time in more than five hundred years, I put my head in my hands and sobbed.

Ren

I was sinking. And sinking. I should have anchored myself in the brilliant empty place Phil showed me when we danced, but I was too tired, and maybe a little drunk. Elise and I hadn't left much in that bottle. I kept sinking. I let all the spaces between things elongate—more air between my muscles' strings, more empty under my skin. I was sinking into sleep, or it was rising up around me. I was floating in it. Like flying.

I wanted to fly.

I drifted, sailing over timeless sweeps of memory. Over Matsu's garden. Ramon's grid. Phil's villa, with its low Roman wall and its prehistoric, terrifying date palm.

His sharp-fronded right-in-front-of-me date palm.

I was sitting in Phil's date palm, stuck too high off the ground on a trunk made of scales, in yards and yards of lilac muslin, my legs spread embarrassingly wide for balance on the foreshortened flat part of a long and very spiky frond.

I remembered that tree from his Las Vegas yard. And I remembered this dress, its well-made, delicate layers of cloth, and the freedom of a dancing gown worn uncorsetted again at last. It was *trés Neo-Grec*, draped after what the dressmakers said was the classic style.

I never told them otherwise; the high waist and low cut were too flattering. But really all wrong for trees.

A man stood under me, looking up my skirts. I yanked the muslin around to cover my thighs, and tore it.

"My dear lady, you have treed yourself," he said. "Will you come down?" His blond hair was cropped close, and his fingers were long and slender—more delicate than mine. "Aristocratic" could be the only word for those pale hands, yet this was Oskar. I was certain of it. Whoever had chosen this Second for him had been teasing just a little, putting his stub into an aesthete's body. He wore a peasant's coarse flax and a red neckerchief anyway.

"Thank you, no. My dog will come," I told him. Oskar had been a woman during *La Révolution*, but had not survived to wear the lovely dresses after. Had he been female since? Not during the buttoned-up days when the high waists dropped again and the corsets came back with a vengeance. But since when did I give so much thought to clothes?

"Aren't you afraid of falling?" he asked.

"No. Not afraid of falling or heights. I'm quite happy up here. As soon as I untangle my dress, I'll fly off again."

"He could have killed you."

"Incrementalists can't be killed," I said. "Not really."

"But you weren't one yet, just a nemone, no memories beyond your one life's brain-bound ones."

My dress was truly Greek now, a woolen peplos. I hiked the skirts of it up and swung my legs around. "You take risks with the nemones all the time," I reminded him.

"Now you sound like Celeste."

I had to think a moment. "I don't know Celeste."

"Celeste of the Little Steps," Oskar's voice was cold. "Stuck in a tree because she won't jump."

"I'm not Celeste," I said. "And legs are broken by bold leaps."

"Progress only happens in leaps. Mutations, not evolutions. Small steps are fine, sometimes. But if you mince when circumstances call for bounds, you hold back progress. Hold it back enough and it goes in the other direction. That's why liberal policies support reaction, however much the liberal may wish otherwise."

I didn't want to fall. Someone was coming. "Lukos!" I called, but saw right away that it wasn't.

"Wolf!" I cried as it got closer, but I already knew it wasn't one of mine.

I—the primal I, the Primary I—haven't had a life without a dog since we first trapped wild wolf pups and hand-raised them. I've called them all "wolf," or the word for it in the language of the moment. Dogs have herded and pulled and hunted for me, with their strong bodies and faithful eyes, creatures well-suited to their lives, time-designed to love and serve.

The Dog of Good Design dutifully began chewing down the tree I was trapped in. "Good dog," I said, and gave Oskar a benevolent smile. He shrugged. I fed the dog a date from the tree he had gnawed down to hip level, and stepped from its leaves into the dusty courtyard. Phil had admired this merchant's villa in his life as a Roman shoemaker and had chosen it as his metaphor for memory when he took the spike.

I left Oskar in the courtyard sampling Phil's dates. The Dog of Good Design and I walked soundlessly out of the courtyard to the red-and-white jungle gym from the backyard of my childhood home. Phil stood on its summit, like king of the mountain, smelling like summer grass and pink lemonade. He jumped down between the bars and turned to face me, Persephone's fruit in his large hands. I wanted to tell him not to eat the dreams, but with his long neck and agile fingers, he looked more like an iguana.

He was no bigger than my dog now, but I knew I was falling for him. I bent down and reached a hand under a horizontal red bar to stroke his lizard's back, scaled like the date palm's trunk. But he shrugged off my finger and shook his wings free. The jungle gym folded into their fierce ribbing and stretched outward. He put a thumbless claw on my shoulder and reached out his serpentine dragon's neck to kiss my ear.

But he bit it instead, with electronic teeth that stabbed into my dream.

I reached out and slapped my alarm clock.

The Winged Iguana of Love kissed me between my eyes and flew away. The Dog of Good Design licked his balls. I guess he was made that way.

I checked my phone.

> **From:** Liam@GlyphxDesign.com
> **To:** Renee@GlyphxDesign.com
> **Subject:** Schedule for today
> Monday, July 4, 2011 8:42 am GMT - 7
>
> Hey Kiddo—
>
> Hope you managed to keep yourself entertained in Vegas over the weekend. Don't do anything I wouldn't. :-) Jorge has rescheduled for this afternoon at The Palms. We're going to finally do this thing! Obviously, I won't be there for breakfast, but have a mimosa on me!
>
> See you by 5:00.
>
> Liam

I didn't admit to myself how pleased I was that Phil had made sure it wasn't Liam meeting me at the 24/7 Café. For all the craziness in the world he'd spiked me into, I knew I was falling in love with him, and Oskar had a point after all. You can't fly if you don't jump. I showered and checked out of New York, New York, Las Vegas and got to The Palms in time to run up to my room and drop off the stuff I'd stolen out of it last night when I was running away from Phil and Irina. I was ready for both of them, if necessary, although I had to fight off a grin when I spotted him sitting alone at the table I'd first picked a week ago as the least likely to attract company.

He saw me and smiled, but stood up slowly looking tired or wary. I smiled back and saw something in his eyes collapse.

Phil

I had apparently stood up to greet her, and since I couldn't figure out why, I sat down again.

"What's wrong?" were the first words out of her mouth.

"Alphabetically or chronologically?"

"Prioritized by crisis level."

"God. That requires thinking."

Kendra arrived and asked Ren if she wanted anything. When she didn't answer, I said, "Tea." Ren looked mildly startled, then nodded. I said, "Dreams?"

When no answer came, I discovered I'd been staring into my coffee cup, so I looked up and she was staring at me; the expression on her face said she had no intention of being sidetracked, but was quite willing to wait all day if necessary. I took a deep breath and let it out slowly. Sometimes that helps. Not usually.

"Well, well, Philip. Who is this?"

Christ Jesus. "Hello, Captain. This is Ren. Ren, this is the Captain."

"How do you do?" she said like a machine. "Captain of what?"

"I've never figured that out. Why did you start calling me that?"

"It wasn't me," I said. "They were calling you that when I met you."

"Mind if I join you?"

I opened my mouth, but Ren said, "Actually, I'd love to talk to you another time. But we're kind of in the middle of something."

I looked up at the Captain and nodded. "Another time, then," he said. "Good to meet you."

He walked away and Ren said, "Did you do that on purpose?"

"No," I said. "I don't think so. I don't know how I'd—no."

"Phil, what happened?"

I was saved again by her tea arriving. If this would just continue, maybe I'd never have to say anything. That wouldn't be good, but it would be better than speaking.

Silence stretched out, and I said, "Do I have to?"

"I think you do," she said. There was something even and strong in her voice. I remembered when I was studying her, considering her as a potential recruit, I'd picked up on that strength. The sort of strength that shines brighter the more things around you fall apart. She'd shown it when she was fourteen and her grandfather had died; she'd shown it when she was seventeen and her father was arrested for fraud. She'd shown it in college when her dormmate had OD'd on Vicodin. I could use that strength just now, if only I could figure out how to tap into it.

I finally said, "It's about Celeste. All right, so she meddled with me. But it turns out that's not all. It seems—"

"Wait," she said. "First of all, who is Celeste?"

I looked up and studied her. No, she wasn't joking. I looked at her some more. She still wasn't joking.

"What?" she said.

"Are you joking?"

"About what?"

She really wasn't joking.

"Give me a moment," I said.

One plus zero is one. One plus one is two. One plus two is three. Three plus two is five. Five plus three is eight. Eight plus five is thirteen . . .

After a while, I said, "Well. And here I thought we had problems."

Ren

I suspected Phil grew his mustache to hide the dimple that lurked just under its outmost edge on his right cheek. It usually did a poor job, but today the inviting little line was fully cloaked. Nothing in his face was giving anything away. Even when he met my eyes, there was nothing I could read in his. But as he sat across the table from me, holding his coffee in both hands and not talking, a bubble of terrible sadness opened up behind my solar plexus.

"Celeste?" I prompted.

He just nodded.

"I'm sorry, I don't know her," I said. "Did you get bad news?"

Worry twitched his eyebrow. "You remember me, right, Ren? And what we've been doing the last couple of days? The Incrementalists?"

I thought about his body against mine, dancing in his little flower-filled house, and about the slow seep of memories getting deeper and deeper in me, of lives I'd lived, some with him. "I remember," I said. "Is Celeste part of that? Something I haven't remembered yet?"

"You used to remember her."

"No, I didn't."

Phil lifted his cap and smoothed his wild brown hair back against his scalp, retwisting the elastic that held it at the nape of his neck. I'd seen the same swift twist tie back periwigs and plaits. Behind him, a blond man walking past the café watched the same gesture with something like the same interest.

I refocused. "Something has happened to Celeste?" I guessed.

"She died."

"Oh, God. Phil, I'm so sorry. She was someone you cared about?"

"Very much."

"Someone you were in love with?" Even asking the question made my stomach twist.

"I thought so."

"Are you still?"

"Good morning, Ren. Phil."

"Irina." Phil kept his voice carefully scrubbed of emotion, but a scowl hovered just above his eyes. "I've got this," he said.

"Is that your objective assessment?" Irina held a little clutch purse in both hands. It was an old-fashioned patent leather thing with a giant gold clasp and reminded me of the bag my nana had called her "formal purse," although I'd always thought of it as her funeral bag, because those were the only occasions I'd ever seen her carry it.

"Go away, Irina."

She ignored him and addressed herself to me. "Has Phil told you about Celeste?"

"He was just doing that," I said.

Irina surveyed the empty half circle of seating between Phil and me.

"You should eat something," she said. "Both of you." It sounded cross, but I knew it was concern. I'd never worried about anyone's health unless Nana was angry about them.

"We've got people arriving from the airport starting at two. Since—"

"People?"

"Salt."

"Christ. Can Ray afford it?"

"Jimmy is covering everyone's airfare and hotel. I've moved to one of the condos in the other tower. Since you're our native guide, Phil, it would be nice if you would stay here to greet them."

"When does Jimmy get in?"

"Jimmy can take a taxi here like everyone else."

"Everyone else can take a cab; I'll get Jimmy."

"In what?" Irina turned an acid smile toward me.

The blond man watching Phil from the tiki-looking bar across from the café caught me watching him and stood up to leave. I knew I had no right to feel possessive of Phil, but I was glad to see that guy go. He reminded me of someone, but I couldn't think who.

"Yeah, sorry about that," I said. "It's valet parked. Ticket's at the hostess stand."

"I got it." Phil's eyes touched mine for a moment and under the mustache, the dimple flickered. When he looked back to Irina, it was gone. "Will we have full Salt by tonight?" he asked her.

"Well that's a tricky question, isn't it?" Irina seated herself by me, forcing me around the bench closer to Phil.

"Is everyone coming in for Celeste's funeral?" I guessed, and was surprised Irina's bony neck didn't splinter with how fast she turned her head to me.

"Celeste's been dead for two months. We're gathering Salt to discuss her missing final memory. Phil should have told you."

"Irina," Phil's voice was low with warning. "Ren doesn't remember Celeste. At all."

Irina's keen eyes swiveled back to me. Her mouth opened and closed, and then she said, "Confirm that."

"I have no idea who Celeste is," I said. "Is that what you want?"

"Not especially."

Phil's face looked so grim that I rubbed my temples.

"Does your head hurt?" Irina asked.

I nodded. "Didn't you say you had something for that?"

Her eyes narrowed, but she said, "Yes. I have to go up to my room; I'll be right back." She stood and the blond man who was absently feeding coins into a machine straightened as well. I was certain I knew him, I just couldn't think how. "Phil," Irina commanded, "for God's sake, bring Ren up to speed on what we know."

She swept out of the café, stopping to say something to the waitress on her way. I watched the blond man keep the visual noise of slot machines and their propitiators between himself and Irina. Given the choice, I'd do the same.

"Thanks," Phil said.

"It's okay," I said. I had wanted her gone as much as he had. I wished I knew how much overlap our reasons had.

Phil took a deep breath and let it out slowly. It seemed to help. "Celeste was an Incrementalist," he said, like reciting his sins. "She died two months ago. Her last memory, which would be of her death or just before it, is missing. That's why our leadership is gathering."

"Irina said that was tricky, why?"

"More coffee?" Kendra gave Phil a generous smile, but her eyes kept darting my direction until she overfilled his cup, and coffee spilled onto the table. "Oh, I'm sorry! I'll get a rag. Be right back."

"Salt is the five longest-enduring personalities. Celeste was one. If her personality doesn't reemerge, we're only four until we put the next oldest in the Salt."

"And?"

"And we have some worries about Oskar."

My feet went cold and my tea got heavy all at the same time. "Oskar," I said. "I think I dreamed about him last night."

Kendra returned with the rag, and by the time she'd mopped up, still smiling at Phil and peeking at me, I was trying to decide whether I wanted to hear the Kendra story or the Celeste one more.

"So you're looking for Celeste?" I asked. It seemed the more immediate concern.

Phil wouldn't look up from his coffee. He nodded.

"You're looking for her missing memory in the Garden, and you're looking for her reemerging personality. Where?"

He met my eyes.

"Oh," I said. "In me."

He nodded.

"More tea?" Kendra reached for my cup.

"No," I said. "Thank you. I think we're good for a while."

Kendra frowned. "The lady said to make sure I kept checking on you."

"Tell you what," I said. "When she comes back, you can come check again."

Kendra nodded and left.

It was my turn to take deep breaths. They must work better for Phil. "But now you're afraid that Celeste's personality may not reemerge in me. Why?"

"I was worried about that before she died. Personalities can burn out over the course of lifetimes. We start to get jaded, which makes our work seem unimportant. But that wasn't happening to Celeste—I think the only reason she came back at all was the work, to fight Oskar, and maybe, I hoped, to try again with me. I guess I just didn't realize how cynical she'd gotten."

"How do you mean?"

"She meddled with me to choose her own Second. If we had any rules, that would be against all of them. Celeste chose you."

"But I don't remember her."

"I know." Phil's hair was coming loose from its knot and he shook his head to free it. He pulled it back again. I was glad the blond guy was gone.

"Hiya, Phil." A young, slender Asian man had spotted Phil through the slatted wall across from our booth and came around it into the café. He didn't sit but stood by our table, touching its still-empty surface with the small, round tips of his fingers.

"Hello, Swede," Phil said. "This is my friend Ren."

Swede studied me for a serious moment from behind his glasses. "Hi, Ren," he said. He beamed at Phil. "Just side-games again this series?"

Phil opened his mouth, and closed it.

"I've been keeping him pretty busy," I said.

"Oh," Swede said. "I get it." He laughed a little. "I'm busy too." His dancing fingertips danced against Phil's coffee cup, spilling some. "I gotta go."

He left.

"Swede?" I asked Phil.

He shook his head. "Long story."

I mopped up the spilled coffee with a napkin, hoping to prevent the return of Kendra and her wiping rag. I was pretty sure that Phil, consciously or not, was creating this French farce of waitresses, captains and Swedes. "Why can't I remember Celeste?" I asked him.

He shrugged. "You shared a genetic link. Sometimes that does things to memory. Creates loops."

"You're afraid you may have lost her."

"If we ever really had her."

"Why did she choose me?"

"I don't know. I thought *I* had chosen you because you were strong and bright, with a history of standing up for what's true, even when it's risky. I thought you were smart enough to manage all the information we have to handle, and beautiful, because that mattered to Celeste, and I wanted us to have a shot at just loving each other."

"You and Celeste?"

"Without Oskar. He was all she talked about the last ten years. She was almost obsessed with stopping him."

"If Celeste doesn't make it back," I said, "that would be good for Oskar, right?"

Phil just nodded.

"Is Oskar blond?"

He looked up. "Are you starting to remember? God knows, if Celeste was going to remember anything, it'd be him."

"Blond and tall?" I asked.

"Yeah. And fucking good looking."

"And walking toward the lobby?"

Phil whipped around to follow my eyes. The gorgeous, tall blond man stepped out of sight.

"Were you watching for me?" Irina slid into the booth beside me and dropped a prescription bottle in my lap. "So," she said. "Are we all caught up?"

Phil

"Oskar's here," I said.

"Where?"

I shrugged.

Irina frowned. "Are you sure?"

"Someone's been watching us," said Ren.

"And he was tall, blond, and big-shouldered, so it's either Oskar or Matt, and if it was Matt we wouldn't have spotted him."

Irina turned her head and looked at Ren. "Did he seem to be making an effort not to be noticed, or was he blatantly staring?"

"He left when I caught him watching," she said.

Irina turned her hawk's eyes to me, as if daring me to brush it off. I had no intention of brushing it off. "That," I said, "is more than a little troubling."

"No shit," said Irina.

Ren was looking at me with an expression of simple trust, like, I know you'll help me figure this all out and see that it comes out all right. Something twisted up in my stomach. Ren without Celeste's memories was different from Ren with them, and different from Ren before them. I had a terrible urge to protect her, and I didn't know from what.

"There is no reason for Oskar to do that," I said. "It's out of character. Oskar is Mister In-Your-Face. Here's what's right, and here's why, and if you don't agree say so and we'll have it out. He is the last one of us I'd expect to be skulking."

Ren was still watching me.

"What's your point?" said Irina.

I shook my head. "Give me a moment, all right?"

And I smelled cherry blossoms and tasted chive, and I pulled a rope, and a length of wall slid back, revealing a circular, stone stairway descending into darkness. A torch appeared in my hand, black smoke curling up, harsh in my nose, walking downward to a hallway, opening up forever; another behind me, the stairs gone, everything extending everywhere, but Las Vegas was this way, The Palms was here, the front desk, yes, right there, there was the computer, that hanging vine, following it up until a leaf looked familiar; such a bright green. I inhaled it, then dropped the torch and let the trail of smoke carry me back.

"What did you learn?" said Irina, but I ignored her and stood up, walked out of the café. Past slot machines synthesizing the sound of dropping coins, and shouting from the craps table. You can always find the craps table with your eyes closed. There was the bank of elevators.

I got off on the fifth floor, turned right, walked down the hall past six rooms, stopped, knocked on the door. It opened at once, and Oskar said, "Shit. I suck at that clandestine bullshit, don't I? Come on in, then."

"You could come down and meet Ren and say hello to Irina."

He hesitated. "Irina," he said. "We aren't getting along so well."

"Oskar, who have you gotten along well with in the last century and a half?"

"Vivian."

"I rest my case."

"All right," he said. He stepped inside long enough to grab his suit jacket.

"Oskar, do you have any idea how hot it is outside?"

"Yeah," he said, and put it on.

About then, my cell phone rang. We shut the door and started walking as I dug for it. It was Irina, of course. I showed Oskar the caller ID. He said, "What, you forgot to tell her where you were going?"

"I didn't forget," I said, and clicked Answer.

"Hello, Irina."

"Phil, where did you—"

"Would you mind getting the check, love? Meet us at the valet."

"Us? Who . . . Oskar?"

"I figured to take us to my place. There are such lovely flowers there, seems like the right place for a chat."

She disconnected without even saying good-bye.

"Flowers?" said Oskar.

I shook my head and got into the elevator.

Ren

"Okay," I told Irina when she announced we were going to Phil's. "But I have to be back here by five. I have a meeting."

She twisted her mouth into a shape that suggested both incredulity and disdain. I wondered how long you have to live behind a face to make it do that.

"My boss is flying in today," I said. "And I'd appreciate it if none of you would mess with that."

"None of *us,*" she corrected me.

"Whatever. My point is, I like my job. I put a lot of energy into finding work doing something I like, and I want to actually get to do it. Today."

"Of course, dearie," she said.

Phil and Oskar were waiting for us by the valet stand. Phil looked tired and a little put out. Oskar looked wary and delicious.

Irina installed herself in the front seat of Phil's Prius, so I got in the back, and when Oskar didn't go around to the other side, I scooted across to make room for him. He smelled nice, but there's no way he could have been comfortable folded up like that. He didn't even try with the seat belt.

Phil swung out of the parking lot and almost ran the red light.

No one spoke. Irina was texting with speed and apparent spleen. Phil launched a sustained but silent assault on the structural integrity of his steering column, and Oskar turned to me with surprising grace for a guy twice as big as the space he occupied. "So," he said, "Ren."

"Yeah."

"How very nice to meet you." He was wearing the kind of seriousness you put on for children whose vocabulary exceeds their pronunciation.

"Were you expecting someone else?" I snapped.

"I was," he said, in the same careful voice.

"Well, sorry to disappoint."

"No, not at all." He leaned back into the seat and, to the extent his size would allow, appeared to relax and enjoy the view.

"Why are you here, Oskar?" Phil asked.

"I believe you invited me."

"I mean in Las Vegas. And don't say poker."

"I read your email. I expected Salt would be gathering, and I wanted to be close at hand. In case I was needed. Looks like I am. Without me, you wouldn't have five."

"We have five with Ren."

"Ren's not in the Salt."

Phil braked hard enough to dislodge Oskar. "We're here," he said. "Welcome to my humble home."

SEVEN

In the Barren Sucking Wasteland

Phil

For some reason, I had expected the flowers to be gone, but of course they were still there. If Irina's whole point had been to keep me irritated, it worked. But I'd have loved to know why. I was not, however, going to give her the satisfaction of asking.

I got Irina a Pernod, and got a couple of Big Sky IPAs for Oskar and me. "Sorry, Ren," I said. "Still no tea."

She looked at me like she was waiting for an explanation of what tea was. When it went on too long, I got her an ice water. Oskar, of course, had taken my chair, so I sat on the couch. Ren sat down next to me, staring straight ahead. Irina was going about the room smelling her flowers and eventually seated herself in the armchair next to Oskar. I wondered if I'd need something more than the little coffee table to keep them separated.

"So," she said.

"So," I said. "I've been thinking. How hard a piece of meddlework would it be to get rid of interleague play?"

"Sorry?" said Irina.

"Baseball," said Oskar, not rising to the bait by gesture or even tone.

"Oh," said Irina. "You'd think someone surrounded by flowers would be more inclined to cooperate."

Oskar said, "No one enjoys having his environment arranged for him."

"Or her," corrected Irina.

"In English," began Oskar, "the non-sex-specific pronoun takes the form . . ." but I didn't hear the rest, because as soon as Irina had spoken, I'd bolted to the kitchen and was digging among my pots. I found the right one, and bits of conversation drifted back to me, but not enough to make out details. It took me five minutes to make the popcorn, which was a loud enough process that I heard nothing. When it was done, I poured it into a bowl, added butter and salt, and came back into the living room.

"Are you suggesting," Irina was saying, "that the words we use have no effect on how we think?"

"No, I'm saying they have less of an effect than a lot of people believe. That other things have a much more profound effect."

"That doesn't mean—"

"Things like unequal pay. Like effective servitude in marriage. Like forced prostitution. Deal with the real problems, and language will take care of itself."

I passed Ren the popcorn.

"Language changes," said Irina.

"I don't question that," said Oskar. "But it changes on its own, according to its own laws. People trying to force their agenda on me by deciding how I'm permitted to speak is offensive."

"Aren't you the one who said the more humanity exercises conscious control over social processes, the better off we'll be?"

I whispered to Ren, "Oh, nice one! Now watch Oskar wriggle."

"There is a difference," said Oskar, "between exercising conscious control and sneaking in an agenda through subterfuge."

"What difference, other than whether you agree with the agenda?"

Ren passed the popcorn back and leaned her head on my shoulder. I hadn't realized what a knot I had in my stomach until it relaxed.

"You're missing the point," said Oskar. "There are at least ten languages, not counting Klingon—"

"Oh, for God's sake."

"—in current use that have a non-sex-specific pronoun."

"Which only proves—"

Oskar held up his finger. "I include Finish, Estonian, Lappish, Hungarian, Swahili, spoken Mandarin, Farsi, Tamil, and Tuda. Can you show me any way in which those cultures demonstrate less oppression of women than those that use the male pronoun as the generic?"

"Point for him," whispered Ren.

"Yeah, but Irina shouldn't have let him off the ropes."

Oskar was still talking. "There are real, actual, material problems in the world. The burden on the working woman is brutal, and yet here come a bunch of *petit bourgeois* academics determined to remove the class content that is the essence of the oppression of women and imagine they are making things better by altering the conventions of the language. It's offensive to women who are actually suffering."

"Done now," I told Ren. "When Oskar uses *petit bourgeois* the conversation is over."

Irina turned to Ren. "What does the only other woman in the room say? Does a man get to decide what's offensive to women?"

Ren cocked her head at Irina. "In general, I'm more inclined to agree with you on the subject. And haven't you—we—all been both sexes? But if you think the sex of the person making an argument has anything to do with the validity of the argument, you're an idiot."

"Have some popcorn," I said.

Ren turned to me. "Was that performance for my benefit?"

"Performance?" said Oskar, looking positively annoyed.

"No," I told Ren. "I'm pleased if you enjoyed it, but, yeah, they're just like that. We all get a bit like that when Oskar starts in."

Oskar looked disgusted.

"Perhaps," said Irina, "we should return to the issue."

"Which issue is that?"

"Celeste's suicide. The alpha-lock on Celeste's last seed. The fact that Ren can't remember Celeste."

"What?" said Oskar. He looked at Ren. "You don't remember Celeste?"

"Celeste who?" said Ren.

"Jesus Christ," said Oskar.

"Welcome to the party," I said.

Ren

I felt like something bad the dog's done on the rug, when everyone gathers round and points at the stinking pile and says, "See what you did?"

Oskar leaned forward in his chair, his elbows resting on his knees, like a very focused king on a stolen throne. "Phil, your email said Ren was the one who realized Celeste had killed herself."

"Yeah," Phil said. "Celeste was very present initially, to both Ren and me."

I was sitting beside Phil, so I couldn't check his face, but I was pretty sure I heard the wry underscore that usually went with a cocked eyebrow in how he said "very present."

Irina chuckled, but Oskar only said, "Oh?"

"Celeste has been dominant in Ren a couple of times, then resubmerges," Phil said. "She gave me quite an earful on the subject of peanut butter. She felt I was culinarily unprepared for a new Second."

"Well, you were," Irina said.

"Yeah, I was. Have you ever had a recruit say yes at the second meet? She wasn't even supposed to believe it yet."

"You must have been very persuasive," said Oskar, still watching me. His eyes were the blue of those jewel-toned frogs, whose skin is too toxic to touch, and who can spit poison at you from three feet away. "How did you know that Celeste killed herself?" Oskar asked.

"Who is Celeste?" I said.

"Ren keeps forgetting Celeste," Phil said. "I've told her twice. It's like the shelf where information about Celeste goes has turned into a vacuum. But just that shelf. She remembers everything else. And sometimes she remembers Celeste."

"What do you remember, Ren?" Oskar asked.

"I remember hearing myself talking and thinking, 'That isn't me,' but I knew who it was. I guess that's what it feels like when your personality steps aside for an older one. The other one—Celeste, I guess—told Phil I wasn't like her, I wasn't a martyr. And I remember thinking, 'That's right. I'm not. Get out of my head, bitch.'"

Irina laughed. "I can't imagine Celeste's reaction to that."

"But the suicide?" Oskar pressed.

"The idea that she had killed herself just popped into my head."

Phil's voice was low and warm beside me. "The idea or the memory?"

"Just the word, actually," I said.

"The word 'suicide'?"

"Vicodin," I said. "My roommate OD'd on it in college after the guy she was dating broke up with her. It was really twisted. She said she loved him so much that if he didn't want her, she'd just take herself out of his way so he could be happy."

"I imagine that put her right centered in it," Oskar said. "Sounds like Celeste. Is that when you forgot her?"

"Who?"

Phil drained his beer. "No, that wasn't when. It was overnight last night."

"Has she tried grazing?" Irina asked Phil. "When I was grazing over here yesterday—"

"She's sitting right here," Oskar interrupted. "Ren, have you tried grazing for Celeste?"

"I haven't tried grazing at all," I said.

It was Phil's turn to be the pool ball. Oskar and Irina gaped at him.

"He hasn't had a chance to teach me," I said. "There's been so much going on."

"It doesn't take teaching. Surely you've remembered how?" Irina sounded cross.

"Ren's not having a normal integration," Phil said. "Celeste's memories aren't creeping back to her. Most of the time, either Celeste is fully present and talking through Ren, or she's just gone."

"But you've been having dreams?" Oskar's voice was a low rumble of worry.

"Last night was pretty wild," I confessed.

"Well, go ahead and show her, Phil," Irina said. "We'll wait."

Phil set the popcorn bowl on the floor and pulled one knee up onto the sofa, turning to face me. He took my hand and held it. Irina yanked her phone out of her bag and started texting. Oskar watched me.

"Close your eyes," Phil said. His back was to Oskar and all his attention was on me. But so was all of Oskar's, and I wasn't sure why that bothered me. I closed my eyes.

"What do you see?" Phil asked.

"Can we go in the bedroom?"

"Sure."

"Phil—" Irina said, warning and question in her voice, but he ignored her and led me across what suddenly seemed an endless stretch of living room rug. Irina went back to her texting with an exasperated sigh, but Oskar sat back in his chair, smiled, and closed his eyes.

"Are you okay?" Phil asked once the door was closed.

"Yeah," I said. "It just seemed like a private thing."

He shrugged. "It isn't really. We graze in front of each other all the time. Sometimes it's nice to have someone to keep an eye on you, when you're gone."

He sat cross-legged in the middle of his bed. "Come here."

I climbed up beside him and he took my hand again. "Close your eyes and tell me what you see."

It was almost immediate. "Your villa," I told him.

"How do you know it's mine?"

"I dreamed it last night."

"That's interesting," he said in his neutral voice. "It probably isn't, actually. We don't experience each other's metaphors. But I told you mine was a villa and Jimmy's was a medieval castle, so your imagination is filling in for what it doesn't know since you haven't created your own yet."

I was pretty sure the villa was his, but I said, "Okay," matching him neutral for neutral. "How do I look for someone?"

"You can't yet, we have to get you located in your Garden first. Once you can navigate your own analogy, you can start manipulating it. What are you seeing now?"

"The mudflats out behind your wall."

"Okay."

"But they aren't mudflats. It's just mud in every direction forever. I don't like it, Phil."

"It's okay, just drift on."

"I can't drift on. I'm standing in the mud. I mean, I know I'm sitting there with you. I can feel your hand still, but when I look down, I'm barefoot and standing in the mud.

"Phil, I can't walk. When I try to lift one foot up to take a step, the other one presses down into the goo. I can't stay here. Open spaces make me jumpy. It's like the opposite of claustrophobia. I want to open my eyes."

"See if you can hold on." Phil's other hand wrapped around the one of mine he was holding. "Just be still," he whispered. "What does the air smell like?"

"It smells like mud," I said testily. "And like the ocean."

"Can you taste anything on the breeze? You're smiling. That's good. What do you taste?"

I had to think for a second to find the name for the fizzy sweet tickle. "Root beer," I said.

"I think this is your Garden, Ren."

"A mud garden? There are no plants, no sun, not a single living thing out here. It's not a garden, it's some kind of special hell for gardeners. Phil, I'm up to my ankles."

"It's okay. This is why Seconds have titans. I'll help you orient yourself."

"Orient myself in the barren sucking wasteland that is my imagination? Wonderful."

"The easiest line is usually 'When.' For most of us, it runs up and down. So look up. Is there anything at eye-level?"

"There isn't anything at any level."

"Nothing raised or lowered?"

"Hang on."

"Nothing growing up out of the ground?"

"No. But I think there's something pressing into it. When you said 'When,' it was like a giant screen dropped down over the mud."

"Good, Ren. Say 'Friday, July first.' "

I said "Friday, July first," and an invisible mesh screen pushed down into the mud. The sunken places looked darker and more solid, the raised places grainier, almost pixilated and dynamic, moving like tiny, color-changing fireflies. Warm air eddied over the endless mud, and brushed the skin of my face and arms. I squeezed Phil's hand.

"Say, 'Las Vegas, Nevada.' "

I did, and watched another screen settle over the landscape. In the cross-hatched places where both layers of filter pushed into the mud, it became clay and a dry powder over my feet. I bent down and brushed off my toes, appreciating their candy apple red nail polish. If my metaphysical self was a terrible gardener, at least she had cute feet.

"Say, 'Phil.' "

"Phil," I said, and watched yet another screen drop over the landscape. It compacted the pushed-down places further and contoured the rest with color.

"It's a bright blue flower in a vase just past my front gate," he said, so I walked along the hard-packed dirt, touching the singing reeds which take root in secrets, each one whispering a story, as they have since King Midas's barber dug a hole to bury what he mustn't say.

A little black-and-white dog with a bow to match my toenails trotted out from behind a clump of reeds and walked along beside me. Then one of the tall, slender leaves sprouted a blue flower and I reached for it.

The reed was as tall as I was and supple, blowing in the warm air. "Hey, little wolf, do you know how to make these things talk?" I asked the dog, but it dropped to its haunches and cocked its clever head at me.

I put my nose to the reed, and it was sweet and grassy, greener smelling than it looked, but inert. I pulled at its roots, but I didn't really want to, and it made Wolfie growl. I put my ear up against it, feeling like an idiot for trying to hear a leaf talk. Wolfie watched me. "I know," I told him. "Look at my Garden. Clearly I'm no plant whisperer." But my thumb hooked in the reed. I followed the furled edge up, and it peeled open.

It wasn't a hollow tube after all, but a tightly curled leaf. I thought maybe, if I could flatten it out, I would see the memory playing out on its surface like on a television screen. But the leaf had other ideas. I pushed apart the two bottom corners, holding them with my feet, and the top rolled up like a window shade. I pushed the right top up and the right bottom down, and the whole left side closed up like a fist.

Wolfie watched me struggle, his face a portrait of canine concern. He barked.

"If you don't have anything helpful to offer, shut up," I said. "Can't you see I'm engaged in mighty combat here?"

He wagged his tail and watched me fight the leaf.

I anchored the bottom of it with my feet and wriggled my hand between the upper corners and pushed. I managed to stretch the furl open at last, my body in a painful *X*, like a racked man. And wedged there. "Great," I said.

"What's wrong?" Phil's voice sounded parched and distant. I let go to look for him, and the leaf snapped in on itself and wrapped me up inside it.

I was in the living room. In Phil's chair. In Phil. The leaf held me motionless, and I watched through him, learned of the ritual he'd done that brought me into this strange world, and heard him talk of my reactions. Then the leaf opened, the reeds dissolved into mud, and I opened my eyes.

Phil was watching me closely, still holding my hand.

"Okay, I can graze now," I said. "But I want pizza."

Phil

Her voice was the same, but there was a glitter in her eyes. She was starting to feel the Garden, and the connection to it, and to all of us. She wouldn't recognize, yet, the feeling of finding her family, but the first hints of it would be making their way into her spine.

There are good parts to this thing we do, this thing we are. Being someone's titan reminds you of that.

"You don't know what you're saying," I told her.

"That I want pizza? I'm pretty sure I do."

There was nothing different in her expression, or her body language, but it was like there was a glow under her skin.

I shook my head. "Think about it, Ren. You. Me. Irina. Oskar. We will starve to death before we can manage to agree on a pizza. Or two pizzas. And I'm too hungry to even get started with them."

"You and I will agree," she said. "Those two can do whatever the hell they like."

I opened the door, stuck my head out, and said, "Ren and I are ordering pizza. Flamingo. 702-889-4554. You two can do whatever the hell you like." Then I shut the door before they could respond. Fortunately, my cell was in my pocket, so I didn't have to ignominiously walk back in there to get it. I ordered us pepperoni, onion and green pepper. When I was done, Ren was looking thoughtful.

"What?" I asked.

"Do you ever agree on anything?"

"Not much, really."

She shook her head. "Then why are you still together?"

"Can't help it."

"That's the only reason?"

"On bad days, I think it might be. But I don't know."

"Two hundred pure-blood altruists and you can't get along with each other?"

"Something like that."

She squinted one eye. "That altruism thing has me stumped," she said.

"How so?"

"Well, are you saying that no one, in all this time, has, I don't know, gone rogue? Used these abilities for himself? Gone crazy? Become evil, whatever that means?"

I started to tell her she'd remember, but then I realized that wasn't a given. "That's all happened. I think of them as the Dark Years. Hear the capital letters? But—" How to put it? "Okay, I said we don't agree on much of anything. But eventually, we did have to agree on one thing: If you're going to live indefinitely, one lifetime doesn't count for much."

She frowned. "That seems like—"

"Let me finish. This is hard to explain."

"All right."

"You live a normal lifetime; actually less, because the first twenty or thirty years you're someone else. Then, pop, you're someone else again, and you can't control who. So, what do you do to try to give your next Second a good life? When you don't have a clue who that Second is going to be?"

She thought for a moment, chewing her lower lip, which I found adorable. "You try to make everything better?"

I nodded. "With as little risk as possible of making things worse."

"So, it's all self-interest and Rawl's veil?"

"Pretty much."

"Couldn't you do more good if you were rich and powerful?"

I grunted. "You'd think so. But most of the time, money and power make you spend all of your time dealing with money and power. If you don't, you tend to turn into an asshole. Most of us make enough to get by and don't worry about anything more. Usually at least one of us is wealthy at any given time, which is a pain for that person, but useful for the group. Right now, it's poor Jimmy. His last recruit invested in Google before taking the spike."

She thought some more, her forefinger tapping her eyebrow. "Self-interest is a little easier to accept." She curled her hand into a fist. "But couldn't a group, a subset, all agree that they were going to become powerful, and give each other powerful Seconds, and—"

"Yes," I said. "Sorry to interrupt. I don't like to dwell on it. That's exactly what happened, and it didn't turn out well. Those memories are hazy, and go back a long, long way, but I know it happened. There was almost a full millennium of fighting among ourselves and making everything worse. I know it was ugly. No one wants to go back there again. We learned."

"God," she said. "I'll remember this?"

I hoped so. "It'll start coming back as impressions and half memories. But you can always go to the Garden and graze for as many of the details as you want. It's a good idea to, actually. I do it from time to time, just to keep myself in line. But don't tell Oskar, it'd make him feel superior."

"Can't have that," she said, and gave me a six-thousand-watt smile that looked nothing like Celeste's.

Her mouth was soft and yielding and strong all at once, and her tongue tasted like lemons and unabashed laughter; her hands on my back felt like she was trying to pull me into her, and one part of my mind wondered if I were crushing her, while another part wanted this to never end. We were somehow both standing up, and I was just starting to think that falling over was a real possibility when she stiffened and pulled her mouth away. I dropped my arms and she took a step back. She fixed me with her eyes like she was trying to see into my skull and said, "I'm not Celeste."

I thought the best thing to do was stand there like an idiot with my mouth open, so I did until she walked past me, opened the door, and went back to the living room.

I wasn't hungry anymore.

EIGHT

How's the Head?

Ren

Three pizzas came. For four people, we got three pizzas in three separate deliveries, and we moved all Irina's flowers from the breakfast bar and sat there and ate. Or Oskar and I ate, Phil and Irina picked.

"You discovered your Garden," Irina said. "Phil stayed with you and guided you. Oskar grazed. I just sent messages. I'm not so hungry."

But she looked hungry, and I suspected she just didn't like pizza, even though she'd ordered her own. Phil sat beside me, and I told Irina and Oskar about my muddy Garden, and they were nice enough not to laugh. Oskar called it "postmodern," and Irina said it wasn't, but Phil said it sounded like Ramon's grid, with its mad swarm of data points filtered by tracking axis lines, which made me feel a little less like a freak. "It's just a signal from noise problem," Phil said. "We all solve it differently."

"Sounds like you all do everything differently," I said, and Irina and Oskar laughed.

Irina climbed off her barstool. "I'm going to put a slice of this in the oven. Is yours warm enough, Ren?"

I looked at the empty box Phil and I'd been eating from. "I'm fine," I said.

"Oh, for the love of all the gods in heaven and all the bullshit on this stupid earth, Phil!"

Phil's eyes got round and he set his beer down softly. "Irina, don't—"

"I made this myself! Her mother's recipe. You heathen!" Irina brandished the mummified tuna casserole at us over the bar. "What did you do, just turn the oven off and leave it?"

"Maybe."

"And you've been eating pizza and Froot Loops since? Are you children?"

"I like sugar cereal," I said. "I didn't get it as a kid, so it feels grown-up to me."

Irina looked from me to Phil and back as though trying to evenly distribute her disdain without spilling any.

"I thought you were just baking it for the smell," I said at last. Which earned me a quick sideways glance from Oskar.

"I wasn't meddling with you!"

"No?" Phil asked her. "With the mint sprigs tucked into the flowers, and the tempting offer of a hotel breakfast in bed tray?"

"No." Irina stood, her monkey hands clamped to her bony waist, and I tried to imagine what she'd been like young. Her personality was a third of the age of Phil's, but she felt like someone's grandmother, and I just wanted to kiss him again.

"Gosh, look at the time," Phil said, and stood up. "I'm going to go pick up Jimmy from the airport. We can run by the store and get you some tea on the way, if you want to come with me, Ren."

"That'd be great," I said. "I have a meeting at The Palms at five."

"Can you drop me off there, too?" Oskar asked, and I was unreasonably disappointed that Phil said yes.

"Well, I'm not going," Irina said. "I have some grazing to do."

We got tea—four boxes, two herbal, two black—at the grocery near Phil's house. Phil also got Lipton instant iced tea, lemon juice, and a lilac-scented candle. But when he caught me looking at the instant iced tea, he said it wasn't for me. After we dropped Oskar at the front of the hotel and pulled back into traffic, Phil reached for my hand. "I knew you weren't Celeste," he said. "I didn't want you to be."

"Who's Celeste?"

He laughed. "Never mind."

So for a few miles, I didn't. I adjusted the A/C vents to point right at my face and leaned my cheek against Phil's shoulder. He put his hand on my knee and squeezed it, and I watched the tropical trees and the brilliant sun, and felt the space between our bodies fill up with wanting and curiosity.

"Celeste was the most recent dominant personality in the stub you got," Phil said after a while. "I was in love with her, or tried to be, over several lifetimes."

"Do I remind you of her?" I asked.

"Not anymore," he said.

"Do you miss her?"

He shrugged, lifting my head a little on his shoulder. "I don't know. She killed herself, and that makes me sad."

"Is suicide one of the things you, I mean we, aren't allowed to do? Like choosing your own Seconds?"

"It's not that we aren't allowed to choose our own Seconds, it's that we can't. And, no, suicide isn't forbidden. In fact, Eleanor and Gaston have stayed together and kept their ages roughly in synch for quite a while that way."

"I can't decide if that's awful or sweet," I said.

Phil chuckled, its rumble amplified in my ear against his arm. It made me want to wrap myself around him and feel his laughter everywhere. "I think it's both," he said. "But with Celeste, it was just sad."

I nodded. "So now Oskar's in the Salt."

"Yeah. Celeste would have hated that."

"She must have been pretty sure she'd stay dominant in me," I said.

"We all were," he said. "First time in a long time I've liked being wrong."

I squeezed his arm and smiled. "I have a meeting with my boss at five o'clock, and then we're meeting with his boss either after that or tomorrow morning."

"Let's make it tomorrow. I'd like to see you tonight."

I nodded. It's stupid how big little things are in the very beginning of anything. "Won't you be meeting with Oskar and Jimmy and Irina tonight?"

"And Ray. But I think you should be there too. That'll make six, which isn't great, but we can call in Matt if necessary; he's next after Oskar."

"Is he on Oskar's side?"

"Now you sound like Celeste."

"Who's Celeste?"

"No, it doesn't matter. We don't really have sides. Celeste thought Oskar was an extremist, and dangerous because of it. He thought she was cautious to the point of irrelevance."

"And you?"

"Different arguments, different points along the axis. On Germany, I was with Oskar; I wanted us to do more. With Fox News, I agreed with Celeste; what Oskar pushed was unsubtle. With Cambodia, we all blew it."

"Suicide seems like a drastic step for a moderate person," I said, as we pulled up along the curb outside baggage claim.

"Yeah," Phil said. "I still don't quite believe it. There's Jimmy!"

I climbed out of the car to find myself folded into a hug like a cashmere coat. Jimmy looked like an Arabian thug but smelled like vintage leather and good wine. A tiny ruby winked in the pierced flesh of his earlobe like blood in black velvet. He kissed both my cheeks, and then hugged Phil every bit as long and as tightly, and kissed him firmly on the mouth. He threw open the Prius's back door and tossed in a vintage Amelia Earhart suitcase. I tried to offer the front, but he refused and positioned himself squarely in the middle of the backseat like a Pasha, completely obscuring the rear window.

"So, Ren!" he said, "How's the head?" and laughed when I groaned.

We laughed and talked our way back to The Palms, and I got out and waved good-bye. Phil winked at me, and I promised to head over when my afternoon meeting ended. Jimmy and Phil drove off and I went up to my room to drag myself back to the real world before I had to meet Liam.

Phil

Jimmy moved into the front seat, twisting a bit so he could come closer to facing me. "You know, I've arranged for a rental," he said.

"Pick it up tomorrow. I want to talk to you."

"So I gathered. All right, what is—"

"I'm falling in love with her. Falling hard."

"With her, or—"

"Her. Ren. Not Celeste. Shit. Got it bad. I kissed her today, and then she pulled away from me like I was poison, thinking I wanted to be kissing Celeste. And then after that, she—crap." Jimmy was silent, looking at me. Then he cleared his throat, and I said, "Jimmy, if I hear '*mon ami*' escape your mouth, I swear to God I'll pull over and punch you."

He chuckled. "All right. I heard she's lost Celeste's memories."

"She's lost Celeste completely, except it comes back sometimes, and—wait. Heard how? No, don't tell me. That lying hen."

He shrugged. "The problem isn't your Ren. Our Ren. So she's not integrating smoothly. All right. We've handled that before. But what Ramon calls the alpha-lock is worrying me. Where is cause and where is effect?"

"You're the grazing shaman, you tell me."

That shut him up for a moment, then he said, "What doesn't Ren know?"

I drove for a while, running that through my head. Jimmy didn't know Las Vegas, so I took us onto the 15 and all the way to Sahara and then to Arvile. I trusted Jimmy and I liked him, and I wanted some time to talk to him before dealing with Irina. I finally said, "She doesn't know about the disconnect."

"The disconnect?"

"That's what I call it. She doesn't understand that we're not really like the amnemones, at some basic level."

"We're just like them at the most basic level."

"You know what I mean."

He said, "Are these dips in the road indicative of bad design, or do they serve some engineering purpose?"

"I don't know. I suspect some of each."

"And did you bring us this way just so I'd bump my head?"

"No."

"All right. You haven't talked about the nemones with her? She never asked what we call everyone else, or how we think of them?"

"I mentioned it in passing, but we didn't actually talk about it."

He studied me. "Has it been getting worse for you?"

I considered. "I don't think so. I had to fight Celeste's attitude at close range for a few hundred years; that pushed me in the other direction."

"Sometimes, you get pushed in one direction, it snaps you back in the other."

"I know—Oskar."

"Sorry. But—"

"No, you're right. I've been trying to watch for bits of contempt creeping into my attitudes. So far, I think I'm all right."

"Okay."

We turned onto Flamingo and I pointed to The Palms. "That's where Oskar and Ren are."

He studied it as we passed by. "They're trying to project naughty," he said. "Why there?"

"It's the best place for my sugar spoon."

"All right."

I turned onto Decatur and took it back to Sahara. We reached the house and got out. Jimmy looked around. "Nice neighborhood. Blue collar."

"A lot of Mormons," I said. "And a lot of Hispanics."

"And, it seems, a lot of foreclosures. Have you thought about meddling with that?"

"Thought about it; haven't come up with anything."

We went in. Irina was on the couch, but stood and rushed into Jimmy's arms. "Ah, my beautiful man! Come to save me from the hostility of those who fail to appreciate my charms!"

"None could so fail, *ma chère,*" said Jimmy. "I must ravish you at once; I cannot restrain myself."

I started coffee while they played out their game. By the time I poured a cup, they were sitting. Since Oskar wasn't here, I was able to take my own chair.

"So," said Irina. "I think the best solution is to just stub Ren and find a new recruit. What do you think, Jimmy?"

Ren

The knock on the door came on the phone's second ring. I was still scrambling to answer one as I opened the other. Oskar filled the opening, a linen-draped waiter's tray balanced at ear level. My phone went to voice mail.

"It's Liam," Oskar said. "He's been delayed an hour. He'll meet you at six in the café. I brought tea."

"I need to call my boss back," I said.

In a single, smooth sweep, Oskar brought the tray from his shoulder to the desk. I called Liam back while watching Oskar pour what I once would have called a Princess Tea: orange pekoe from a silver pot into porcelain cups, milk first, sugar after, and a plate of finger sandwiches and little pink cakes, with Chopin lilting from an iPad on the room service tray. I dialed both of Liam's numbers, and then my voice mail. He'd been delayed. He would meet me at six in the café.

Oskar pulled out the desk chair for me and placed a delicate cup in my hand. I smelled the tea before I drank it. "So you know my mom's an anglophile," I said.

"Phil was very thorough." Oskar stretched himself on my bed, propped on one elbow, like a formally dressed version of a teen idol beefcake shot: jacket artfully opened, in conservative, tailored trousers and a classic black T, with the rebel's red necklace cord peeking at his throat.

I sipped my tea. "I don't think tea is a switch for me."

"It isn't. It was one of Celeste's."

"Who's Celeste?"

"Don't you ever get tired of saying that?" He lifted his cup from its saucer. It looked like a golf ball in a backhoe's claw.

"I do, actually," I told him. "But she's all anyone seems to want to talk about, and I don't know who she is."

"How frustrating for you."

"What do you want, Oskar?"

"I want to talk to Celeste."

"Get in line. But I meant, why are you here, in my room?"

"Because I think you can help me. Pass the cakes?"

I waddled my rolly desk chair over to him with the tray. He took one, and bit into it, looking at me. It was an overtly sexual bite, and corny as hell, but it ran a shiver through me anyway. He looked like my first celebrity crush, with his hair slicked back the new way he was wearing it.

He dropped his voice to a deep whisper, and I had to scoot forward in my chair just to hear him. "Have you ever really wanted something, Ren?" he asked. "Have you ever worked, and ached, and struggled after the same one thing over long reaches of time? Did you ever suffer without that one thing you desired, only to find it suddenly, tantalizingly near to hand?"

"The Fisher-Price Little People Play Family Castle," I said. "Saving up allowance was never going to get me there. I almost gave up, until I thought of Santa."

Oskar assessed my face. Yes, I'd wanted other things more, but he got that I wasn't just joking. He twisted to sitting in one fluid spring. "I've wanted in the Salt for forty years." His voice was a deep growl in his chest. "And now it's so close I can taste it." He smiled briefly, showing strong, sharp teeth, and I thought he would not so much taste as devour with his kind of hungry.

"I know why I wanted the castle," I said. "It had dragons. Why do you want in the Salt?"

"Because they're doing it wrong," he said, not needing to consider the question for even a moment. "You weren't born yet when Nixon resigned. It was like a victory that ended the war before it was won. All the passion, the need for change, the hope, just left. The kids who were fixing the world went home. They busied themselves with neo-paganism, positive thinking, identity politics, and organic food co-ops. But they could have done it. They almost did. It was our fault. I told Salt subjective idealism—I told Salt they needed our help. They didn't listen, and I want them to have to. Incrementalists can cause real change. We can make things better. It's wrong to be able to do that, and to not do it. It's just . . . it's wrong."

"Maybe it's getting near Christmas," I said.

"It's July."

"Your birthday?"

I started to roll my chair back to the desk, but Oskar caught it by its padded armrests and shook it. "Celeste would never have let this happen. She despises the nemones, and she would never permit us to so much as inconvenience ourselves to help them." He pulled my chair right up against the bed. "Celeste's not gone. Celeste would never just go. She's hiding."

With my knees between his, and his shoulders filling my field of vision, I couldn't think of anything to say. Oskar brought his forehead to mine. "I'm here to coax Celeste out."

"I'm here on business," I said.

"You're here because we brought you."

"Well, there is that," I admitted. "Also the poker."

"You don't play."

"The shows?"

"You haven't seen one."

"The food?"

"Ren!" He stood up, towering over me. I backpedalled my chair, but he sat down again, watching me through narrowed eyes. "You should want this too," he said with something like menace in his voice.

"To be in the Salt? Nah, I hate politics."

"For me to find Celeste."

"I thought you wanted her out of the way."

"I do." His face left no doubt about the depth of that desire. More than dragons.

"Enough to break rules?" I asked.

"We have very few."

"Did you kill Celeste?"

Nothing moved. In the poison-blue of his beautiful eyes, I saw Desire roll onto her back.

"Stubbing Incrementalists is not against the rules," he said. "We don't like to do it, but we have before, and we can again."

"See?" I said. "More things I haven't remembered about us."

"We have to protect against dementia and chemical imbalance to keep inadvertent falsehoods out of the Garden. Man knows of the world what his senses tell him, but our senses are interpreted through our material brains, and a sick brain can bring bad information. Paranoids can record dangers that aren't real. Brain injuries alter personalities. We are not charioteers to spur forward or rein back the brute beasts we ride upon." He pulled my chair closer, touched his fingertips to my cheek, and smoothed my hair back from my temple. He leaned in toward it. I spun the chair toward the armrest he'd released and jumped to my feet.

"More tea, Chiron?" I asked from back at the desk.

He stood and carried his cup to me. Maybe he wanted the tea. Maybe I was looking particularly Sabinian. I was as tall as his shoulder.

"So Phil has introduced you to what happens when our temples touch," Oskar mused. "Has he told you what can happen when Incrementalists make love?"

"No, why would he?"

"He might think you'd appreciate the warning. He wants you, you know."

"I know he was in love with Celeste," I said, but I had to bite my lip to keep from smiling.

"Now you remember her?"

"I remember people talking about her."

"Phil was in love with Celeste for a long, long time."

"Sounds like it was a rocky relationship," I said. I poured another cup of tea, forgetting the milk.

"All Celeste's relationships were," Oskar said. "But Phil never saw that. He lost his objectivity. It's possible you have lost yours as well." He reached across me and took the creamer by its slim handle.

"Phil knows Celeste meddled with him," I said.

"Celeste was subtle." Oskar poured a thin stream of milk into his empty cup. "It suited her for Phil to adore her. It kept him timid. Love does that, you know." He lifted the teapot as he poured, drawing a long curve of the steaming stuff so the smell filled the space between us. "Not at first, of course. At first love makes us wild. Reckless." The sugar tongs looked like tweezers between his fingers, but he wielded them like a surgeon. "In the first throes of love, we leave homes and jobs, abandon lives and cities." He stirred the cup, looking into it thoughtfully. "But later, after the flames of love burn down to embers, love tempers us." He handed the cup to me. "Love domesticates us until we fear the feral passion we remember." He pressed me tenderly into my chair and leaned on the edge of my desk. "So we corral our love with rules and ethics. We pen love in, clip its wings, and castrate it to keep it safe from itself. Tame, and moderate."

I looked at him over my teacup. "So what, love no one? Is that the wisdom of your accumulated years? Play the lone wolf?"

He dropped a finger sandwich, whole, into his mouth. "Wolves are family creatures, but they don't tolerate a challenge. I would not be welcomed in the Salt, even if your personality's dominance over Celeste's were strictly to form. As it is, they may dispute your spike, argue it was a broken stub, or that Phil was too involved to choose a suitable recruit. He doubled the genome with you, after all, and you're not integrating. And people were loyal to Celeste." He drained his teacup. "Do you know who you need most, Ren?"

"Santa?"

"You need Celeste. You need enough of her to prove she's still around, just not the dominant personality any longer. You need to demonstrate you got a viable spike. I can help."

Oskar leaned across me and took the teacup from my hand. He touched a button on the iPad, and Leonard Cohen's voice lapped over my shoulders. Oskar straightened and held his beautiful, empty hands out to me.

I picked up my teacup, sipped and returned it with unshaking hands. "You know, Santa brought me Barbie's Dream House that year, and it wasn't the same at all."

Oskar enveloped one of my wrists. "But you played with it the day after Christmas, didn't you?" He pulled me to standing.

"Yes," I said.

He carried my hand to his shoulder. "I don't want to see Celeste when I look at you," he said.

"You want in the Salt."

"I do." He took my other hand in his. "And I want you in the Incrementalists." He rested his fingers on my waist. "And I think you want that too. You must have had something really big in mind to take the spike as quickly as you did."

I nodded.

"I like big," he said, and actually blushed when I raised my eyebrows at him. It was adorable.

"I know you've been you for a couple of hundred years," I told him. "And I know you've wanted something big for that long, maybe longer. But it wouldn't have hurt you to want some*one* in all that time as well."

His blush deepened. "I've had lovers."

"Not the same thing," I said. I reached up on tiptoe to kiss his cheek, like the oversize little brother he suddenly seemed. "I gotta go," I said.

"I'll wait for you, Ren."

"Yeah, but my boss won't."

"I could make sure he would." His sweet smile flashed a wolf's teeth at me.

"I could too," I reminded him. "But I'd rather just do what I promised."

"Because Santa won't bring anything nice to wicked children who break their word?"

"Or who kill people and make it look like suicide."

"Santa doesn't bring anything to anyone."

"Harsh," I said. "I'll see you tonight when they gather Salt."

"Oh, do you think so?"

"I promise."

Phil

In the early '60s, I played a lot of Texas road games. After the first time the game was hijacked, I started carrying a gun in my pocket. I never used it, even the second time we were hijacked, but during those times it reassured me to have it there. My hand twitched, going for that pocket from fifty years ago.

Jimmy said, "I've learned, Irina, not to play your games before I know the rules. I don't believe you're just trying to get a rise out of Phil, and I don't believe you're just playing head games with me. So, what is it?"

"Maybe," she said, "I actually mean it."

"Bullshit," said Jimmy. "We call it stubbing, but the police call it murder."

"We've meddled with police before. And juries, if it comes to that."

"You can't be that stupid."

"Not stupid. Scared."

"Of Celeste?"

"Of Oskar."

"Christ." Jimmy looked at me. "How high have you gone so far?"

I was at 17,711, but it wasn't working. I said, "I have no interest in stubbing you, Irina. But if there was a way to kill you, I'd do it."

She sniffed. "If that were possible," she said, "none of us would be around by now. So, I take it you want to find a different solution?"

"Yes," I said.

"Then do it," she snapped. "Come up with something. Celeste stubbed herself, which is entirely out of character. Oskar is stepping in the Salt, without the mediating influence of Celeste. Meanwhile, the nemones are on the brink of either destroying themselves—and us—or creating a world where forty thousand years' worth of problems might actually get solved. Theirs and ours. And this is when we lose the most stable voice in Salt and replace her with the most unstable. And—"

"Oskar," I said, "is not unstable."

"He's drunk the Kool-Aid. That makes him unstable."

"Unless he's right."

"Do you think he's right?"

I hesitated. "I don't know."

"Will you gamble humanity's future on it?" When I didn't answer, she said, "I didn't think so. So there we are, and if that weren't enough, we have a big, fat alpha-lock in the Garden. How many times in the last forty thousand years has that happened? Four times?"

"Twice," said Jimmy quietly.

"Good luck convincing me that's coincidence. So, yes, Phil. If we can solve this by stubbing Ren, then that's what we do. You'll be miserable for a hundred years, and hate me for a thousand, and I can deal with both of those consequences, unless you can find a better idea."

She finally ran down, and no one said anything.

My cell phone rang. I answered it, and Ray said he was at the airport. I suggested he take a cab over, and he said he would.

Part of me wondered if Irina would still be alive when he got here.

NINE

We Can Do Better

Ren

I got in the elevator fervently visualizing Oskar standing by my desk, alone in my room, eating the last two sandwiches and letting himself out, but when I looked back down the hall, it was a uniform row of closed doors. I thought about marching back and throwing him out, but I was already late to meet Liam, so when the elevator doors slid open, I got in.

The mirrors on the four walls showed multiples of me, and it felt entirely too apt, an infinite regression of me's, only not identical. Different since Phil drove the flaming stake between my eyes. Different since I found my Garden, with its sucking mud and swallowing reeds. Different since Phil kissed me, and I wanted him to, even if maybe it wasn't me he wanted. Different again since Oskar tried to seduce or threaten or meddle with me, I still wasn't sure which or in what combination. And it might have been different like Nana got in the end with husband, son and grandson all refracting in my little brother's face if the elevator hadn't stopped and opened up the real world of fake trees and artificial coins in synthetic slots.

Liam looked just as lifelike in the café, mercifully seated at a non-booth table, which was spread with what looked to be one of everything on the menu.

"Orgy?" I asked, seating myself opposite.

"Peace offering. I feel like crap about keeping you stranded here all weekend."

"For crap thou art, and unto crap shalt thou return." I gave Liam my brightest smile.

"Want tea, Ren?"

"Thanks, Kendra."

Kendra gave Liam a long, sideways look.

"Kendra, this is my boss, Liam, from Phoenix."

"Hi, Liam from Phoenix." Kendra gave me a wink that shrugged away her suspicions I was two-timing Phil. I was still curious about that story after all.

"So you've been making friends?" Liam observed.

"Well, you did abandon me out here. What's a girl to do?"

Liam assessed me with the squinty eyes of lurid curiosity.

"You've made a special friend," he guessed.

"I didn't," I said without glancing up from my nibble feast.

"Then you're pregnant."

"That's not funny."

"Well, I'm sorry, but you're glowing, and I've never seen anyone actually do that before. Emma just threw up."

"I'm not glowing."

"Yeah, you kind of are. I like it. It suits you. You met someone."

"Maybe."

"Well, you're way too cheery for a sales meeting. Glum up, kiddo. Who is this guy?"

"Just a guy."

"Oh, dear. A Vegas guy? Renee, this is serious. Worse than musicians."

"You have no idea," I said. "And on your head be it."

He laughed and moved plates around to accommodate the eleven-by-seventeen booklet of documentation we would leave with Jorge after the pitch.

"Talk me through this one more time," he said.

The book started by introducing a cast of archetypal RMMD patients, and even though I'd okayed the artwork myself, every one of the models looked wrong. The man we'd cast as the Doctor bore no resemblance to Jorge. The Patient was female, yes, but entirely too young and curvy to put him in mind of his aging and increasingly forgetful mother.

We went through the book, me explaining our ham-fisted attempts at persuading Jorge to spend extra time and more money than he'd planned on features he hadn't asked for. But his own research had been clear. If RMMD was going to tailor a remote medical monitoring device to the growing population of Alzheimer's patients, this was what doctors and patients wanted. Like the standard RMMD, it reported vital signs to medical staff and family members, but it added cognitive metrics to allow for the assessment of lucidity. And our proposal included the creation of an externalized memory component, with GPS-driven alerts, icons customizable with family photos, and meticulously designed auditory prompts. RMMD's research into memory and music had made me cry twice while reading, and yet audio was nowhere in the project scope.

Audio would cost more and take longer, but every justification I'd built into the book looked to me like a blunted, blind stab at meddling. We'd made a pitch book of blatant manipulation. And Jorge would know that. He'd come to the meeting expecting us to try and nudge him into spending more money and taking more time to make a beautiful, streamlined, light-weight device that would save time, money and lives over the next five years, but cost him his quarterly goals now. Wherever he was, he was already working on the counterarguments.

Liam loved it, but the ants of shame were crawling on my arms. "We can do better, Liam."

"No, this is great!"

"I can improve on it. A lot. I know I can. Give me a week to redo the book. Let's show Jorge that we're willing to do exactly what we're asking him to. Sacrifice a deadline to quality. Eat the extra expense to do it right."

"How much extra expense?"

"We need to reshoot all the Use Case scenario photos. And rewrite some of the copy. I can do it all myself, I just need time."

"But he's flying in tonight. We can't just not show up for our own meeting."

"Buy him a nice dinner," I said. "Let him play poker. Tell him you need time to understand his needs and values. Stall."

"Ren—" Something in the way he was trying to read my face reminded me of Phil, and the whole web of the Incrementalists lit up under my skin again. I took a deep breath and let it out, feeling just a taste of ocean air on my lips. I gave Liam a hint of a smile with a trace of worry in my brows. How had I learned to do that?

"You're the boss, it's your decision," I said. *You hired me because I'm good at this, remember? If you trust your own judgment, you should trust mine.* It wasn't meddling, but it also wasn't how I would have played it a week ago. I would have still been explaining.

"Can you do the work from here? If Jorge doesn't go for it, I want us ready to roll."

"We'll be ready whenever he is," I said, and stood up to go.

"All right," Liam grumbled. "But I want to meet this new guy of yours. He's done something to you."

I had to bite my lip the whole way out of the café to keep from laughing. Yes, Phil had done something to me. But so had Oskar and the Garden and Irina, and it buzzed and hummed and rattled me. And it made Liam and Jorge and Kendra feel far away and dull. I cared about RMMD. I still did, but I had bigger work waiting. And I had missed my new world as soon as I stepped outside it. But mostly I missed Phil, who centered it.

I wanted to follow the thread of him into the labyrinth of days, to discover each next turn with him, to watch the walls of our baffling history slip by under his fingers, and to feel those fingers on my skin.

I took the elevator back to my room. Oskar was gone, but except for his iPad, nothing else. Not even the sandwiches. I ate one wondering if my distrust of Oskar was residual Celeste blinding me to help I should heed. Was it stupid to trust Phil when he'd been ready to sacrifice me for Celeste? When he could love her that untamedly over that many years? Or was that the only reason I had for trusting him in the first place?

I rode the elevators and navigated the lobby to the taxi stand. I didn't know what I'd find when I got to Phil's, but I was going with my shampoo and my phone charger and my laptop, and I didn't care how late the Incrementalists stayed and fought. I'd fight with them and outstay them until it was just the two of us.

Phil

If there's anything we're good at, it's reading people; if there's anyone we're good at reading, it's each other. Jimmy studied my face, then said, "Irina, let's take a walk."

She shrugged and said, "All right."

I don't think their walk took them far from the house, because about three-quarters of an hour later, when Ray knocked on the door, they were right behind him. Anyone else would have noticed that, perhaps, all was not well; Ray either didn't notice or didn't care. He said, "Where's Oskar? He should be here."

"He'll be arriving shortly," said Jimmy. "What have you learned?"

"What have *you* learned?" said Ray, his voice, as always, clipped and precise and almost without inflection. "You're the grazing shaman. What did you find out that you haven't seeded?"

I'd have taken the last bit as a reprimand, but Jimmy either knew Ray didn't mean it that way, or didn't care.

"This is the third time we've had an alpha-lock," he said. "The first one was during the Dark Years, about six thousand years ago. The other was seven hundred years ago, more or less."

"Causes and cures," said Ray.

"Which would you like first, Ramon?"

Ray frowned, then scowled when he realized Jimmy was needling him. Jimmy said, "The second time was pure fluke. One in, I don't know, millions. A pretty standard seed of a pretty standard piece of meddlework having to do with taxes for infrastructure in a small principality in India. The Focus changed his mind just as we were working, because a pretty girl asked him to; the Incrementalist considered the Why as he was seeding, and his Second turned out to be epileptic and had a temporal lobe seizure at that exact moment. The causal chain was short, the brain twisted it up, the Why became determinate."

"Interesting," said Ray, and I could just see him trying to figure out if there was a way to duplicate the effect under controlled conditions.

"Does Vicodin cause seizures?" I asked.

"It can," Ray said.

"The temporal lobe kind?" I asked, but Irina talked over me.

"What about the other alpha-lock, Jimmy?"

"Not as clear. We were at each other's throats then, and everyone was forging alliances and counter-alliances, making deals and breaking them. People were trying to seed false memories, and one of those memories looped around itself and became the answer to its own Why. I can't be more precise, because that one is still locked. It was isolated, and big warning signs put on it. If you want to look at it, it's the picture book on the small side table in the back corner of my library."

"Excuse me," said Ray. "But how can you know where it is, if—"

"Sorry," said Jimmy. "That isn't the memory, that's a memory of the memory."

"Ah, all right. What of the cures?"

"For the first one, there wasn't any. It's still locked and off somewhere. For the second, the seeder re-created the memory with the same

Who and the same Where, but a different When, then we tricked the seeder into believing it was the same When as earlier, and got the two seeds close enough that the Why of the original became undefined, so they were able to locate it. My basement, broom closet, piece of paper under the oil can."

"Who did them?" said Ray.

"Who?" Jimmy frowned. "You mean the Primaries? Does that even mean anything, after all this time?"

"I wouldn't think so," said Irina.

"I wouldn't mind knowing," said Ray.

"All right," said Jimmy. "It's going to take some time, especially for the first one, to go through everybody."

"Maybe not," said Ray. "Just yes or no. Was it Celeste's Primary?"

Jimmy cursed under his breath, scowled, grunted, and finally closed his eyes. But as soon as Ray had asked the question, I knew what the answer would be.

Less than a minute later, Jimmy opened his eyes and nodded.

Ren

I meant to call Phil on the drive, but the cabbie wanted to talk about the Fourth of July in Vegas, so I just turned up on the doorstep. I expected no shortage of pyrotechnics. Phil answered the door, his face an unreadable tangle of welcome and worry. He had moved all Irina's flowers back onto the breakfast bar, and his living room, now packed with people, was both emptier without the blooms and full of a tension almost as vibrant.

Irina was perched on one arm of Phil's love seat in her gauze and turquoise, while Jimmy reclined into its depths in his linen and flesh—the ascetic and the sensualist side-by-side on the sofa. He as swollen as she was shriveled, every pound of the man a proud testament to past pleasures and current appetites. "Ren!" He held out his arms, and I bent over him to take a kiss on both my cheeks.

"Hello, darling," Irina's hands lifted from her lap in what I'm sure she thought was a regal gesture reminiscent of rings kissed, but reminded me of the stiff elbows and fallen wrists of zombies. I held her brittle fingers and met her eyes, like little pointed shovels, peering into mine. "Meet Ramon," she said, waving to the man beside her.

He was tall, black, and thin, his face all sharp angles, his head almost shaved. He stood with his arms crossed over his chest, his back to the curtained glass doors. He stepped forward smoothly to shake my hand, his clothes almost monklike in their austerity, but exquisitely made of something sheenless and soft. Simplicity, not poverty, if he'd taken any vows at all. "How are you, Ren?" he asked.

And because he seemed genuinely interested, and because he hadn't said it, I said, "I feel like someone put a flaming stake through my head," which made him laugh. Which made me like him.

Irina offered to help Phil make us all drinks, and Oskar stood in a single, fluid gesture, to give me his chair. It put his powerful body, of which we were both conscious, closer to mine than necessary, just in case I'd missed the point that it was beautifully formed. I hadn't, but I plunked into his vacated seat unceremoniously.

Phil's empty chair was on Ramon's left, across from Irina, and separated from me by a small coffee table. Oskar drew up a barstool to close the circle. He'd changed out of his T-shirt and sports coat into an open-necked light blue linen which showed a bronze fuzz of chest and a low-hanging charm on a red thread. I wondered what superstition or sentiment a man like Oskar wore over his heart.

"Now we are six," Irina observed, handing me tea in a dainty porcelain shamrock-painted teacup whose gold trim gave the tea a metallic edge.

"Yes," Ramon agreed. "Until we've located Celeste, I think we must have both Oskar and Ren with us."

"Then this isn't Salt, just a gathering of friends," Irina said raising her glass. "Should we call Matsu as well, to keep the number prime?"

"I don't see why." Oskar matched Irina's casual, breezy tone.

"Ren, you know, don't you," the calm in Ramon's voice was real, although anything but easy, "that you have become the pivot of a rather weighty teeter-totter."

Lucky me. "Could I play on the swings instead?" Even my tea tasted bitter.

Ramon smiled politely. "Celeste is the only Incrementalist to ever successfully alpha-lock a memory," he said. "You have her stub, and we can't find her final memory."

Jimmy, Irina and Phil all looked at me.

"You do know who Celeste is?" Ramon asked.

"I know better than to ask."

Ramon nodded, satisfied. "Very well. The rest of us—all of us—have our memories of Celeste, but we have none of her memories. And you—the one who should have not only her memories but her personality—can scarcely remember her name between hours."

"Is it because she committed suicide?" I asked.

"We don't know," Phil said quietly beside me. "Maybe."

I wasn't sure if it was grief for her or fear for me that kept his voice subdued, but I couldn't afford to be delicate. "Because I was wondering," I said. "What if she didn't?"

"You're the one who said she did." Irina's voice was clear and hard. Something had shifted since I'd seen her last, and I didn't think it was just the currents of strength I could feel her drawing from Jimmy.

"I know," I said, still talking to Phil, but something had changed in him too. He felt steeled, but I was just going to pretend it couldn't possibly be against me. "I know I said Celeste killed herself, but I told you why I said it, and I've been thinking more about it since." I could feel Oskar coiled on his stool behind my shoulder. I didn't want to, but I turned my eyes from Phil to Ramon, still standing motionless between Irina, fidgeting on her sofa arm, and Phil, rigid in his easy chair.

"Maybe I got it wrong," I said. "Everyone keeps telling me how out of character suicide would have been for Celeste."

Phil nodded, and I met Irina's cold eyes. "What if someone killed her?" I asked. "I understand that's not against the rules."

Irina flinched, and something in Phil let go, but Ramon just shook his head. "It is not strictly forbidden," he said. "It used to happen more, but no matter how hot we all may burn at times, few would choose the cold of isolation over the friction of our fellows. To undertake such clumsy work is to be tribeless until the Second dies."

"And after?" I asked. "Do you ever just leave someone in stub?"

"No." Oskar's voice was a raw growl.

"Almost never," Phil said. "And then not forever. Doing that now, even for a few years, would mean leaving the stub so lost in how things have changed that it would almost guarantee dominance of the new recruit."

"But often the recruit chosen for such a stub is a very powerful personality." Ramon's professorial tone didn't waver. "Perhaps someone somewhat unyielding. The personalities integrate, of course, and the stub retains the memory of their reasons for killing and its consequences, but frequently the personality is so broken by them that it does not seek dominance, even with a relatively pliant Second."

"And that Incrementalist still usually spends that second lifetime alone," Jimmy said. "Certainly he tends to stay distant from the new Second of the Incrementalist he stubbed."

"Or they marry," Irina said softly.

"Yes," Ramon agreed. "Or they marry."

"And you do the opposite if you're in love?" I said, putting down my fragile teacup carefully. "Do you recruit a Second whose personality is weak and more likely to be dominated by the stub's?"

"No," Ramon said. "That would be discouraged." He uncrossed his arms and clasped his hands behind his back. "We always select for strength. How could anyone unresilient, incurious or dogmatic bear up under the weight of what we are? Ren, you know what you've been through."

"Is still going through, Ray," Phil cut in. "It's only been four days."

"I am sorry, Ren." Ramon inclined his head toward me just fractionally. "It occurs to me that Celeste might have nudged even me a little, in this regard. I did not read the file Phil seeded. And I always do. For some reason, with you, I was looking away."

"We all were," Oskar said.

"I wasn't." Jimmy's voice was soft. He was looking at Phil.

"Jimmy sent me," Irina said.

"Not until it was too late." Oskar stood up from his barstool. "You chose Ren, Phil. But you may have underestimated her strength."

"Celeste chose Ren," Irina said.

Oskar started to demand something of Phil, but Phil's voice cut over Oskar's. "Maybe I didn't," he said. "Maybe I knew exactly how strong Ren was."

Oskar barked a laugh and sat back down. "You would never have done that," he said. "You loved Celeste. You followed her through how many Seconds? Two? Three? Trying to get back those couple of good years the two of you had before the Great War. But everyone had good years then. It wasn't Celeste, Phil. We were all happy then. Happy, and paying as much attention to the nemones as we do when we are. Which is never enough. And you're still clinging to that dream of Celeste because you can't give up. You never could. You've never known when it was time to let go of an unrealistic dream."

"And you never knew when it was time to wait for one," Phil told Oskar. "You want to reach into the womb of dreams and tear yours free before it's fully formed. That's why you found yourself skulking around The Palms even though you're worse at subterfuge than I am." Phil closed his eyes, his eyebrows like a fist.

I remembered the way their tough hairs felt under my finger and against my face, and I watched the work of Phil mastering himself, dragging self-control up the sheer face of rage and fear and something stronger. It must have cost him everything he had, but when he opened his eyes and found mine, they were the same warm brown they had been when he first touched me. "Ren," he said quietly, like there was no one else there. "Do you think someone killed Celeste?"

I wanted something profound to match the depth in his eyes. "Maybe," I said.

Oskar made a Viking noise in the back of his throat. "That's stupid," he said. "Who, beside me, would have anything to gain from Celeste's death?"

"Matsu would be next in the Salt after you," Ramon noted.

"Matsu will scarcely come to a gathering when we beg him," Irina said. "He has no interest in, or talent for, this messiness."

"But he would step up," Jimmy said. "Remember Seville? Matsu has never lacked for courage. And certainly, in tribute to Celeste, he would do what was needed."

"True." Irina turned to Jimmy, nodding. "He was one of those who always got on with Celeste."

"Because he never loved her," Oskar said.

"Ren," Ramon asked me, "why do you doubt your memory of Celeste's suicide?"

"Because it was never really a memory," I said, and took a swallow of tea. "It was just an idea triggered by her word 'martyr.' But I'm guessing my roommate's OD was in Phil's file. Anyone could have known that I'm twitchy around that idea, and it seems like everyone thinks my head is a fine place to tinker with the future."

"Not the future," Ramon said. "No one believes we know that."

"But Ramon, there is so very much at stake just now," Irina whispered, studying her hands. "Humanity is poised to upend its mad pyramid of needs and wants and dreams, and drive itself, and us, back to berries and caves. Or to build a new structure on something quite near to that order, inverted."

"Humanity has long fancied itself thus teetering," Jimmy said.

"But this time it's true." Oskar spoke without moving. "Man has found a mirror. He looks into the clear glass of science and sees his own face for the first time. Neuroscience will show all of us who we are, who we have been, and how we might become who we long to be. Soon, a profile of fourteen neurotransmitter levels will not only explain, but predict behavior."

Someone scoffed, I'm not sure who. Oskar ignored it. "And consider this: We already produce enough for everyone to have nutritious food, good health care, and decent housing, with only the distribution system standing in the way of panhuman post-scarcity. The new content is there, but needs to break out of its old forms. And we could help, if we were willing. We've tweaked oxytocin levels to build trust, and boosted dopamine to generate reward since the days of angels and devils. Let's use our scientific magic to destroy the blockades of greed in the distribution system and let profit-based deprivation finally die. Or Big Pharma and, hell, advertising, will start using our tricks to drive sales."

"He's right," I said. "There are already half a dozen big neuromarketing firms out there working to nudge people any direction retailers want them to go."

"How can we stay hidden," Oskar demanded, "when our tribe's gift is exploited to rake in wealth for a few rather than distribute it to the many?"

"Exploited by whom, dear Bronstein?" My voice cut across Oskar's.

My voice, but not my words.

"Who are these rake wielders of whom you speak? Capitalists? Producers and consumers? You are too eager, my dear boy, to tell another man's story in just one word. When you assign *-ist* to anyone, you throw all our years of accumulated nuance away."

"Celeste?" I could feel Phil next to me, but I couldn't make my eyes move from Oskar's pale face.

"It is not our ideologies, nor our chemistry, but our memories that tell us who we are. We disclose our histories to our lovers, so they will know us from our infancy. We create ourselves, telling our biographies to strangers, and construct our morality from the same narrative. 'I could never,' we say. 'I'm not the kind of person who,' and 'I always.' But how long is a memory, Oskar? How long is yours?"

We were both standing, Oskar lean and wary, Celeste towering, furious and powerful, inside my smaller body.

"Humanity swims in the shallow skin of an ocean that is infinitely deeper, more complex, and more chaotic than we can bear to look into," Celeste said. "We develop unique tastes—this kind of food, that kind of sex—and try to satisfy our need for meaning by consuming what we like, not creating what we love. We name ourselves by these petty dispositions: by what we won't eat—Vegan." Celeste pointed my finger at Irina. "Or for whom we will not vote—Radical." She drew my finger to Jimmy. "Or by how, and with whom we make love—wife, sadist, bisexual, polyamorous *amante.*" She stroked my fingers down the length of my throat, and turned my eyes to Oskar. "But how could I have loved you for so many years, dear boy, if I did not keep looking for your other selves? I worked to find them out. Punk, romantic, warrior, child. I wonder, can you see anything but Moderate in me?"

Oskar closed the distance between us, glaring down into my eyes. Celeste raised my face to him. Far away, I knew everyone in the room was on their feet. "Your neurochemistry is crude sonar, nothing more," Celeste whispered up at Oskar. "It graphs a black-and-white outline of the ocean bed. It shows you nothing of the water's clarity or temperature, speed or salinity. Nor any information about the slippery little fish of meaning."

Oskar stood over me and smiled the wolf's bare-fanged smile of a clean, swift kill.

"All of those things are knowable, Celeste. You try to drown yourself in your unknowable sea, thinking nothing will disturb you in its depths. You speak of an ocean in which you're afraid to swim. But truth is real, and it is objective, and it will find you sooner or later. You chose a poor analogy in the ocean, because I do know something of its Salt. I know you're out of it." He dropped my eyes and reclaimed his barstool as though newly crowned. "Celeste has been hiding," he said to Ramon. "Ren is a viable spike. Celeste is recessive in her, and I am in the Salt."

"That is the tradition," Ramon noted. "If Celeste is simply lost in Ren, there can be no debate."

"There can be all kinds of it," Phil said, standing and coiled. "And I can promise you there will be. On every front. Of every kind. Debate is what we do. But not about this. Not now."

Ramon put a hand on Phil's arm, and I thought it brave of him, considering. "There must be nothing—no decision made, no judgment passed"—he said—"until we find and free the alpha-lock."

I sat down.

"I feel like shit," I said.

"Finish your tea," Irina suggested.

"You people are nuts," I observed. "And I have a headache."

"We have asked too much of you, *ma chère,*" Jimmy said.

I finished my tea, pulled myself out of my chair, and got my bag from where I'd dropped it under the Kovacs painting by the front door. "I'm going to go lie down," I said. "I have a couple things I need to do for work, and then I'm going to graze for Celeste. If she is hiding, I want to know where."

I met Phil's questioning eyes with my swimmy ones.

I walked between Oskar and Jimmy, past Irina and Ramon to take Phil's hand and squeeze it. "I'm okay," I said. "Take your time. But wake me when it's over."

I walked back through the web of unspoken questions whose answers belonged only to us, and went into Phil's bedroom. I shut the door, undressed, and climbed into his bed.

Phil

"Phil," said Jimmy for the second or third time, and I finally looked away from the bedroom door.

"What?"

"Are you all right?"

"No, Jimmy. I'm not all right. Any other questions?"

"What's wrong?" said Ray.

I didn't answer. Irina said, "I proposed stubbing Ren."

Oskar said, "Really! You're that afraid of me?"

"Yes," she said.

"Then you don't know Phil as well as I'd thought you did, or you'd have proposed it with him out of the room and never seeded any of it until after the fact."

"Why?" said Ray.

"Christ, Ramon," said Jimmy.

"What?"

"I think," said Irina, "that we ought to at least discuss it," and there was a little pulse at her throat, which might have been enough, but she brought her knuckle up to rub her upper lip as she spoke, so I couldn't have missed it if I'd wanted to.

"You folks carry on without me," I said. "I need to putter."

I went into the kitchen and poured some lemon juice and water into a soup bowl, heated it in the microwave, then soaked a washcloth in it. I put some butter on a piece of French bread, sprinkled garlic powder on it, and heated that. I made a glass of instant iced tea. I lit the candle. I set all of these delicacies on a tray, then found "Childhood's End" by Pink Floyd. I turned the volume down to a whisper, and set it to playing in the living room while I carried the tray in. I put the tray in front of Irina, picked up the washcloth, smiled, and ran it gently over her forehead. The conversation stopped, everyone watching me.

"What did you do to Ren?" I asked her.

Her eyes widened, and for a second she tried to fight it, but it was too sudden, and too complete. "I put concentrated benzodiazepine and opium in her tea," she said.

"Jimmy—" I said.

"On it," he said, and closed his eyes. A horribly, horribly long ten seconds later he opened them and said, "Flumazenil. Point two milligrams in saline over fifteen seconds to start, repeat at one-minute intervals if necessary."

Ray stood. "We have time. I'll graze for a pharmacy on the way and have it back here before the EMTs could figure out what to do."

I tossed him my car keys. "Go," I said.

He went.

Jimmy said, "Irina, leave now," at which point I realized that Jimmy was standing between me and her.

She stood up without a word and left.

He should have told her to take her fucking flowers with her.

Ren

Phil's bed was soft, and his room was dark, and I was miles more tired than I had been even an hour ago. I could remember Celeste's anger in my chest, but not her words. Or even Phil's. She had churned the whole casing of my torso and left it pulped and muddy.

I didn't know if I could graze. I turned my cheek into Phil's pillow to touch my temple with the back of my fingers, but my head wouldn't turn and my hand didn't move. I wanted Phil's arms and our dancing. I wanted him to come to bed.

But he would be talking. With the rest of them. Always talking. And where was the little dog with the red collar to match my ghostly toes already sinking into mud? I would have called him, but my lips were numb.

And I did not know his name. He was never one of mine. They never are, my nightmutts in the garden of good and plenty. But he was black and blond, like licorice.

But where were the overlays that candy-coat this black goo? What had Phil told me to say? What does he say when he closes his eyes? I would take even his Jurassic date palm.

It had been about that long. Sad.

But my jeans were rolled up too high, like clam diggers at the beach with my dad, because the mud was touching them. We made mud angels, like the snow ones but harder to get out in the laundry, and Mom said it was disgusting. But I knew that memories should wrap me up, cocoon me, and the beach and the green bucket of clams were only words.

I lay down in it.

How deep did the mud go? What did it hide?

"Ren!"

His bark was calling out of the sky a long way above. No dogs on the sea air.

"Ren!"

My pink-and-blue dragon without her Play Family Castle, my poky puppy with his muddy paws, and the gold tags like a tiny charm on a red cord.

Silly puppy, tricks are for pigs.

"Ren, listen to me. You're in trouble. I need you stay awake, okay?"

Big dogs tell no tails.

"Ren, stay with me. Can you open your eyes?"

My hair was in the mud. I did not like it in my ears.

"That's good, Ren. Can you see me?"

Yes, with your sweet puppy mouth of wolf teeth.

"Stay with me."

I said that to someone once. But the puppy left. Maybe the vulture got him in her sharp brown claws and ate him with bright red poppies and mint. But my ears were full of the mud now so it did not hurt. And heavy on my chest. Too much to breathe in. And vast and empty, circling over me, the carrion sky.

TEN

A More Reasonable Question

Phil

I held her hand while Ray administered the injection. Her hand was limp, which was bad, but warm, which was good.

"Is that enough?" I asked him.

He gave me that look professionals get when amateurs question them.

"All right," I said. "Do we need to get her to the hospital?"

That, apparently, was a more reasonable question. "I'll watch her. Avoiding the hospital would be better, or she'll spend the next three years meddling just to get her life back."

"Unless we tell them what happened. Then Irina will."

"No, then we all will."

Jimmy came in and handed me a glass of ice water. A little later Oskar came in, put a comforting hand on my shoulder, and left.

Ray checked her pulse, put his head on her chest to listen to her breathing or heartbeat or something, and grunted. I drank some water. You can repeat that sequence several more times.

Eventually, Ray looked up and said, "She'll be okay. She's just sleeping now."

"Thanks, Ray."

"It's Ramon," he said, and left me alone with Ren.

I took a breath and let it out slowly, closed my eyes and put my temple against hers. I was not, goddammit, going to cry twice in two days. One day? Three days? How long had it been since I'd walked into that café to do a typical first interview with a potential recruit? Was the WSOP over? How were the Pirates doing? Christ. Too much to handle; Fibonacci couldn't deal with all of this, with Celeste, with Ren, with Irina, with the goddamn mud sucking at my shoes not wanting to pull me down as much as to keep me, to make me stay, one place, one goddamn fucking place just for a little while, was that so much to ask?

I'd loved Pittsburgh with her steel mills and her frame houses and theaters and restaurants in the back of people's homes, and Vienna with her tiny winding streets like Baghdad, which they fucking bombed and was that coffee shop with the fat man who always shook his head when he laughed, was it still there, or had it been bombed we should have stopped it God help me maybe Oskar is right, but the Sahara is so fucking hot I'd promised myself never again that far from lakes and rivers and oceans and here I am in Las fucking Vegas, but where next I just wish I just wish I just wish I could stop, make it all stop, but screens filter out everything in the mud that isn't alive, and what's left keeps me moving, pushing, play the next hand, the next session, the next day, the next lifetime, yes life, it really does mean that much, whatever else you do to someone, the end of life is the end of hope and hope can't can't can't end so pick your feet up out of the mud and wave to the living things but pass on.

You want to know what sucks? Pope Gregory VII was real. You want to know what doesn't? So was Spartacus. And even, in a way, Robin Hood. I mean, sort of. Yes, we Incrementalists made him up, but not out of whole cloth. And we had nothing to do with the popular reaction to him. Resistance to tyranny takes many forms, and the fact that we—Incrementalists and amnemones alike—make heroes out of those who resist, says something fine about us all and is one of the things that keeps me pulling my feet out of the mud.

But what is tyranny, anyway? It's just the result of ambition pushed a little too far. And ambition is how we all got out of the mud.

Here's the thing, though: Small changes are just what lead to big changes. Can't help it. That's how nature works. Water gets a little hotter, and a little hotter, and a little hotter, and then you have steam, which is a pretty big change if you happen to be a water molecule. So even if you try to do something small, you'll end up doing something big, and if you do something big, then people are going to get hurt. God help me, maybe Celeste is right.

Ren took my hand to pull me out of the mud, and suddenly it wasn't holding me, but we were skating along atop it, me in my slick shoes, her in her bare feet, and we were twirling, and we were laughing, and when we fell down we got up again, still laughing. A dream created within a construct of the mind? Go ahead, interpret *that,* Sigmund. But I was good with it, because I was moving again, and I realized that I was never going to stop moving, and that would be all right if I had someone to move with me.

"Phil?" said Ren for the second or third time.

"I'm right here, my love," I told her. My voice sounded harsh in my own ears, but her hand felt so good in mine.

"I'm glad," she told me. "Come to bed."

Ren

I threw up. Then I lounged for a while on the clean solid tile wearing Phil's robe, twitching with cold and slick with sweat. Then I threw up again.

I answered Jimmy's discreet knocking with a mumble, and he came in and started reading the bottoms of Phil's tiny shampoo bottles. He selected one and poured its contents into a little paper cup he found on the sink. He filled the cup the rest of the way with water and handed it to me.

"Medicine," Jimmy explained, "distilled from your previous healing and personal comfort. They take a long time to formulate, so good titans build their pharmacopoeia as they do their research, well before contact with a recruit is made."

I nodded and drank. The water was cool and tasteless, and it lay still in my twisting stomach.

Jimmy studied the rows of little bottles. "Huh," he said. "This must be the first time you've encountered something for which Phil had prepared."

"Poisoning?" I croaked.

"Nausea."

"Thanks, Jimmy," I said. He inclined his head gallantly and seated himself on the tub edge. "Did you sleep on the barstool all night?" I asked. "I saw you when I came in to puke."

"Yes. I wasn't sleeping."

"But you knew I'd want the first few minutes on my own?"

He nodded.

"Why'd you stay?" I asked him.

"It was the only way Phil would sleep."

I pulled his robe closer around me to feel wrapped in his body. "It's lonely being poisoned," I said. "I needed him. Thank you."

"It was nothing."

"Why else did you stay?"

His bleary eyes focused. He shrugged. "To persuade him to, if the comforts of his bed were not enough to keep him here."

I waited.

"Ramon argued against any further delay. To him, lifetimes out of tribe, rage, loyalty, and revenge are trivial compared to the alpha-lock. He suggested we make peace with Irina. Matsu is on his way."

"It was Irina?"

"She spiked your tea."

I used a bad word.

Jimmy smiled without humor. "Phil said much the same."

I sang, "So why'd you put that poison in my tea?"

"Hmm?"

"Nothing. Never mind. Flash Girls song. I'm going to throw up," I said.

"Are you a leave-me-alone-when-I-vomit person, or a stay-and-comfort—"

"The former."

"I'll go." Jimmy stood, filling the space between tub and sink. "But I will make eggs for you unless you tell me you want ham."

"Eggs are good," I said.

Jimmy left. I threw up. But it left me feeling better, so I turned the shower on. Phil had great water pressure and right then, that alone would have been enough to make me love him.

I stood in the drenching heat and remembered his body sliding into bed beside mine, his arms shaking, and my face against his long throat. We slept together the same way he had put a flaming stake between my eyes—with no difference between what was real and what was symbolic. Our bodies were extraneous, boats on the unmanageable ocean, but we could swim. If we could filter all the material out, take the dust from the mud, we'd have been water, but my body in the water whispered "bullshit." It wanted him. I wanted him. In a real and material, not-metaphorical way.

I turned off the tap and dried myself off. Wrapped in Phil's bathrobe, I ate eggs while Jimmy scrubbed out emptied flower vases. I passed on the tea. He made coffee. I carried two cups with my laptop into the bedroom. Phil was shirtless in jeans and a Gordian knot of bedding. I plumped up pillows and wedged my back against the headboard with my hip against his back. I alternately Googled and grazed for switches that would work as RMMD icons or audio, and I stroked the gorgeous place where the top of Phil's biceps swallowed the end of his collarbone and the start of his shoulder blade, not because it was beautiful, but because it was his. No, because it was him.

Phil

The smell of coffee and the touch of her hand woke me up, which is a far, far better way to wake up than many others. After what seemed a long time, I said, "If I sit up and drink coffee, will you still be able to do that?"

"It will challenge me," she said, "to find something else."

I sat up, took the coffee, drank some, and set it down. I looked at her. "Thank you. How are you feeling?"

"The headache's gone. You saved my life."

"We all did. Jimmy found the antidote, Ray procured and administered it. Welcome to the family. We work together and hardly ever try to kill each other. I'm sorry that happened."

She put a hand on my leg over the blanket; it woke me up faster than coffee. "You told me before that it was rarely dangerous. I guess I'm just lucky."

"I should have added that it's regularly dangerous to your peace of mind. But peace of mind, as Oskar would say, is a bourgeois luxury."

She gave a gentle laugh. It sent shivers through me. "He would say that."

"Do you remember who Celeste is?"

"No. Should I?"

"In some sense." I drank more coffee. Saving someone's life is a wonderful feeling. Try it. You feel like, if you don't mind a TV reference, a big damn hero. I've done it before. I've also been saved. The latter is not always such a good feeling. You're glad to be alive, and the gratitude you feel isn't feigned, but it can make things weird with your rescuer. Especially if your rescuer is someone you very badly want. Your head plays games, and your rescuer's head plays games, because you might feel obliged, and the rescuer might be afraid that you feel obliged. Lust and obligation have a tendency to get in each other's way and mess up both. In the worst case, it turns into a battle of obligations. More than a few marriages have broken on those rocks.

So I enjoyed her touch, and enjoyed the coffee, and only clenched my jaw metaphorically, and shifted my position very slightly so what I was feeling wasn't quite so obvious. From time to time her hand would move when she had to type something, but then she'd bring it back to my leg. I studied her face. What I'd first thought was American Indian could also be a touch of South Pacific Islander. Or, God knows in this country, anything else. She was fully concentrating on what she was doing, and her total focus reminded me of Ray.

Given an endless supply of coffee, I could have just stayed there indefinitely, even enjoying unfulfilled lust. But as I was staring at the empty cup and weighing my options, there was a soft tap on the door.

"Come in," I said, and there was Jimmy.

"Matsu is here. Take your time, we're filling him in."

He shut the door.

Ren was looking at me. "I don't remember much about Matsu," she said. "He's a fighter, isn't he?"

I nodded.

"Are you expecting a fight?"

"No. But he's almost Salt, and he's not stupid, and he has a good perspective on things. And he gets under Oskar's skin the way Oskar gets under everyone else's. These are all good things. I'm going to get up and face the world now." I kissed her cheek and got out of bed. I grabbed underwear, socks, and a shirt, then took myself to the bathroom to prepare to face the world.

She was wearing my bathrobe, so I had to use a towel to dry myself, but eventually I emerged, coffee cup in hand, ready for human society. I went past everyone, straight to the coffeemaker, got the last cup, started another pot, then came back.

"Hello, Matt."

Matt is as blond and blue-eyed as Oskar, but a bit shorter and considerably leaner. He radiates calm the way Oskar radiates intensity, and is reserved the way Jimmy is effusive. I can't think of anyone

I've known for as long and know less about. In this Second, he was about forty years old, which put him right at the peak of his abilities—his body had by now caught up to his knowledge, but hadn't yet started to degenerate. He rose and smiled and gave me a hug that was at once warm and reserved.

I sat down on the couch since Oskar had my chair again. Matt sat across from me and said, "I'm looking forward to meeting Ren."

"She's working, but I'm sure she'll be out soon."

"Working?" said Jimmy. "On what?"

"I imagine her sugar spoon, or else she's gathering switches for some meddlework I know nothing about, or grazing for Celeste."

"Yes," said Matt. "Celeste. That is a problem, isn't it?"

"So is Irina," I said. "Would you mind stubbing her for me, Matt?"

"I won't do that, no."

"Just asking."

Ray said, "Celeste, Irina, and the alpha-lock. All related problems. How do we address them?"

Oskar said nothing; I suspect he was trying to control his annoyance at having to share the same air as Matt.

The door opened, and Ren emerged, and my heart did a thing. I guess it showed, because I looked over and caught Jimmy watching me. He said, "I don't know, but permit me to suggest that stubbing Ren is not one of the options."

"Glad to hear it," she said, and sat down on the couch next to me.

Ren

It was a formidable group of men to greet in a bathrobe, but my hair was clean, and Phil introduced me to Matsu, sitting cross-legged in an office chair someone had rolled in from Phil's office, while Jimmy refilled my coffee.

I sat on the sofa by Phil, where Irina had perched on the armrest last night, and tried not to feel some residual sinister pall over the cushions. Ramon was standing by the glass doors again, but their curtains were open to reveal the date palm and the scraggly yard. With Oskar in Phil's chair and Jimmy in what I'd already started to think of as mine, we were a stranger, sleepier reprise of last night.

"It's good to see you looking well," Ramon said, and I remembered Phil's litany of the people who'd saved my life, and how I'd gone to bed naked, and felt my face pink up.

"Thanks," I said. "Thanks, all of you." I looked at Oskar and Jimmy. "That was scary."

Phil squeezed my knee. Jimmy nodded.

Ramon said, "Indeed," while his eyes searched my face and hair and fingers, then he said, "We can wait for you. Or work without you."

"I'm okay," I said.

"Very well. You suggested the hypothesis last night, that perhaps rather than suicide, Celeste's death had been murder."

No way I was going to say, "Who's Celeste" again.

"Were you perhaps intuiting Irina's attempt on your life and misinterpreting?"

"I don't think so," I said. Having been on the receiving side of a murderous hatred, I felt sorry for Celeste suddenly, whoever she was.

"You believe she was killed, and the notion of her suicide suggested to you by someone with access to your memories?"

"It's just that I don't remember Celeste," I said. "So before everyone else remembers her as a suicide, based on something I've said, I needed to say I didn't remember."

I had the uncomfortable feeling of having just made very little sense in front of a lot of very smart people.

"Oskar," Ramon said, "this casts suspicion on you, of course. You had the most to gain from Celeste's death. You should, perhaps, excuse yourself."

If I'd held everyone's eyes before, Oskar now had them eyes, ears, and curly hairs.

"Fine," he said, disgusted.

"Hang on," Phil said, almost on his feet. "If we're going to start excusing people, we need to do better than casting suspicion around like fishing line."

"It's okay," said Oskar, rising to his full height.

"It's not," Phil said.

"No, it is," I said, "because Oskar knows he can get into your Garden."

Oskar, very slowly, sat back down.

"No, not really," Phil said. "It doesn't work like that."

"I'm sorry, Oskar," I said. "You reached out to me last night, and it saved me, your voice telling me to stay awake when breathing seemed like more trouble than I felt like taking, but I already knew."

"No," Phil said again.

I said, "Have any of you seen him in your Garden?"

Ramon reached into the neck of Oskar's shirt and studied the gold charm on the red cord. He dropped it and straightened. "I have seen him in mine."

"I haven't," Matsu said.

"Nor I," said Jimmy.

"I'll just go then," Oskar volunteered.

Matsu stood, and Oskar stayed in his chair.

Jimmy dropped his head into his hands. "The whole Garden is running amok or breaking down. It's all going alpha. All the noise is signal. Everyone's meddling with everyone else. It's like the Dark Years, but now we're all too agile to catch."

"And it's no longer just us," Oskar said. "Don't forget the nemones are meddling too."

"We must find the alpha-lock," Ramon said.

"There's ritual," Phil said.

"Or sex," Oskar's voice was almost a whisper.

"Irina is Salt," Jimmy said. "And we need five."

"Oskar and I will stay behind." Matsu's voice was a threat and a promise. "We are not."

"Ren?"

"For this," I said, "I should get dressed."

"Phil?"

Phil

"No," I said.

Ren looked at me, startled and worried.

Ray said, "But—" and I held a hand up.

"Sorry," I said. "I didn't mean no to going. Or getting dressed. I meant no to Oskar and Matt staying behind." I had everyone's attention, except for Ren who ducked into the bedroom. "First of all, fuck tradition. Second, fuck ritual. There's no law that says it has to be five, it's custom and you all know it. Jesus, our only rule is that we have no rules."

"But—" said Ray.

"I want us all to meet in my Garden to see where Celeste's final memory should be. I want Matt there because I trust him and because I'm betting he fights as well in the virtual world as he does in the real world."

Oskar said, "You think—"

"And," I said, steamrolling him, but so caught up in the moment that I couldn't enjoy it, "I want Oskar there because this is all directed at him."

I stopped there, waiting to see who'd speak first. It was Ray. "You know this, how?"

"Oh, come on, Ray. You can see the pattern, can't you? Who was Celeste afraid of? Where is all the suspicion pointing? Who did you just suggest couldn't be here?"

"The argument that suspicion points to someone is not, in itself, proof that—"

"Oh, bullshit, Ray."

He muttered something I didn't understand, probably in Catalan, then he said, "It's Ramon."

Oskar was utterly still; what else could he be?

Jimmy said, "I think you're right," which caused some confusion because neither Ray nor I were looking at him. "You, Phil," he added. "It looks more than anything else like Celeste trying to—"

"Celeste is dead," said Ren coming back from my bedroom wearing clothes.

"Valid point," said Ray.

"You remember?" I said.

She nodded.

"Then," I said, "let's go now, while you still do."

We all looked at Ray. He hesitated, then nodded. I think his driving motive was curiosity, but I was fine with that.

Oskar said, "Someone needs to explain it to Ren. She still hasn't had the memory rush yet."

"Explaining it to me would be nice too," I muttered.

"The Garden," said Jimmy, "is whatever you want it to be. Your individual Garden is a product of your subconscious, but everything else is arbitrary. You can fly. You can walk through walls. You can create or destroy objects at will.

"When someone else brings you into his or her Garden, it works a bit differently. It's a shared, imagined world. You see it as that person imagines it is, but you can't hurt someone else's actual Garden, or make permanent changes. You can move or change a seed, but it'll revert when you leave. And you experience the memories more viscerally when you take them in their native symbol. When I, in my Garden, drink as wine a memory Phil seeded as a flower, I know the information that memory contains. When he allows me to pluck his blue bud, I live the experience as he did."

Oskar coughed, Ramon studied his boot toes, and Jimmy covered the awkward silence by plowing on.

"What we're going to try to do now is all of us reach Phil's Garden. We'll all be in this room, and we can talk to each other, and we'll simultaneously be there, individually, and can look over—"

"Wait," she said. "Individually?"

He nodded.

"So, I won't see any of you there?"

"No, but we'll be right here—"

"Is it possible to be together there, too?"

Jimmy looked at me. Ray said, "It's possible, but unnecessary."

"If you'd be more comfortable," said Oskar, "that's fine."

"I would," she said.

I stood up. "All right." I opened my arms for her. She stood up and walked into them, with no trace of self-consciousness. I felt everyone else's fingers touch my temple.

"Is everyone ready?" said Jimmy. When no one spoke, he said, "Leaving now."

Ren said, "What do I do?"

"I'll show you my favorite way," I said, and kissed her. I could feel the moment when, "I'm kissing someone in a crowd of strangers I don't trust," turned into, "To hell with them anyway." She kissed me back.

Her skin smelled like cherry blossoms and her mouth tasted like chives.

ELEVEN

The Easy Way

Ren

Ocean air and root beer, sweet and salty, and wrapped up in Phil. Phil, and four other guys. Weird. Not bad, but weird.

I opened my eyes, and almost screamed. Phil's villa must have been in Pompeii; it was hip-deep in black sludge and everything—the walls and trees, the courtyard and fountain—were coated in, or melting into, the ashy mud. Phil made a noise between a whimper and a moan, his mouth reaching for mine. I couldn't talk, only try to kiss comfort onto his lips for the destruction of his Garden. He took it hungrily.

"It's fine now, Phil."

"No sign of Ren's Garden bleeding over anymore, Phil."

"Yup, nice and solid here."

"Oh, for the love of God, Phil!"

I lost Phil's mouth and opened my eyes. Jimmy had one beefy hand on my shoulder and one on Phil's, his substantial bulk imposed between our bodies. "That should do nicely, thank you, you two," he said.

Phil beamed blearily at him.

Oskar had stalked off to one end of the courtyard. Matsu

wandered to the other. Ramon was still standing near us, studying his nail beds with unwarranted interest.

I looked around. "I've definitely been here," I said. "Oskar too. I saw him eating dates."

Phil tipped his head up, considering the fruit hanging from the branches over our heads. "They're olives," he said. "Dates are at the Las Vegas house."

"Ever have a long argument with a Praetorian just before the war with Parthia, say 161 ACE, as they count the years now?" Oskar asked.

Phil looked up again, then at Oskar. "What about it?"

"That wine was awfully bitter."

Phil exhaled slowly. "Damn," he said.

"How did you get into his Garden?" Ramon asked Oskar, something almost like passion in the tart clip of his words. "And mine."

"Celeste taught me."

"Celeste?" It's possible we all said it together.

"I caught her in mine."

"And you threatened to tell the rest of us about her new ability unless she shared it with you?" Matsu guessed.

"There was no threat," Oskar said, sounding annoyed. "I caught her, asked her, she told me."

"You were lovers," I said, remembering how he'd asked if Phil had told me what happened when Incrementalists made love. "Oh, shit," I said. Oskar had been trying to see if Phil had made a similar deal with Celeste. Because Phil and Celeste had been. "You didn't know. I'm sorry, Phil."

Phil untied the knot holding back his hair and retied it, considering this new information about the man he'd just defended and the woman he had loved. He took my hand. "It's okay," he said, and somehow, I believed it was. "Let's go find her last memory."

Still holding my hand, he led us, strange parade that we were, past an orchard and out through a broken wooden gate to a little hill behind his house where a simple stone bench sat nestled in a modest grove of olive trees. "According to my Garden, this is where Celeste's Garden begins." He pointed at a hole in the ground. "That's where her stub was," he said. "And that pomegranate is her next-to-last memory. And that," he said, pointing at the empty place between the hole and the fruit, "is where a *kithara* isn't."

We all gazed seriously at the thing that wasn't there.

"Kithara?" Matsu said at last.

"Stringed contraption," Jimmy explained. "Like a lyre."

"Liar?"

"Never mind."

"Well," Ramon said after serious consideration. "It's not there."

"Right," Phil said.

"The Y axis is gone."

"Right," Phil said again.

"All we know for certain is the X."

"The X is Celeste," I said. "She's dead."

Phil looked at me a long time. Then he looked through me. We stood around Celeste's missing memory like mourners graveside until Phil's eyes refocused. "Gone," he said. "But not forgotten."

"I'm listening," said Ramon.

"We don't have Celeste's memories, but we have our memories of Celeste. Could that be enough? Could we create her out of our memories of her?"

"Jimmy?" Ramon said.

Jimmy shrugged. "That's not a grazing thing. Matsu's the pattern shaman."

I said, "Can someone please explain that?"

Matsu opened his mouth, closed it, and shrugged. "All right." He pulled a handful of olives from a tree. "If I have six black rocks," he said, placing six olives on the bench seat where they obligingly darkened from green to black and turned to stone. "And six white rocks." Six neatly placed olives bleached to white pebbles. "And I arrange them in four rows of three each, three black above three white rocks, above three black, above three white; the rocks, the design, the space between the rocks and the activity of arranging them are all pattern. As is the set of three columns of alternating black, white, black, white rocks, or the diagonal. The pattern can be perceived and described different ways, but the act of patterning, both being and creating, is where my art lies. Do you understand?"

He pulled six more olives from the tree and divided them between his hands. "Three more black, three more white." He opened his hands and held the bleached and blackened pebbles out to Phil. "The knowledge you have that the white go together in a row beneath the black is the voice of pattern. If we collect and bring to this place, as Phil suggests, our memories of Celeste, it's possible that I could hear her pattern speak."

"Or I could show you how to break into her Garden," Oskar said.

Phil

I clamped my jaws together to keep from laughing. "What?" I said. "The easy way? We never do that."

Ren had her hand on my arm. If I could have, right then, I'd have kicked everyone out, I mean, forever, and given up on everything, and grabbed Ren and pulled her to the bed that I'd wished I'd had two thousand years ago.

"That's a good idea, Oskar," said Ray. "How do you do it?"

"Be clear on what we're doing," he said. "You want to get inside an analogy that isn't your own without being drawn into it by the creator. It's like walking around in someone else's dream."

I nodded, as did everyone else. Ren's brows were furrowed; she was listening and absorbing. "That's what you did," she said. "You were in my dream, when I dreamed Phil's Garden. That's why the olives were dates."

Oskar nodded. "Right. You pick a memory seeded by the person whose Garden you want into. Any memory. Doesn't matter. Then, just when the memory is starting to come clear, you superimpose your sense triggers over it, and try to force your metaphor onto his memory. It doesn't work—the memory doesn't change, and it's not easy. But if you grit your teeth and hang on long enough, it's like it pulls you back to the seeder, and you'll start to get sense triggers that aren't yours. You grip those, and follow them, and eventually there you are. Yours," he said, looking at Jimmy, "are the taste of old shoe leather and the sound of a Mozart concerto played on a piano that's just the least bit off from true."

"You've been in my Garden?" said Jimmy.

"Have you eaten a lot of old shoe leather?" I asked Oskar.

Oskar ignored me and answered Jimmy. "Not far. Just to see if I could. Your images, Phil, are the taste of chives and the smell of cherry blossoms."

"I knew that," I said.

Jimmy said, "Will it be more like dropping into my own Garden, where I can do or create anything and nothing can hurt me, or more like being drawn into someone else's analogy, where I can't affect anything, but experience memories like they're mine?"

We all looked at Oskar. "I have no idea," he said. "But I know what dinner with a Roman guard tastes like."

"Well," said Jimmy. "Shall we try this then?"

To answer him, I nodded toward Ray, who was standing with his head bowed and his eyes closed. I looked at Ren, and she was looking at me. She nodded once. All right, then. I put my arm around her and led the way back into the villa, and down the stairway to the room that never ends. We all have one of those rooms, in one way or another, where the past lives, and where the dust of history fades gradually, almost imperceptibly, into what came before history, and where we can search for, and sometimes even find, the scattered consciousness of who we were, who our friends were, who we thought our friends were, and what they thought.

That's where we keep our own master index, organized however we organize it. There are, at present, something like a billion memories seeded in the Garden. If you're going to have any chance of finding one, you need a method, and you need organization. This was mine.

We could each find our own memory of a memory Celeste had also seeded, except for Ren, who should have had all Celeste's memories as her own. Well, that was fine; she could have one of mine. She had once asked me who I was. Now, when she hadn't asked, I thought she wanted to know. And I wanted her to know, because however necessary lies may or may not be to keep love alive, if you build love on a lie, you're an idiot.

If you're going to do this, Phil, do it right.

A narrow, rickety wooden table arose and on it were scrolls bound in white ribbon, each labeled with a neat, precise glyph of the kind used in Sumeria five thousand years ago. For just a moment, I thought about Livianus, who held this consciousness before me. I'd vowed I wouldn't forget him, and I haven't, quite. He wasn't much like me; he spoke less and thought more and had a passion for Greek poetry. He'd held that stub for more than three hundred years. Then I came along, and he was gone.

"Phil," said Ren. "What—"

I shook my head and she fell silent.

I'd kept his filing system, if you can call it that, as a sort of tribute, as he had kept it from his previous, and so on back to before there was farming. I no longer remembered how to read the glyphs, but I didn't need to. I found the one I wanted by touch, and it led me to another set, and another, until—

"This one," I told Ren.

"I can't read it."

"Just touch it," I said, and opened it.

And there I was.

I called myself Carter, and I sat in my tiny room at my tiny table and wrote on coarse paper with cheap ink and a poor excuse for a quill. The execution of Guy Fawkes was still recent, and it seemed to me I ought to be doing something besides playing noddy and draughts. There was Ireland, and there was King James, and there was the printing press, and it all spelled trouble for anyone with the misfortune to be Catholic. But what could we do? I didn't know, but I was worried, and so I seeded my worries on coarse paper until there came a knock at the door.

I stood up and opened it, my thick shoes loud on the floor.

"Celeste," I said. "Enter and be welcome."

She did, walking briskly and sitting down without an invitation, her light green skirts giving life to the fire that had almost died. She said, "I have one last question, of all the questions there are, and if your answer should engender yet more questions, as your answers are wont to do, why then, these newborn questions will pour forth in a torrent until you, dear devil, are so mazed you cannot answer, upon which I do purpose to laugh at you, both cruelly and in friendship, and possess myself in patience until you are possessed of yourself again."

I sat down, facing her. She was so lovely; a dimple on her cheek, her fair hair curling, and mischief in her eyes. "Ask, then," I said.

"That wight whose—I have forgot the word; what called you it?"

"Souche," I said. "In English, it is 'stub.' "

"Yes. That wight. Betsy. An it become me, what doth become of her?"

"As best you may, remember her."

"She is known to you?"

"For many a year, Celeste. She is my steadfast friend. An you take her place, I'll mourn her."

She looked at me, her head tilted charmingly. "I would be a steadfast friend," she said.

I smiled. "And so?"

"Yes," she said. "I will do't. You are a dicer, is it not so? I will roll the dice. I see but the smallest part of what may come, but it doth fill my heart with such ardor as I have not known. I might not bear myself, did I say no, and so I do say yes."

I let that memory go instead of playing it out, and Ren said, "Phil? That isn't her memory, it's yours."

"But she will have made a congruent one," I said. "Her first seed.

As you should seed your memory, by the way, of taking the stub. The point is, now we can find hers. December 4, 1606. Welcome to the group, Celeste. What did you write on your fine lady's paper with your expensive quill?"

Ren squeezed my arm as I found the scroll.

"When I open this," I said, "as we start to fall into the memory—"

"I know," said Ren.

"All right."

I unrolled it.

Ren

Phil unrolled the parchment of Celeste's first seeded memory, still smelling softly of her uniquely compounded pounce. I closed my eyes. I could still feel Phil standing near me and the wooden table of white-tied scrolls. Nothing was happening. It wasn't going to work.

I opened my eyes to ask Phil what pounce was, and realized I knew. Vellum was greasy no matter how high quality, so you kept a muslin bag of powdered pumice or fishbone, or Celeste's peculiar blend of ground incense and egg shell, to dust over and rub into it. I also knew that Celeste felt fairly confident Phil was the devil Mephistopheles whom she had seen onstage not more than a year or two ago in Mr. Marlowe's scandalous play about Dr. Faustus. But she didn't care. She had lost everyone she loved to the plague three years back.

I tried to read the looping, sloping hand unrolled before me. I could pick out letters: a capital A, the word *you,* but it distracted me from the memory seeping, not in images or smells, but in clumps of fact, into my awareness. Celeste preferred a swan quill. Phil lived alone in rented accommodations. It had taken extraordinary cunning to meet him here, at night, alone. Even before the flaming stake, Celeste hadn't been certain she would survive the night.

She didn't remember the ritual any more than I did, but Phil had carried a white, two-handled milk pot to her from the fireplace when she first woke, and had alternately fed her posset and answered her questions. And I knew I could keep telescoping down into the memory until I knew every question verbatim and its answer. This was Celeste's memory; it would never become something I experienced, only something I knew, unless I got the rest of her stub. I closed my eyes.

I knew Celeste had worn her new shoes with cork heels, but I tried to see my mudflats. I knew Celeste had stepped in something foul on the way up the back stairs, and for a moment, the stairs were muddy. But it felt like trying to imagine Cinderella while your dad reads *Treasure Island* aloud. Or the trick I'd seen on a science museum wall once when I'd gone with my little brother. They had painted the color names—red, blue, green, black—on the wall, but in different colors. The word red in blue paint, green in yellow, with the instruction to say what color the letters were, not read the word they spelled. I'd laughed that he couldn't do it, he was such a good reader, even then, but I couldn't do it either, and I remember realizing then that I had no idea how my brain did anything, saw color, or read words.

Or remember Celeste, or feel Phil beside me, even with my eyes closed.

I must have been chewing my lip with the effort, hard enough to have bitten it to bleeding. It tasted like hot wine in pewter tankards, blood on the sides of my tongue. But the smell was of cloying spice and fruit. Pomander. I'd found Celeste's sense triggers: blood and pomander.

Phil

"What now?" I said, just to be saying something.

"Let's look around," said Ray.

"Just pick the first memory you come to."

"Celeste must have been an apothecary," Ren said, eyeing the wooden counters and row upon row of wooden tubs, glass bottles and stoneware jars. Above that, dried herbs, flowers and moss hung on strings from the ceiling.

"Not necessarily," I told her. "My Garden is a merchant's villa, and I was a shoemaker."

"And I'm guessing you didn't come from the swamp," Oskar said.

"Yeah, okay," Ren said. "Is everything in here a memory?"

I felt a flash of anger at Celeste. Ren should know this by now. This all ought to have come back. It was like she'd been blinded.

I said, "Yes, in one way or another. You can create anything you want in your Garden, if it amuses you. But only three things remain when you're gone: seeds, stubs, and hedges. Seeds are memories you or someone else deliberately put there, stubs are the memories of a Primary waiting for a new Second, and hedges are information that just made its way into the Garden from some other source. The hedges are what you use—"

"—for finding switches," she said. "It's coming back. And you can tell the difference by looking at them or touching them. These are all seeds."

I smiled. "Yes," I said. "Good."

"And that's Jimmy's skill, isn't it? Grazing hedges to find what he's looking for?"

"We can all do it, but he's especially fast. I'm glad you're remembering."

I realized that everyone was standing around waiting for me to finish talking. I said, "Jesus, guys. Just grab one. Any one."

"The same one, maybe?" said Ray.

"Why?"

"Better control," he said. "So we get the same data to work with, the same time."

"All right," I said. "Here's one. This jar, the blue one with white designs. Let's do it."

"I'll remind you," said Oskar, "that it's different when you graze in someone else's Garden."

I stopped, my hand just above the jar. "Remind me more."

"It's like grazing your own seed. You don't just get the facts. You relive it. I was there at your meal with the Praetorian, like I lived it."

"That could be interesting," I said, and put my hand in the jar and let it happen.

Stupid move.

I sat there and let it play out, living it, living Celeste. Everyone else experienced it, too. They all saw us argue, saw my eyes abstract and twitch, running the Fibonacci sequence. They all saw Celeste's imagination paint a bull's-eye on my forehead.

Not my best day.

But, okay, it was over, and no one has ever died of embarrassment.

Jimmy said, "She really did a number on you, didn't she, my friend?"

"Yeah, that wasn't a good day."

"I don't mean that day," he said. "I meant what it's done to you."

"What the hell are you talking about?"

He said, "Matsu? Think you can try? He trusts you."

I did, now that Jimmy mentioned it. I trust Matt more than, perhaps, anyone else. Odd that I'd never thought about it.

Matt said, "You've spent long enough as Celeste's target, Phil, don't you think?"

"What the hell—"

"You know what I'm talking about."

"I really don't."

"Who are you, Phil?"

"That's a stupid question."

"Maybe, but you're the one with Celeste's arrows in you. And now they've hooked us all. Who are you?"

"The sum total of all that I've done, all that I haven't done, all that I've wished I've done, all that I'm sorry I did—"

"Who did Celeste think you were?"

I wanted to say, "The center of her concentric universes," but that wouldn't have helped. I said, "Evidently, she thought of me as something to take aim and fire at."

"She defined you in terms of your relationship to her."

"Don't we all do that?"

"Yes," he said. "But the other person doesn't usually accept it and make it part of his own identity."

Oh. That's what Jimmy had meant. And I could answer Matt now, too. I was comfort for Celeste. A soft, marked hay bale, a familiar destination. Comfort, in the sense of having things stay the same, of knowing she could count on her life from year to year, and day to day, anchored in me. And she had rejected me because I was always moving, and it's hard to hit a moving target, but she had kept me around, because knowing I was there made her comfortable.

I turned to look at Ren, and she was looking back at me, steadily, and a little sadly.

"What would you like me to be?" I said.

"We're still working that out," and I mentally kicked myself, because now everyone was looking at her and she was getting a little red. But she held my eyes, and took my hand, squeezed it, and held on. Fibonacci, you have no clue.

Ren

"So how do we find Celeste's last memory in all this mess?" I asked, still holding Phil's hand. We were standing around a broad, raised wooden table, cluttered with brass scales, Pyrex beakers, empty gelatin capsules, stone mortars, and knives ranging from dull copper to surgical steel—clearly Celeste's lab bench. On either side of us wooden shelves reached to the ceiling without any sign of organization by historical period, or material, or size. Unless they were arranged by use, they just weren't arranged. It made me impatient. How would you find anything in such a jumble?

"Celeste's memories were always recorded like recipes," Jimmy said. "Or an alchemist's notes."

"Ray?" said Phil.

Ramon shrugged. "That was long ago. And no two alchemists kept notes the same way."

"Anyone remember the formula she gave for the *kithara*?" Phil asked.

"It was a rosemary bush in my castle garden," mused Jimmy. "For remembrance."

"As she gave it?" Matsu clarified Phil's question. "Yes. It was, 'Decant four gils of brandy, having crushed together some oil, some bitumen and a pinch of cinnamon with four drachmas earth of Chios. Having melted chocolate, spread upon it the earth of Chios and stir in such a way as to mix them. Burn it on wood of juniper and extinguish in some buttermilk slightly thick. Season with salt to taste.' I grazed for it before I followed you here."

"Right then." Jimmy was back in charge. "Let's each just pick a spot and work outward searching for anything on that list."

I said, "But, why would anything on the list be here, if these are all memories?"

"They won't," said Phil. "Nothing on the list will be here. But if you concentrate on looking for those items, you'll notice any seed that embodied any of them when she created it. Does that make sense?"

"I think so."

"All right. Then let's start looking."

"Maybe we should stick together," I said.

It all felt too Disney-spooky, with the dust-mote sunbeams streaming in from high, opaque windows to risk flaunting the horror movie rules.

"We are together," Phil reminded me. "We're all still standing in my living room."

"It's bad," Oskar said with a chuckle, "when Vegas is your safe place."

But Phil stayed near me, even in my imagination, and we struck off together, down one narrow corridor of bookcases. "I imagine she'd keep the oldest memories here," Phil said as we walked. "Like my scroll vault."

I nodded.

"I'm sorry if I embarrassed you back there," he said.

"You didn't."

"You were blushing."

"I wasn't!" We reached the end of our row and turned the corner to find Matsu reading spines in the next row. We walked over to the next aisle and started up it, watching for anything hidden in the shelves.

"What is it then?" he asked. "Or do you enjoy making me guess?"

"I'm not being coy," I said.

He cocked the wild eyebrow at me.

"I'm not!" I said, then realized I was. "I guess I just didn't realize how much power she still has over you."

"Celeste? She's dead, you know," he said, trying not to smile, but dimpling.

"So I've heard," I said, feeling like I should drop it, but not quite able to. "But it was like you didn't know who you were without her."

"Matt's question just took me off guard, and I answered it."

"Right, but what you said, about being the sum total of everything you've done or not done, that's not a self. That's a jumble."

"You're critiquing my UI?"

"You kept being an object to her. You're so much more alive than that."

I was trailing my fingers over the dry spines of books and he took my hand and turned it over. He spread my palm open and placed a gentle kiss in its center. "Loving someone arms that person against you. I loved Celeste for lifetimes; she had a lot of time to pick up ammo."

He pulled me against him, and I leaned into his chest.

"Quiet, everyone!" Ramon's voice was cold and urgent. "There's someone else here."

Phil's arm hardened behind my back. "Where are you, Ray?" he whispered.

Nothing.

"It's Irina," said Oskar. "Try not to let her see you. She must have had the same idea."

"How do you know it's her?" Jimmy asked.

"She's the only other person Celeste taught to move through people's Gardens." Oskar's voice was heavy with anger. "She's down here trying to re-create Celeste's last memory just like we are, only she's doing it because she believes the memory will be of me killing Celeste, and seeding it properly will be enough to keep me out of Salt."

"It doesn't look like Irina," Ramon said, keeping his voice low even though Irina's actual ears were miles away at The Palms.

"Where are you, Ramon?" Phil asked again, something cold and wary in his voice.

"I was trying to find the outside," Ramon whispered.

"Celeste's Garden doesn't have one," Oskar said. "At least not that I've found. It's all ladders and hatches."

Ramon's voice was a taut whisper. "I went through the back door," he said. "From the workroom."

"The door by the stacked barrels?" Phil was already headed back the way we had come.

"Phil?" I said, following him. Something in the set of his shoulders worried me. That he didn't reply worried me more. "Phil," I said again, touching his arm. He pulled up short and caught my face in his hands. My anxiety dissolved under his eyes' warm scrutiny, until I thought he would kiss me. He dropped his forehead to mine. "I love you," he whispered into my hair.

"Ramon, can you see what Irina is doing?" Jimmy asked.

The silver impact of Phil's words slid over my breasts, clashing with the persistent gnawing in my belly that something was badly wrong.

"Yes," Ramon whispered. "She's stirring something in a pot."

"Phil?" I said, looking for his eyes again.

"Wonderful!" Jimmy exclaimed. "Maybe she's already done the

work of collecting ingredients for us, and we can simply sweep in and eat the memory."

"Phil?" Matsu's voice was right beside me, but Phil was striding off across the dusty workroom floor.

As Phil and I stepped through the back door, I turned and caught a glimpse of Matsu sprinting noiselessly into the workroom. "Phil, wait!" Matsu whispered.

"Phil," I said, "Matsu's calling you." I stopped to catch the door so it wouldn't slam, and held it for Matsu. He came across the workroom floor with astonishing speed, still not making a sound, but when I turned back, Phil was gone.

"Wait," I called, bypassing worried and afraid, and going straight into terrified. "Phil!"

Jimmy muttered, "Oh, God."

"Fuck," Oskar said.

"I'm on it." Matsu stopped beside me. "Did you see which way he went?"

I shook my head.

"Ramon?" Matsu was motionless, his voice tight and brisk. "Think. Through the back door from the workroom, four stairs go down, then there's a left and a right branch. Which?"

"Left."

Matsu leapt over the stairs and vanished.

"I'm on my way," Oskar said.

I ran after Matsu, but he wasn't waiting for me. I didn't want him to.

"There's a raised hatch," Matsu said.

Ramon was quick. "I went down it."

Ahead of me, Matsu dropped out of sight.

"Phil." Jimmy held his voice deliberately low and calm. "Phil, my friend, stop a moment and think what you are doing."

With eyes that weren't blinking and a belly made of rock ice, I ran down the hall—some sort of dank root cellar with crude wood-doored cubbies dug into the earth. I was so afraid, I wasn't even thinking in words anymore. I was just running. When I reached the hatch, I peered into the hole beneath it, but it was entirely dark. "Matsu?" I called into it. My voice sounded breathless and too young.

"You can't kill her Phil," Ramon said. "This is just an image of her."

Nothing. From Matsu or Phil.

"Actually," said Jimmy, "we don't know that."

"Ramon, how deep is the cellar?" I asked.

"There's a ladder on the near side."

I felt with one hand along the lip of the hole. Well, that was stupid. People trying to access the cellar would need to hoist the door, then turn away from it and back themselves down. My knees were shockingly wobbly.

"Phil's with me," Ramon said.

"Let me through." Phil's voice was hoarse with warning. "She tried to kill Ren."

"But she didn't succeed," Jimmy soothed. "And killing her here may accomplish nothing."

I paused at the bottom of the ladder to get oriented. The stone under my feet was cold, or adrenaline had claimed them, and a few yards ahead, the silhouettes of Ramon and Phil squared off against a warm glowing backdrop of firelight. A shadow moving quickly along the black wall toward Phil was all I could see of Matsu.

I couldn't move.

"Phil," I said, but he faked left and stepped right, slipped by Ramon and lunged out of sight around the corner.

I ran full tilt and would have rounded the corner not much behind him, but Ramon caught me and pinned me against the rough-hewn wall.

"Ren."

I fought against his hands on me. I couldn't breathe. Phil was in trouble. I battled Ramon for all I was worth.

"Ren." Jimmy's voice was still falsely calm. "We can help Phil best if Irina thinks he's alone."

Ramon grunted as my elbow connected with his ribs.

"Almost there, Ramon," Oskar said.

"Matsu's here," Ramon said.

And he was. And somehow, without hurting me, he caught my flailing hands and pinned them to my hips. I could flop forward or back, and that was it. I tried to kick, but he pushed my wrist gently into the opposite hip and I staggered to keep my balance.

Then Oskar reached us too, and I quit fighting. It was pointless, and I didn't want Oskar to touch me.

Matsu opened his hands until they merely circled my wrists. "You will stay hidden?"

"I will stay hidden," I said.

We peered around the corner, and all four of us took a startled breath.

"What?" demanded Jimmy. "What are you seeing?"

"Well," Oskar said. "Phil's right on target again."

"And Irina's beautiful," Ramon whispered, something like reverence in his voice. "Her hair is loose and flows like water, but it's brilliant, bright fresh green. Her skin, even in this unworthy firelight, is radiant white, purer than the thinnest teacup, with such a tender pink at the edges. And her body moves with slender, boneless grace, like the spring air."

"Jesus, Ramon!" Jimmy said. "Pull yourself together. Stress has reduced you to poetry. Tell me what's happening!"

"Irina's got Phil in her sights again," Oskar said. And she did. She drew a delicate silver bow from the pocket of her apron and fitted it with a slender arrow, smaller even than the single brass key and sheathless bone knife looped to her apron by its strings. I wanted to hurt her. I wanted to make my will into a weapon, or force her own knife to cut her. But most, I wanted Phil away from Irina, away from the curved walls and low ceiling that gave him no space to maneuver as he tried to get around her.

Matsu wasn't moving, but I've never seen a less restful stillness. My body, in contrast, was twisting and dodging involuntarily in pointless synch with Phil's delicate combat. He dodged, but Irina fired and skewered him to the wall with a glittering barbed arrow through the armpit of his shirt, quiveringly close to his heart.

Matsu caught me again and held me. Irina nocked another arrow into her bow and drew it. I could see her lips moving, but couldn't hear her. Then Matsu picked me up and chucked me over his shoulder. He headed, fast and soundless, back to the ladder while I slugged him right where I figured I'd find a kidney. He climbed us out in three fluid steps.

Jimmy was waiting at the top. "I'm sure Ren will come the rest of the way of her own accord," he said. "It's time to wake up."

"I'm not leaving without Phil," I said.

"He's probably already awake," Jimmy said. "He won't stay in Irina's clutches."

"That's not Irina," I said. I knew tears were running down my face, but I couldn't unball my fists enough to wipe them.

"What do you mean?" Jimmy's voice was wary.

"Of course it is," Oskar said.

I swallowed air. "Irina?" I said. "With chive hair and cherry blossom skin?"

"Fuck," Ramon said.

"It's Celeste," Jimmy whispered.

"She's coming up the ladder." Matsu's voice mastered our collective shock. "Wake."

With the bones in my body, and my voice—there and here—all saying "No, no, no," I opened my eyes.

TWELVE

Raggedy Ann

Phil

One plus zero is one. One plus one is two. Two plus one is three. Three plus two is five.

Yeah, so, okay, sometimes the universe sucks. Sometimes you have all the odds on your side and all the chips in the middle, and the other guy spikes the miracle card. It happens.

Five plus three is eight. Eight plus five is thirteen. Thirteen plus eight is twenty-one.

Or maybe you lost because you played like an idiot. Doesn't matter; same result, same solution.

Twenty-one plus thirteen is thirty-four. Thirty-four plus twenty-one is fifty-five. Fifty-five plus thirty-four is eighty-nine.

The solution? Simple. Play the next hand. That's all you can do anyway, as long as you're in the game. So play it, and play it right. And if you're pissed off at the dealer, or your opponent, or yourself, or the world, you aren't going to play it right.

Eighty-nine plus fifty-five is one hundred and forty-four. One hundred and forty-four plus eighty-nine is, uh, carry the one, two hundred and thirty-three.

So the first step is to get your head in shape to address the problem. The next step is to look at the situation; don't blow it up bigger than it really is, don't minimize it. Look at it. The next step is to remind yourself that you can't control either the decisions your opponent makes or the deck; you're dealing with unknowns and with random numbers. So you cut down the unknowns as much as possible, figure a way so that as many of the random numbers as possible work in your favor, then you make the play.

Short version: It doesn't matter how many bad decisions you've just made, your job is to make the next one correct.

I tested myself against the three arrows pinning me to the wall and took a moment to stand in the cellar of Celeste's Garden and think.

First, let's see if I could cut down on some of the unknowns. As she'd shot the second arrow through my other shirtsleeve, she'd said, "Sorry, Phil. I just need a little time to work."

And it went *thwik* into my head, in time to the arrow, that it was Celeste's voice.

How could it be Celeste? Celeste was stubbed, and then put into Ren. Ren had Celeste's stub. Ren—

Couldn't remember Celeste, most of the time.

Because Celeste's memories were floating around the Garden.

She put her bow back in her pocket and took the pot she'd been stirring off the flame.

The arrows weren't real. They couldn't hurt me, couldn't even immobilize me, unless—

Unless I was willing to subordinate myself to her. Unless I saw myself as a reflection of her. Unless what defined me as me was my love for her. Then the arrows could hold me, because I would choose to let them.

"When I come back," she said over her shoulder, "we should talk, dear." And she left.

Just like her. But how could that be? The Garden, however real it feels, is a mental construct, created by us back in the beginning, when we first used symbols to communicate and needed a place to store the information so it wouldn't be lost. Information, ideas, do not have an independent existence, except insofar as someone expresses them. We had seeded with ocher on cave walls, with sticks on sand, with chisels on stone tablets, with styluses on clay, with ink on paper, with electronic signals on Sony's latest laptop. We became what we created, self-perpetuating memories, and we were forced to commit acts of altruism from fear of what would happen if we didn't.

Because, when you stop and think about it, fear is the driving force behind so very much of what we human monkeys do. We work from fear of being without what we need. We fight from fear of what will happen if we don't. We love from fear of being alone. Okay, maybe that last is a stretch, but it's what Celeste thought, and she wasn't entirely wrong. I've been around long enough to know. In any case, fear was driving Celeste. All right, fear of what?

She was terrified of Oskar, afraid he would do something that would upset the comfortable life, or lives, we'd all been having. So Oskar had to be kept out of Salt. Which was silly in its own way; it wasn't like we had absolute power in the group, or even that much relative power. Oskar wanted in because he wanted some control over the discussion. So what? Is that a big enough deal to meddle with a lover, and several other people as well, just to ensure your personality stays on top to keep him out?

Oh, of course. Looked at that way, no. Oskar had nothing to do with it. Celeste wanted her personality to stay on top because she wanted her personality to stay on top. Because she didn't want to die. It was that simple. Oskar served to have someone for us to focus on, to suspect.

And then—what?

She had chosen Ren because of blood relationship, and because she thought Ren was someone she could overpower. She'd miscalculated, and Ren's personality came out on top. Why wasn't that the end of it?

Because Celeste had a backup plan. Celeste always had backup plans. Okay, then. What would she do if plan A didn't work? Best thing would be to arrange for a different Second, but that's not so easy since the failure of Plan A alerts all of us to what's going on.

So? So you make a copy of your stub, a memory of all of your memories; you replay them, seed them, and to make sure no one finds them except you, you alpha-lock them. How? By seeding the moment of your death, and looping it back to your own stub, even as you die. Hence, the need for suicide. And the result being, as long as Celeste existed only in the Garden, Ren could remember her. When Celeste existed in the real world, the memories were with Celeste. She'd probably been doing this for lifetimes, but we'd never seen because her personality had always been dominant, until now. But this time she knew, almost right away, that she'd miscalculated; that Ren was strong enough to assert control.

How could she exist in the real world? A confederate, of course; probably an unwilling one. Irina. Now Irina/Celeste. It would be uncomfortable, but still good enough until they killed Ren and found a new Second. Which one of them had tried to kill Ren? Irina. To get rid of Celeste.

All of which brought up the eternal question: Now what?

I could open my eyes and be back in my house in Las Vegas. That would be the safe play. I have nothing against the safe play; a lot of the time, the safe play is just another way to say the money-making play; the safe play is usually to throw away pocket 3s in early position.

But then there's the rest of time. The safe play is to overbet the pot, make your opponent fold, and get what's in the middle right now while it's yours. Often the right play is to entice your opponent to make a mistake—to bet enough so that it's a mathematical error for him to call, but little enough that he wants to anyway. If you do that, he'll draw out on you and you'll lose a good number of times. But, over the long run, it's the way to make the most money.

Make the right play.

"I am who I am," I told the empty room. "Not who Celeste wants me to be."

I walked out of my clothes pinned to the wall of Celeste's cellar, out of Celeste's cellar, and in three steps brought myself back to my villa, wearing my old Roman clothes, because this was the Garden, and your own metaphor is always there, under everything. The first thing I did was seed my deductions and leave them in my atrium in the form of a Raggedy Ann doll hanging from a noose. Then I went out front and stood before the place where Celeste's last memory should have been.

The Y/When and Z/Where were known quantities; X/Who was, quite appropriately, undefined.

If this didn't work, Celeste might know what I'd tried, and then we'd be off to the races again. But you always play the odds. Even when you're playing the other player, that's just another factor in the odds.

I said, "Why, Celeste? In order to make sure your personality was dominant in the new Second, you self-centered, heartless bitch."

Then I picked up the *kithara* and strummed it once.

Ren

We were standing in a ragged circle, leaning into one another like tepee poles. Oskar yawned. Matsu shook himself and bounced lightly on the balls of his feet. Phil, his eyes closed and his face slack, didn't move.

"He didn't come back!" I reached for him. "We have to go get him."

"That's not how it works." Jimmy gently took my hands from Phil's arm. "Think, Ren. We don't know if he's in Celeste's Garden or his."

Matsu moved behind Phil and crossed his arms over Phil's chest.

"He can open his eyes whenever he wants," Jimmy said. "Or put himself in his own Garden, if he chooses. If he hasn't yet, it's because he's not done."

"But Celeste trapped him!"

"I'm sure," said Matsu, "that Celeste thinks she did. I'm just as sure that she's wrong. He is now aware of how she controlled him. The awareness will be enough."

"Are you *sure*?"

"Yes," he said.

Matsu moved Phil's inert body expertly across the room. Nothing I'd seen from Irina came even close in zombiness. I couldn't watch; it was too eerie to see him in motion but vacant inside. I shivered. Matsu eased Phil into his chair.

Oskar came back from the kitchen with a monster-size bag of Doritos, a box of Nilla wafers, a packet of Oreos, and two sacks of pretzels. He tossed them one-by-one to each of us as we shambled into chairs around the room. I was starving, but nearly as empty inside as Phil. The hollow in both of us kept me from eating.

Ramon took his accustomed spot by the glass patio door, but seated, leaning against it rather than standing. Oskar and Matsu shared the sofa, like twin hand grenades on plaid foam. I wanted to crawl into Phil's lap and wrap my arms around his shoulders. "I don't know what to do," I said, holding the Doritos.

Jimmy led me gently to the chair by Phil's and pressed me into it. "I know what Phil would do," he said, dropping into the office chair beside me.

"What?" I asked.

"He'd run the Fibonacci sequence until his prefrontal cortex engaged," Ramon said with a chuckle.

Oskar and Matsu nodded.

"I'm not that strong," I said. "Or that good at math."

Jimmy cracked the bag of Oreos and slid out the flimsy tray. "Phil thought otherwise," he said.

"I can't," I said. "I can't just be still and calm down. I have to do something."

"What do you mean, Jimmy?" Ramon asked.

"I think Phil chose Ren specifically for her strength," Jimmy said.

I laughed dully. "Celeste chose me."

"I don't think so," Jimmy said.

I dropped my head back against the chair, but Ramon folded his legs up under him and leaned his elbows on his knees, suddenly alert.

"Celeste chose Ren, and meddled with Phil, and with us, so no one was watching," Oskar said.

"Jimmy was watching," Ramon said. "And . . . Jimmy?"

"And I wrote Phil and asked what he was up to." Jimmy split open an Oreo.

"And . . . Jimmy?"

"And when Phil didn't respond, I got in touch with Irina. We had all seen the signs in Celeste, right? She was losing her curiosity, showing all the indications of a personality in decline. When I saw what Phil seeded about Ren, I thought he was trying to hurry Celeste's exit up as a coup de grâce, a stroke of mercy, to save her from the ugliness of it." Jimmy regarded the two Oreo halves. The filling had come apart cleanly in a single white cushion on one side. "Phil knew Ren was strong," he went on, looking at me. "He called it out specifically. And like Matsu said, we always select for that anyway, but your real power wasn't obvious. It's more endurance than fight, isn't it? Not the kind of strong personality we tend to recruit when we select for dominance."

"Like you would have done with my stub, if Celeste had managed to pin her death on me," Oskar said.

Jimmy stuck the two Oreo halves back together and popped the whole cookie in his mouth. He chewed and swallowed. "I do think she was hoping for that."

"We never doubted you," Matsu told Oskar.

"Ren did."

"Yeah, I did. I'm sorry." I was fighting to follow the conversation, feeling light-headed with worry and exhaustion, and battered by my struggle with Ramon in Celeste's cellar. When you're trespassing, I guess other people's analogies *can* hurt you. I wanted to throw everyone out of Phil's house and just hold on to him until he opened his eyes. But these were his friends, and I knew they wanted him safe as much as I did.

I knew Phil did math to settle his mind. I couldn't do that, but I remembered what he'd said about how loving Celeste had given her ammunition against him. I wanted to arm him.

"Oskar," I said. "I really am sorry I believed what Celeste was feeding me."

Oskar shrugged, and the anger went out of him. In its absence, I saw the pain Celeste's betrayal had caused him. Good. He loved her too.

"What do you think Celeste will do next?" I asked him.

"Take a bath?" Oskar shrugged again, his large shoulders hunched over his knees. "Celeste loved luxury. Any little discomfort—a shoe that didn't quite fit, a slight head cold—would make her furious. She always wanted to be comfortable, but she never felt safe."

"That's true," Jimmy said.

"Phil was probably as close as Celeste ever came to safety," Ramon said, and Jimmy and I both winced for Oskar.

"Jesus, Ray," Jimmy said.

"What?" Ramon countered. "It's true. If Phil had said anything to her about how bitter she was getting—"

"He told me they fought about everything," I said, cutting in. I needed them focused on learning what we could do, and quickly.

"They surely did," Oskar chuckled. "Every solitary thing."

"Was there a core to their disagreements?" I asked. "Did all their fights boil down to the same differences? Matsu, was there a pattern?"

Matsu closed his eyes.

Oskar studied the rug. "I'm not sure why," he said, "but for as long as Phil's been doing this, he has never lost his love for the work."

"I asked him about that once," Jimmy said. "He said he always wanted to know how the stories ended."

"But what I'm trying to say is that Phil's basic impulse was towards stuff," Oskar said. "Towards the nemones, towards new technology, new recruits. Towards me, even when you were ready to leave me behind." Oskar's gaze took in Matsu and Ramon.

Ramon nodded vigorously. "Just so," he said. "And Celeste's basic impulse was just the opposite. She never moved toward anything, only away from things."

"She was always afraid."

"So she's afraid, and now she knows Phil's in her Garden. What's her next move?" I said. "What will she do now?"

"She's dead," Jimmy said. "I have no idea how she does anything."

"How does someone that fearful kill herself?" I said, fighting frustration and incomprehension. "It still doesn't make any sense to me."

"Oh, Celeste wasn't afraid of dying." Ramon waved a hand dismissively.

"What?" I said, boggled.

"She was just terrified of pain," Oskar said.

"She would never risk heartbreak or injury," Matsu agreed.

"She carried a stockpile of medicine everywhere with her," Ramon put in. "Everything from antacids to Xanax."

"Vicodin," Oskar said grimly.

"I still don't understand." I was somewhere between wanting to scream and starting to cry.

Jimmy put a steadying hand on my arm. "The fear of death is easy to cure. All it takes is faith. Religions have known as much for millennia and have sold their respite dear. But faith in reincarnation, or in the resurrection of the body, or in ultimate immateriality, or even in your fellow Incrementalists is enough."

"Celeste was afraid of suffering, but not dying?" I said.

"Right." Jimmy gave me a kind smile and ate another Oreo. "Not of her body dying, anyway. Not if she—that strange alchemy of memory and habit, inclination and aptitude—survived. It is that—the unique self, personality plus memory—which we save in stub and create in Seconds."

"And that's what you think Phil saw fading in her?" I asked.

"We all did," Ramon said. "We can see pivots, remember, because we know so intricately the pattern of what makes up a personality. Pivots are frontal assaults on the self. They call for change so significant that the old personality effectively dies. That's why we all—Incrementalists and nemones alike—fight against the turning points in our lives that change who we are, or how we understand our world. Big leaps in growth aren't growth. They're stub and Second."

"Jimmy?" Matsu said.

Jimmy was tipped back in Phil's office chair, eyes closed. He sat up. "Phil's cracked the alpha-lock," he said. "Holy fuck."

"Yeah," Phil said. "Let's eat."

Phil

Ren was in my arms, kneeling in front of the chair with her arms around my neck. I held her. When I glanced up, I saw that Oskar was looking away, Jimmy was smiling, Matt was staring off into space, and Ray was looking thoughtful. He finally said, "How did you—"

"There's a Raggedy Ann doll hanged by the neck until dead in my atrium. Help yourselves. We're going to figure out what to eat."

Actually, we did a lot of holding and very little figuring while they all grazed.

"Clever," said Ray, which was about as close as he could come to giving me a compliment.

"Thanks."

"Risky," said Jimmy. "If it almost worked, but didn't quite, Celeste would know what you were up to. She'd have come up with something different that we wouldn't know about."

I shrugged. "Seemed worth the gamble."

Ren kissed my neck. I squeezed.

Oskar said, "I'm good with the eating idea."

"On me," said Jimmy. "Best place in town."

"But old Vegas style," Ren said. "Not slick corporate."

I stroked Ren's hair and said, "Is that all right with you, Oskar? I mean, it's going to be bourgeois and all that."

"I do not object to eating well. I object to how many people can't."

Sometimes it's just impossible to bait him.

I called the Four Queens, had them transfer me to Hugo's, and got reservations for half an hour. We took Jimmy's rental because it was the size of an ocean liner. Ren and I claimed the backseat.

"I was worried about you," she said.

"Who is Celeste?"

She frowned. "I don't know."

"I'm worried about you, too. But we'll come through it."

Downtown was a bit of a pain, but we got there. Hugo's Cellar was well named, because it was in a cellar and felt like it, but a rather pleasant cellar. Ren was given a rose as we entered, and she seemed startled and pleased. Eric was our waiter. Jimmy had the Kona coffee with me, and we shared some snails. I like snails. I had the rack of lamb, Ren had the Beef Wellington. Jimmy, after a long conversation in French with John, the wine steward, decided on a couple of wines that were good, though I suppose I didn't appreciate them as much as he did.

Chef Jason came out while we were eating and clapped me on the shoulder.

"You do know everyone, don't you?" said Ren.

"Jason, this is Ren, Matt, Oskar, and Ray. Everyone, this is Jason. My God, Jason, but you've gotten fat."

"Would you trust a skinny chef?" he said.

We gave him the requisite compliments—sincere, by the way—and when he left, Ray said, "All right, Phil. What was in the *kithara*?"

"Let Jimmy graze it; I don't want to spoil my dinner."

Jimmy was quiet for a few minutes, then he said, "It's as we thought. There is little there, just taking the pills and plans for the alpha-lock. And—"

We all looked at him.

"There is another alpha-locked memory out there. Hidden."

"Of course," said Ray. "Her stub. She made a copy and alpha-locked it. There might be dozens; one for each life as long as she's been doing this."

"Now we know, at least," said Oskar.

"And so," said Ray, "what's next?"

"Once we've eaten," I said, "we need to find Irina, now also known as Celeste, and finish this."

"Finish it how, my friend?" said Jimmy quietly.

I looked at Matt, who looked away.

"However it takes," I said.

Jimmy said, "Stubbing her—"

"Won't solve the problem," I said.

"Just so you know that."

"I do," I said, and ate some more lamb.

Ren

I could almost feel the meat nourishing me. It climbed through my veins, sweetly—incrementally—nudged along by wine. Phil's knee pressed against mine, and whenever he didn't need it for his food, he'd slide a hand under the table and squeeze my thigh. Loved and safe, exhausted and sated, I savored every sip and laugh. This was good, and had history, which grounded me somehow. Jimmy delivered an impassioned paean to his duck flambé, and even Ramon came out of his head long enough to experience rather than dissect his supper.

It wasn't until after the chef, who'd made us all howl with a story from his *sous chef* days under a terrifying Frenchman he claimed bore an uncanny resemblance to Jimmy, had blown us all kisses and left, and Ramon asked Phil what was next, that I realized how not-done the day's work was. And I resented it. I wanted the Incrementalists to go away, leaving Phil as Phil and not the fulcrum of some weighty operation. I wanted him alone, smiling and pleasure-soaked as he had been the minute before. But all the indulgence and languor was gone in the exchange of glances between him and Matsu. Resolve circled the table like a breadbasket. Whatever we would undertake tonight, although none of us were certain what that might be, we were united in it.

I would have said we were unstoppable, but I would have been wrong. We finished our meals in subdued solidarity, and ten minutes after Ramon's practical question, we were saying good-night to the waiter. Whom Phil knew by name. We left in a unified clump, so I could have ducked down among the tall shoulders. Or I could have backpedalled to our private room. All the posh spots have secret doors, and Phil's waiter-friend would have smuggled me out. But sometimes you just have to brazen up and take the bullet.

I waved.

God, was it only this morning I'd advised him to take Jorge to dinner?

Liam waved back. "Ren!" he called, beckoning, and I watched his face melt from pleased, to confused, to surprised, to a little bit frightened as I, along with Phil, and Jimmy, and Ramon, and Oskar, and Matsu obeyed his summons.

"Hi, Liam," I said. "Great to see you, Jorge. These are my friends." I introduced them by name while Liam tried wildly to ask, in a truly bizarre eyebrow and soundless-mouth semaphore, which of these men was my new special friend. I smiled blandly. "Jimmy recommends the duck," I said.

"Won't you join us?" Jorge asked.

I was already shaking my head, when Jimmy spoke up. "I know Phil has a poker table waiting for him," he said. "World Series of, don't you know. And I believe Matsu as well? But Ramon, Oskar and I would love a chance at the third Chilean red. We quite liked the first two. If I could persuade you gentlemen to join us for a glass?"

Phil managed to catch my hand in the confusion of accommodating me plus three additional rather large men at Liam and Jorge's tiny two-top. "Call me when you get out of here," he said.

"Sure," I promised. "Gonna teach me to play poker?"

"Not tonight."

And he was gone.

Oskar offered me a chair between him and Jimmy, with just enough formality to derail Liam, who had pegged Oskar as my most recent and extreme flirtation with the bad boy type. He squinted at Jimmy.

Jimmy raised a glass of the newly poured Chilean. "To the simplicity and refinement of truly excellent wine," he said.

Jorge smiled and we all touched glasses.

They both ordered the duck. Jimmy introduced Jorge to a varietal Carménère he'd never tried, and I realized yet another layer of what it meant that Jimmy had been watching Phil and that, when Phil hadn't wanted to leave Vegas during the World Series of Poker, Jimmy had been the one who did the additional research needed to delay Jorge in New York and bring me here. Jimmy knew all about my work and my bosses. He knew how music, even more than smell, could trigger memory, and that allowing patients to select the tunes assigned to reminders might make the difference between remembering medication and forgetting what the damn monitor was for in the first place. He knew why I did the work I did. And I watched him translate it into wine.

Jimmy was funny and subtle, and Liam and Jorge laughed and nodded along as he wove a body-anchored web of value statements and sense memories detailing the virtue of patience, of care and precision. "Smell the wine," he insisted. "Cherry and earth," he said. "Tobacco, dark chocolate, leather." I made a mental note of Jorge's scent switches.

Jimmy told a hysterical story about sloppiness punished, and with one finger, ever so slightly touched Jorge's head, just by his ear. "This wine is made by a vintner who has achieved through his work, from the vines he plants, to the time he waits, not success, but mastery. A life given to worthy work, is itself, a work of art," he said.

I could almost hear Jorge's mental oath to become not successful, as he had always and easily been, but masterful.

Whether its story was true or not, the wine tasted good, so I drank it and watched a meddle master work. Oskar put a brotherly arm around me and I hugged his wrist between my cheek and shoulder. We were forgiven. Liam was intrigued. I drank my wine and winked at my boss.

I missed Phil, and wondered how he and Matsu were doing, and whether they were playing poker. I figured Matsu was pretty good insurance, but no matter what Ramon said about the body only housing the self, I wanted Phil whole, house and occupant. House and home. And I figured even Matsu couldn't keep an eye on Phil if he didn't want to be watched.

Phil

Matt and I found a cab next to Binion's and went through the ritual: The doorman asked where we were going, I said, "The Palms." He leaned over and told the cabbie, "Two for The Palms," and we were off. Matt didn't say a word during the drive, and neither did I.

Once we were out, with no one around us, he said, "What do you hope to accomplish?"

"To find the next layer of her plan."

"How, meddle with her?"

"Who? Celeste or Irina?"

"One will cover the other. Unless you can surprise her again. If you can do that, either will work. If not—"

"Can you think of a way to do that?"

"No," he said. "Then how?"

"I don't know."

We entered the lobby. "You wait here," I told him.

"No," he said.

I exhaled slowly. "All right."

We took the elevator to eight. Mom and Dad and two kids in wet swimming suits and towels joined us for the ride along with a girl who looked about nine and didn't appear related to any of them. They all continued up after we left.

"You see it?" he said.

"The way everyone was afraid of Mom? Yeah. Want to fix it?"

"If you'll come with me."

I shrugged. "The abuse isn't physical."

"So that's all right, then?"

"Nothing is all right."

"Is all right the goal?"

"The goal is better."

"Yes," said Matt. "It is."

I knocked on the door.

The peephole went dark, then light, and then there was a delay of a good ten seconds before Irina opened the door and said, "Phil. You bastard."

She crossed to the other side of the room, leaning against the desk; there was a couch and a pair of stuffed chairs next to the table. Matt and I came in. "Good to see the two of you, as well. Which one am I talking to, or is it possible to decide?"

"Celeste," she said, furious. "Celeste, stuck in this old lady's body with no one for company except—"

"Oh, hush," I said. "No one feels any sympathy for you except maybe Irina, so don't talk trash about her."

"You fucked up everything," she said.

"If I were sure that was true," I said, "I wouldn't be here."

I sat down, Matt remained standing.

"What the hell are you talking about?"

"Your next plan. Where you go from here."

"Why? So you can stop it?"

"Yes."

She laughed. "If I had a plan, I certainly wouldn't tell you, dear Much the Miller's Son. In fact, I'd make bloody damn sure neither of you interfered with it."

"Not that easy," I said.

"But it is," she said, and about the time I realized she was holding a gun, it was already pointing at me; and about the time I realized it was pointing at me, it was flying through the air, and Irina was on her knees clutching her wrist, with Matt standing next to her.

I caught the gun, more by accident than design. A revolver, Smith and Wesson .38. A big gun for such a frail old lady.

"You broke my wrist," she said.

"No," said Matt. "I didn't. It's just bruised. Alternate cold and warm, half-hour inter—"

"Shut the fuck up."

She rose shakily to her feet and glared at me, still holding her wrist, as if everything she'd done had been my decision.

"I have," I said, "only one thing to threaten you with, Irina. You're old; you're going to need a new Second soon. And everyone will know about this. The harder you push, the more unpleasant we can make things. Want to sleep through the next hundred years? How about two hundred?"

"You Judas!"

"Shut up, Celeste. I'm talking to Irina. Help us out, Irina. Tell us what Celeste is planning."

"I can't." It was Irina speaking now; I could tell from her inflection. She was pleading.

"You can. You're strong. Fight her. Or you can take the consequences if you don't."

"Why are you doing this to me?" That was Celeste again, dammit.

There were so many answers to her question, I could have recited them for a day. I settled on, "You tried to kill Ren."

"That was Irina," she said. "But I had a backup for that. Besides, I've always hated the little cunt."

One plus zero is one. One plus one is two. Two plus one is three. Three plus two is five. Five plus three . . .

"Celeste? I can't remember. How much is five plus three?"

Before she could answer I shot her in the face.

THIRTEEN

Keep Walking

Ren

By the time Jorge and Liam were done eating, my planned rewrites and new photo shoot were irrelevant. Jorge would call tomorrow, I could see it, and in a brief but pivotal conference call, explain to me, and to my boss, that of the three ideals—high quality, quick delivery, and low cost—we mere mortals could expect only two. Quality, nay artistry, was nonnegotiable to RMMD, and because elderly patients can only wait so long, speed was literally vital as well. He would open the budget and let us tell him what we needed. I could almost hear the gears in him turning. But Jimmy caught me checking my phone for anything from Phil, and with a brief digression over half a glass of Tokay on the virtues of and history behind the hot water spa, Jimmy moved the call back a day. Jorge was going to take tomorrow off, and so should Liam and I.

I still hadn't heard from Phil by the time we reeled out of Hugo's. His phone went straight to voice mail when I called him. We ambled through the night oven and parried invitations from Liam and Jorge, arms slung around each other, to shows, or drinks, or the zip line overhead until Ramon managed to peel them away. He piled them into a cab with override instructions to the cabbie not to leave Liam and Jorge anywhere but their own hotel, no matter where they went between here and there.

Ramon gave the driver two hundred-dollar bills and his business card. "Call me tomorrow," he said. "I'll double this when I hear from my friends that they are awake and well. No penalty to you for hangover, but keep them from thieves, photographers and beautiful women."

"What are you?" The cabbie chuckled. "Their goddamn fairy godmother?"

"Almost exactly that." Ramon closed the cab door, and we waved good-bye.

"Thanks," I said.

"Jimmy will reimburse me."

"Then thanks to you both."

Ramon silently inclined his head.

"What now?" Jimmy asked me.

"I'd like to find Phil."

"He plays poker at The Palms," Ramon said.

I shuddered. "Irina's there."

"It's a big place," Oskar told me. "And you're not alone."

"It still gives me the willies," I said. "But let's go."

Jimmy pointed out that none of us should be driving, so we took a cab ourselves. For as late as it was, traffic was grindingly slow, and by the time we turned onto Flamingo, our cab wasn't outpacing the drunks weaving the sidewalk, so we paid up and got out. From the walkway it was easy to see why the cars weren't moving. A welter of ambulances, fire trucks and cop cars was balled in a clot ahead of us.

"I think they're in front of The Palms," Oskar said.

I shivered, looking at the impassive facade and the wheeling red-and-blue lights. "You know, when they're hightailing it down the road, and need those people who are not in their mad dash to rescue someone or apprehend someone else to get the hell out of the way, I'm sure those lights are just right. But even the anemic fluorescent bulbs in coffee shop bathrooms are wired with sensors and switches to plunge their perhaps too-stationary occupants into darkness requiring the coffee-filled and jittery to pee in the dark, or pray that seated, their flailing arms reach high enough to count as present to the censorious sensor. If toilets can interpret sheer inactivity as a Darkness Now directive, could not the flashy chariots bearing our dear extinguishers of flame and catchers of criminals not be similarly equipped with light-stopping technology? Would it not be to their advantage, even, to cease calling such grotesque attention to themselves, advertising the life-and-death excitement of whatever incident has brought them screaming forth? Would it not perhaps afford the stricken and maimed they've flown to some pretense of privacy or at least peace in the disorienting post-life moments should our stalwart foes of Death and Chaos have come too late?"

It seemed we had stopped walking. Jimmy and Oskar were staring, and Ramon was shaking his head. I was holding a rose, though I didn't know where it had come from. I smiled uncertainly, not quite remembering what I'd been yammering on about.

"Sorry," I said. "I had quite a bit of Jimmy's gorgeous wine. And fucking Phil has just fucking killed me."

Jimmy staggered. Oskar caught his massive shoulders and steered him to a planter. Jimmy sat, not on the edge, but in the dirt.

"I'll get us a suite and computers," Ramon said. "We'll need an ops center as close as we can manage." He vanished.

Jimmy looked up at me. "Celeste," he said. He dropped his head into his hands and started to sob.

I looked at Oskar, pale and motionless, and clearly *en guard,* and whispered, "Who's Celeste?"

Phil

If you're going to play the "Pick a moment, call it now" game, I suppose it would be when I settled down enough to realize what had just happened. I don't mean shooting Irina-Celeste; that part was sculpted in marble and would no more fade than my first death, coughing blood and cursing God. I mean that I became aware that we were walking towards the west door, which led to the parking ramp. That took us past the poker room, and I realized someone had said hello as we walked by. Matt had said, "Keep walking."

Matt had been taking care of things. He wiped the gun clean, he got us out of there, and he had been talking to me the whole time. And I'd responded.

"Almost out," he said. "Now, again, what do you say if you're arrested?"

"I need to speak to my attorney, and I do not consent to any search."

"Good."

"When do we call the others?"

"As soon as we're out the door."

"The family on the elevator are witnesses. Are you going to meddle with them?"

"Of course. Me or someone."

"Can you fix Mom while you're at it?"

"I'll try."

No one stopped us from leaving. No one needed to; this was a casino. There were more slot machines than cameras, but only just barely. It was a question of when, not if.

Las Vegas's heat hit me in the face. We walked out into the parking lot next to the ramp. We stopped right there, and Matt said, "Give me your phone."

I did. "I can't believe someone heard the shot," I grumbled. "You'd think they'd have better soundproofing."

He spoke on the phone and I walked away, because I didn't want to hear one side of it. The conversation went on for a while. He came back still holding on to my phone, and said, "They're getting things started."

I nodded. "What's my job?"

"Go home. Stay there until you're either arrested, or we know you won't be. If I put you in a cab, can I be sure you'll go home and stay there?"

"Yes," I said. "But you'll have to take the long way around getting a cab. The cops—"

"I know, Phil," he said patiently. "This isn't my first rodeo."

"Sorry. And thanks. For. You know."

"You're welcome. Ren will be joining you."

I closed my eyes and nodded and almost cried.

"And Phil. Celeste is back sporadically. In Ren."

"All right," I said, meaning it wasn't.

He used my phone again and arranged for us to be picked up at a convenience store on Decatur. It was a long, long walk on a hot night.

As we walked, Matt said, "If you do get arrested, what—"

"I need to speak to my attorney, I do not consent to any search."

"Do you have an attorney?"

"I have the Garden, Matt. I suspect I can manage to find a fucking criminal defense lawyer. This isn't my first rodeo either."

"Can you afford one? How's your sugar spoon been?"

"There are public defenders, if it comes to that."

"We'll ask Jimmy to—"

"No."

He didn't answer, which didn't mean he accepted it. It's not often someone in the Salt has money. It's hard not to take advantage of it when it happens. Besides, I had money; it's just that the money I had was my bankroll, and spending that meant being out of action, with no way to make more. Funny how it's the bullshit that occupies your mind when you don't feel like thinking about things that actually matter, such as—

"You know, Matt, I'd feel better about what happened if I weren't so afraid I did just what Celeste wanted."

"Me too," he said.

The cab was there. Matt put me in and said, "Drink lots of water."

"You too," I told him, and gave the cabbie my address.

Ren

"What?" I said.

Jimmy was sitting in the potted tree, not even trying not to cry. Ramon was gone.

"What?" Oskar demanded, body curled around the phone he clutched to his ear. "Right. Got it." His eyes scoured my face. "Stay here," he said. "Don't move. And don't try to comfort Jimmy."

"Okay," I said.

"But you can sit next to him."

I perched on the edge of the cement planter and watched Oskar run. He was a large man and not at all averse to using his size to make a statement, but when he ran, it was pure efficiency—graceful, powerful and fast.

I sat next to Jimmy in the too-hot night and pondered what I had meant by saying Phil had killed me. It was a stupid expression, "He kills me," right? And what had I been ranting about before that? And why had it upset Jimmy so? The wine and the heat made a sleepy combination, but a quick spike of adrenaline, remembering the last time I'd felt so unnaturally weary, popped me back awake.

I scooted fractionally closer to Jimmy, to touch my side to his shuddering one thinking about a night in Dublin when I was on exchange during college. A man, goaded by calls to "give us a song!" had stood up at his table and done just that. And another man at a table several over, who didn't seem to know the singer, had put his head down on his table and wept. My boyfriend had leaned over to me and whispered, "In Texas, they'd get a beating for that."

"For singing or crying?" I'd asked, and he'd just nodded. We watched another guy clap the crier on the shoulder and kiss the top of his head, as he passed.

"Him too," my boyfriend noted.

Oskar pulled up beside us, driving a limousine. He slammed his door, flipped his middle finger at the honking car behind him, and stalked around to open the rear passenger door. He looked again at the driver now waiting quietly, seized Jimmy by the jacket lapels and heaved him to standing.

"Look at me," he demanded in a gruff whisper.

Jimmy took a shuddering breath and met Oskar's eyes.

"I can carry you or you can pull yourself together and walk with the dignity you deserve." He let go of Jimmy's jacket front slowly enough to verify the man would stay standing, but didn't move from their navel-to-navel pose.

Jimmy took a brisk breath in through his nose and shook his head as though knocking water from his hair. He smoothed his shirt over his globe of body, stepped delicately around Oskar, and moved with studied precision toward the limo. Oskar touched my arm tactically, and we followed Jimmy, me into the back with him, Oskar to the driver's seat, and pulled back into very well-behaved traffic.

"I'm taking you to Phil's house," Oskar said, maneuvering the obscene length of a car like a kayak.

"Okay," I said, and tried not to smile. Jimmy and I were sitting side by side, our backs to Oskar, facing empty seats.

"I'm going to leave you there and come back here with Jimmy."

"What's going on?" I asked. "Did Phil call you? Is he okay?"

"No."

"Oskar." I was starting to get angry, but something in his profile stopped me, and we drove in silence until Jimmy's phone rang.

Jimmy listened for a while and said only, "Okay." Then he turned around to Oskar and said, "I must make a call." He spoke in swift, clipped French, the rest of the drive.

Oskar beached the limo outside of Phil's house.

"Should there be lights on?" I asked.

"He's home." Oskar turned in his seat to look at me. "Phil says you're strong." He didn't sound like he believed it.

"And cute, too!" I said, trying for a smile that wasn't ever going to come.

"Phil's in trouble," Oskar said. "Maybe police trouble, maybe not, but bigger trouble either way."

"Oh, shit." This was not the night I was hoping for.

"Phil's life is in the balance, just as much as yours was the other night when Irina poisoned your tea. If this breaks him, he won't come back out of stub. And we need him. We need Phil, not somebody else in his Primary, do you understand? Phil."

"I understand."

"So you better be as strong as he thinks you are."

I returned Oskar's steady glare. "I am."

"Every time I've heard you let Celeste through it was because you were excited about something."

"Celeste?" I said.

"When you talk, and it's not you, when you hear yourself saying things. When you get carried away."

"Okay."

"You must not let that happen. Not tonight. Not ever again. But absolutely not tonight. It would kill him."

"Okay," I said again.

"So whatever it takes, you keep calm. Choose your words and make damn certain it's you choosing them. Or stay silent."

"I will."

"We must go," Jimmy said.

"Yeah," Oskar said. "Yeah, I know."

I said good-bye and walked up the drive to Phil's door. It was open before I reached it. And I was in his arms.

Phil

After what seemed a long time but not long enough, she said, "We're letting all the A/C out."

I nodded and moved back so she could close the door, then held her again. Can I be trite? It was like she was my anchor on reality, like she was keeping me from flying away into IwishI and whydidn'tI. In two thousand years, you build up a lot of regrets. It doesn't make the generation of a new one any easier, and when you've just done that, there's nothing, nothing, nothing like the touch of someone to whom you matter more than whatever your latest fuckup was.

"What happened?" she said after a while.

I disengaged and went and sat on the couch, hoping she'd take it as an invitation. She did.

"I shot Irina," I told her.

"Are you all right?" She took one of my hands in both of hers.

"If you mean physically, yes."

She nodded. "Why?" There was no change in how tightly she held my hand.

"I was angry. Furious. There was a gun—Jesus. I'm a walking cliché. There was a gun in my hand and it went off. Christ."

I had all of her focus, like she could keep me tethered to the ground with her eyes and her hands, and it almost seemed like she could.

She said, "I've never been, well, in whatever position you were in."

"So angry you couldn't count to eight? I don't know, Ren. I'm afraid I did what she wanted, which is worse than what I did. I feel like, I don't know, like I've ruined everything."

"What do you need right now?"

"I need you doing just what you're doing. Holding me, touching me, convincing me that—shit. I don't know what you're convincing me of, but it's a good thing, and it's working."

"It's not that hard," she said, rubbing her forehead against mine, just a few inches from the Incrementalist Handshake.

"Celeste was never a good person," I said. "You probably don't remember her right now, but it doesn't matter. She was never what I would call good. But the point is, it's like, she didn't have to be good for me to love her. She was just her. She got there, somehow, into me, and that was that."

"That's—"

"Let me finish, Ren."

"All right."

"My point is, now I'm in love with someone who is good. And I like that. Turns out, that isn't a problem for me." She pressed me a little closer. "The problem is, I don't want to fuck it up. I'm scared. I'm more afraid about you, about losing you, then I've been—"

"Phil."

I stopped. "Yes?"

"I adore you. I love you. But, Jesus Christ, sometimes you talk too much."

She stood up and reached a hand out. I took it, and she led us into the bedroom.

Ren

I deposited Phil at the foot of his bed and went back to close the door. He stood where I'd left him, eyes held to mine like an umbilicus. I leaned against the door and considered whether I was being pigheaded. Maybe I should wait for a better time for our first time? Maybe a night when Phil wasn't afraid, and I wasn't half-listening for cops at his door? Maybe after a nice dinner-and-a-movie, rather than dinner-and-a-murder. Yeah, bullshit, Ren.

I straightened up and pulled my shirt over my head.

Phil dropped my eyes. "Gha," he said.

I walked to him and felt his eyes creep back up to my face, but what he most needed to say there aren't words for, so I just watched the fragile hollow where the strong cords of his neck and the hard bones of his chest met, not quite hidden in the few slender, curling hairs. I kissed him there, and he raised his chin and let his arms hang at his sides.

I unbuttoned his shirt and slid it off him, letting the tips of my breasts brush his chest. It hitched up his breathing when I kissed him—his chin and nose—and tasted his lips, like Jimmy's wine, in thoughtful, elongating mouthfuls.

I was pushing him. I knew I was. I was egging him to some sort of breaking point, and for a terrible moment I thought it was that other person of whom Oskar had spoken reaching her needles through me. But he put his hands on my hips and pulled away to look into my eyes. And that was her. That was the other. That gesture. I was reaching out, and he was pulling back. Not from me. But because of me.

I wasn't going to tell him who he was, but I knew he wasn't that. He wasn't someone who sat out games.

I held his eyes and smiled. "I love you," I said.

His smile wobbled.

He could cry or he could fuck me, I didn't care. I just wanted whatever it was dammed up in him to break. But fucking would be more fun.

"I love you," I said again.

He closed his eyes.

Then, because he couldn't yet pull me against him and hold me like I knew he needed to, or because I could see he was starting to believe it, or because there's some stupid fairy-tale magic to saying anything three times, I said, "I love you," and his phone rang. And of course he had to answer it, because jail would be even less fun than crying.

Phil

I just never learn: When you're about to finally get what you've been wanting, and when it's what you need like you've rarely needed anything, turn off your fucking phone.

The caller ID said it was Oskar, who was just exactly the person

I least wanted to talk to, but I had no choice. "Yes?" I said, trying to keep my voice normal.

Oskar said, "We need to know who saw you. I mean, people who know you, between when you entered and left The Palms today."

I pulled the phone away from my ear and stared at it. Ren's head was on my shoulder, my right arm around her, and her breasts pressed against my chest. And Oskar expected me to tell him what?

"All right," I said. "On the way in, Richard Sanderson and Yehia Awada waved to me. On the way out, I have no idea. Someone said something as I passed the poker room, but I don't know who."

"Crap," he said.

"I'm not done. You'll need the security tapes, or CDs, or whatever they use, which are going to be damn near impossible to get."

"That doesn't help."

"I said damn near."

She moved a little, rubbing against me, and I almost squeezed the phone in two.

"Go on," said Oskar.

I reached in front of me and unsnapped Ren's jeans, then slid my hand down to grab her ass. She made little mewing sounds and pressed against me harder.

"The guy who can get them for you is Andy Harmon. All of his switches are in the red ceramic jar next to the hand pump in my kitchen. Getting him to give you access, especially now, is going to be major work, but—"

"You just happened to have his switches?"

Ren started kissing my collarbone.

"Head of security at the place I count on for my sugar spoon? Yes, I just happened to have his switches."

"Are you all right, Phil? Your voice—"

"Jesus, Oskar. I am not all right. But I'll be much better the instant you hang up."

"All right," he said, and disconnected. I turned off my phone and threw it over my shoulder. I ran my hand along Ren's scalp, grabbed hold of her hair, and brought her head back and my mouth down on hers.

Ren

After that, I didn't need to push him.

FOURTEEN

Love Is Only a Game

Phil

I remember the '60s, which, according to Wavy Gravy, means I wasn't there. I remember being accosted on Forbes and Murray in Squirrel Hill by a Buddhist who expressed a desire to know if I wanted to be at peace with myself. I didn't answer him, and I didn't think much about it until I was reminded, thirty or forty years later, by a rant on the subject in a trashy sci-fi novel I happened to read. In general, I agree with the author of said trashy sci-fi novel: I don't want to be at peace with myself. I want to be fighting with myself, struggling, looking for answers; I want to be discontented and busy making my discontentment into something worthwhile. It is our discontent that drives us.

But, every now and then, after being whipsawed by life, and betrayed by those you love, and smacked down hardest by your own irrationality, well, a bit of peace isn't all that bad a thing. She moved a little in my arms, shifting closer to me, and her face twitched as she slept. I brushed a hair away from her eye and watched her for a while. Her hand moved, looking for mine. She found it and rested her cheek on it.

A little later she woke up partway, and pressed back against me, and I wasn't at peace anymore. But that was all right, too.

Ren

There was a funny-colored stream of light coming through the outdated curtains of Phil's bedroom window; I loved that he had bad curtains. I closed my eyes and wrapped my body around his, feeling the way the relaxation deepened, even from sleep, being closer to him.

In a hotel room not that far away, four men were probably still working, having worked through the night, fighting to keep Phil out of trouble. I felt bad for them, and indebted to them, but not guilty. Without our night, theirs would have been wasted.

But all of our nights were well into morning by now, luxury slipping toward decadence. I got up and found the phone Phil had pitched against the wall last night. I turned it back on and put it on the mattress next to him. He opened his eyes.

"Looks like you've got some voice mail," I said.

He grunted.

"I'm going to make coffee," I told him. "It's ten." He caught my wrist and pulled me back to sitting on the bed beside him.

"Mmpht," he said.

I stroked his hair, smoothing it away from his face, running my fingers over his temple. He reached a sleepy hand out for my breast. "But your coffee's awful," he said.

"Then you get up and make it."

He was on his feet so suddenly it almost knocked me off the bed. I laughed. "Don't tell me you're secretly a morning person."

"Have no fear," he said. "I've sprung out of bed, in two thousand years of mornings, exactly never." He stalked out of the bedroom naked.

I opened the curtains and found my phone and climbed back under the light cotton blanket to check my messages and email, thinking that, even after too much and too long, goddamn if love really can't make everything new.

Clear morning light filled the room, and my first email was from Jorge proclaiming the salubrious effects and noble history of a good hot water spa. He was scheduling an important call with Liam and me for tomorrow. I opened the first of three nested emails from Jimmy, and the doorbell rang.

Phil

I put on some boxers and prepared the words, "You could have bloody called," with which to assault whoever was on the other side of the door. I opened it, and it was Jimmy.

"Sorry I didn't call," he said. "I was afraid you wouldn't want to see me."

"I don't. Come in. Coffee?"

He came in. "Phil, why won't you let me buy you a French press? The coffee is so much—"

"I'd never use it. I don't want to spend loving attention on making my coffee perfect; I want to have it there so I can pour it and drink it."

He shook his head. "Where is Ren?"

"In bed. She's awake, if you need to talk to her."

"Maybe in a bit."

He took his coffee, and I took mine, and we sat on the barstools. He said, "It looks like you're not going to be arrested."

"Good," I said. "Thank you."

"You owe Oskar."

"Maybe it's not too late to be arrested."

"Phil—"

"Yeah, all right."

He drank his coffee, and he studied my face, and I knew he could read me pretty well, and he gave a little nod of approval. I was glad he approved. No, I'm not being sarcastic; I really was.

He cleared his throat and said, "I'm still worried about Celeste."

"Who's Celeste?"

He glanced at me quickly, his eyes wide, then they narrowed and he said, "That's not funny."

"Sorry. I'm worried too. If she really did trick me into killing Irina, we need to know why, and what—"

"We don't think she did."

I stopped. "All right. I'm listening."

"Matsu seeded the memory, and we all checked it. If you want it, it's a purple-and-gold lady's fan just to the right of his north fountain."

"Maybe later. What did you learn?"

"That Celeste was trying to kill you. Actually, she wasn't aiming at you, she was trying to shoot Matsu, because if she'd gotten him first—"

"I know."

He nodded. "Matsu only got there in time because he was watching for it, and he was watching for it because he noticed that her desk drawer was open. It was a close thing. She was starting to pull the trigger."

"Maybe she'd have missed."

"Maybe."

"But all right. Good. I mean, not good, but I'm glad at least that I didn't play into her hands. But—"

"But, yes. Why did she say it? None of us are comfortable with the idea that it just slipped out. She knows you. She knows you better than anyone. She knows you so well—"

"I get the idea, Jimmy. Jesus."

"Sorry. Our current theory is it may have been Irina pushing through, seeing another chance to free herself from Celeste."

I let that seep in and nodded. "Not at all impossible." I sighed. "That reminds me that we have to start looking for a recruit for Irina's stub."

"We talked about that, between talking about what happened and meddling with investigating officers and witnesses."

"Busy night. Have any of you slept?"

"All of us. In shifts."

I nodded.

He said, "We've asked Ricardo, Tina and Sally to start looking."

"Sally?"

"Karen's stub."

"Ah, right. They should be fine. Shame about Karen. She had the fire, you know?"

"I think Sally does too. This should help settle her in."

I nodded and we didn't speak for a while. I refilled my coffee and, at Jimmy's nod, his. I sat back down again.

Ren came out. My heart did a flip-flop to see her, though part of me was disappointed that she was dressed. "Good morning," she said. "I heard voices."

"And a delightful good morning to you, charming lady," said Jimmy. "You look well-laid."

She laughed and went into the kitchen and started boiling water. Jimmy can get away with comments like that; I'm not sure how.

"So the question is," said Jimmy, "is Celeste now actually gone?"

"Oh, no," said Ren, turning around holding an empty mug. "She's in the Garden."

Ren

Phil looked about to puke. Jimmy looked constipated.

"You remember Celeste?" Jimmy said the way you'd ask a jumper if he remembered his chute. I'm pretty sure Phil was adding three and two and five and three.

"Hang on." Jimmy dialed a number and watched me as he waited for someone to answer. I decided against tea and took the kettle off the stove.

"Ramon, when did Ren first start forgetting Celeste?"

Jimmy listened to Ramon, but Phil was watching me. "When did you remember Celeste?" he whispered.

I came around the bar to him and tried to wrap him in my arms, but he caught my hands. "When?"

"Oh God, no," I said, understanding. "No, sweetheart. Not last night. Or this morning when we—"

Jimmy was watching us, listening intently. "Go on," he said.

"I didn't think about Celeste until I was getting dressed just now," I said.

Both men nodded. Jimmy clapped a bracing hand on Phil's shoulder. "We had thought Ren might be forgetting her during the periods that Celeste shared Irina's body. When Celeste grazed, Ren remembered her. Irina's death and Ren's remembering coincide enough to mostly confirm that."

"Okay," Phil said, but his hand still wasn't steady when he picked up his mug again.

I thought this was not the time to ask about the "mostly."

Jimmy's eyes searched me. "How do you know she's in the Garden, Ren?"

"I just do," seemed like a poor answer, so I tried working backwards. "I heard you knock," I told Jimmy. "So I got out of bed to get dressed." Any coyness around my activities the previous night seemed futile at this point. "And I saw Phil's robe on the back of the door. It's such a great robe, and I thought about putting it on, which reminded me of something I'd wondered the first morning I woke up in Phil's bed after he'd staked me."

Jimmy's eyebrows shot up.

"Not like that," Phil said. "Flaming spike. In the forehead." It made me almost giddy to see the dimple uncloaking. "Every bit as life-changing as the other," he said. "Much less fun."

Jimmy laughed outright and I curtsied.

"Go on, Ren," Jimmy said.

I walked back into the kitchen to forage for breakfast. "When I wore Phil's robe the first time, I wondered if Incrementalists could squirrel away stuff, favorite clothes, keepsakes, photos, that kind of thing for themselves and their Seconds to create some sort of continuity between bodies. That morning I wondered whether Celeste had saved anything for me. This morning, I knew she hadn't."

"How did you know?" Jimmy asked.

"I remembered being her, and I knew I hadn't."

"Oh, thank God." Jimmy let out a breath so profound I didn't know how he stayed on his stool. Phil, on the other hand, was alert as a prairie dog on his. "You think Celeste's memories have just gone back to the Garden like a normal stub?" he asked Jimmy. "And Ren has them now?"

"Ren, do you have Celeste's memories?"

"I think so."

"So maybe we're just picking up where we left off?" Phil said. "With Ren integrating memories from Celeste's stub and from the Garden."

"Maybe," Jimmy said. "Let's go have you sit on the sofa and get comfortable for a bit, Ren. See what happens if you try to remember some more."

"But I just found oatmeal," I said, holding up a paperboard canister of a red-cheeked religious radical.

"Ren, I will take us for something glorious in an hour, but we'll all enjoy peace of mind and better digestion if we know Celeste is truly back where she belongs," Jimmy said, and stood, and we all heard his stomach register a loud and lengthy disagreement.

"You're hungry," Phil observed.

"Yes." Jimmy sat back down, chastened. "Oatmeal would be lovely," he said.

So I put the kettle back on and found cinnamon and brown sugar in the pantry, both unopened, and a box of raisins. Say what you want about Irina, but she knew how to lay in provisions against a siege. Phil and Jimmy sat on stools, Jimmy quizzing me on what I remembered, Phil mostly just watching, but when Jimmy misremembered Celeste's middle name, Phil corrected him.

"Are Celeste's personal, life memories different from what you remember in general?" Jimmy asked as the water started to boil.

"They have more emotion to them," I said. "And more images. They don't bubble up to the surface of my mind, the way the others do, but the bottom keeps getting farther away."

Jimmy nodded. "That all sounds right," he said.

Phil came in and got the coffeepot to top us all off, and kissed me as he walked by.

"What was her social security number?" Jimmy asked.

I told him, and put the three bowls of oatmeal on the breakfast bar.

He sniffed his happily. "How many children did she have?"

"None," I said, and opened the fridge to look for milk. The oatmeal was too hot to eat and I was hungry too. "But she was close to her nieces and nephew, and then their kids, and they thought of her as another grandmother."

"What did they call her?" Phil asked, smiling.

I pronounced the silly word gravely. "Except one," I said, remembering as I shut the fridge door. "There was one little girl who wouldn't say it, and called her Great-auntie Cece instead."

Then I had to sit down.

"Oh, fuck," I said. "Oh, no."

"What?" Phil was crouched in front of me, hands on my knees. "Ren, what?"

All I could think was that, if the fridge door had still been hung backwards, I wouldn't have whacked my back on the handle. "She was mine," I said.

"What?" Phil demanded.

"Celeste was my Great-auntie Cece."

"We knew that," Jimmy said. "And you used to. Did you just remember again?"

But I could only shake my head and remember one summer when it was so hot out at the lake house that we'd nailed tied-together bedsheets up as hammocks on the second-floor porch. One of those torpid nights, glamorous Great-auntie Cece, who never noticed children, came out into the moonlight after all my cousins were asleep.

Leaning against the railing, with her elegant bathrobe billowing around her like white smoke, she had told me a story about a powerful magician who fell in love with the little bird who loved to fly up and sing at his window in the tallest tower.

One day the magician caught the bird in his hand and spoke to her. She must have been enchanted, he told her, for he could see that, hidden within her, there dwelt a dreaming princess. In order to return to her true form, she must eat, from his hand, the seeds of a pomegranate. For pomegranates are poisonous to singing birds, but juicy and sweet enough to feed a princess on.

But the bird thought, *It is true, I have sometimes felt I was not truly a little bird, but I do not think I am a princess. I too much love to fly and sing. This man wants to make minced bird soup of me,* and so she flew away.

Long after, after she had forgotten she was ever anything but a songbird, a woodsman set a trap for her. He baited its trigger with the dried seeds birds love, but which no princess would consider food. The little bird saw that there was no sweet fruit to eat, but she thought, *This man loves my songs and flying,* and so she let him capture her. The woodsman sold the little bird at market, and she lived in a cage and did not sing until she forgot how to fly.

"I ate the fruit and not the birdseed," I said.

Phil was holding my knees and shook me by them, but all I could see was the moon-bleached face of my beautiful aunt who leaned down over my makeshift hammock to kiss me with cool lips, and whisper, "Someday you will meet someone who shares your hidden dreams, who knows, even before you do, when you're ready to become what you are inside, not because he can see the future, but because he can see you. Whatever he offers you, even if it looks like wicked fruit from a poisoned garden, take it. Until then, learn yourself well enough to know what truly sings inside you. Because once you do, it will take only one other in the whole world who hears it to set it free."

"I ate the fruit because she told me to," I said.

"Ren, you have to make sense for me."

I managed to get my eyes focused on Phil, on his handsome,

powerful magician's face. "You asked me why I didn't have to think about taking the spike," I said.

He nodded.

"It was because of Celeste," I said. "She prepped me to take it."

"Jesus Christ," said Phil.

"I was ten, and she meddled with me."

Phil sat down against the cabinets.

"She all but programmed me to take her stub," I said. I looked at Phil.

I didn't want to say it.

"And to love me," he whispered.

"Yes," I said.

Phil

Some people say life is a game. Maybe that's a good attitude, I don't know. Maybe it keeps them playing their best, enjoying it the most, taking pleasure in the drive to win. But life really isn't a game. Poker is a game. Life is life.

If I were to win a big pot, and then find out the guy had deliberately misplayed the hand because he wanted me to win, I have to say, it wouldn't bother me a bit. I'd be curious about why he did that, and if the opportunity to ask him came up I would, but I'd take the money and be happy. I play poker against the worst players I can find, and there's a reason for that.

But poker is a game.

Life isn't a game.

And love is only a game if you're an asshole.

The weird part is that I actually felt nauseated. I know the expression about something making you feel sick, but I can't recall ever having had the experience before. You're never so old that life can't surprise you. Isn't that grand?

Ren was looking at me, and her eyes were watery. For just a

moment, I was able to pull myself out of my self-centered, self-created pool of misery to get a glimpse of how this must be for her. She hadn't asked for any of it, and the way she felt about me, well, that was real to her no matter how it had been done.

I said, "I wish Celeste were alive, so I could kill her again."

Ren tried to chuckle, but it didn't come off so well. Still, I appreciated the effort.

Jimmy spoke softly. "It is evil, what we do."

Ren and I didn't say anything. He said, "We have good reasons, and we always hope to achieve good effects. But it is evil to meddle with people, to change who they are, to force them to our will, giving them no chance to even know we are there. It is evil. Perhaps the good we do makes up for it. I hope so. But we must never forget the violence, the violation, of our methods. And should we ever use them for even small things that do not make the world better, surely we deserve nothing but curses and contempt from those around us, and from ourselves."

Still no one spoke.

I took Ren's hand, turned it over, and kissed her palm. Then I stood up. "If you need me," I said, "I'll be at The Palms. Call the poker room; my cell will be off."

I put on my cap and walked out of the house.

FIFTEEN

Staying Matters

Ren

"I don't want you to go," I said.

"He's left." Jimmy's voice was colorless and dull, but he tried to fake some energy for my sake. "He'll come back."

"Coming back doesn't matter," I said. "Staying matters."

I closed my eyes and listened to my mind scrambling, like dog claws on ice, for a toehold, spinning out into the vacant cold. I quit trying not to cry.

"I feel like Goldilocks," Jimmy said from the middle stool between the three bowls of oatmeal.

I stood up. "Can I see your phone?"

He handed it to me, and I pulled up his contacts, scrolled down for Oskar and dialed.

"Hey, how's it going, Jimmy?" I could hear the smile in Oskar's voice.

"It's Ren," I said.

"Oh." Oskar was now on full alert. "Where's Phil?"

"He's on his way to The Palms for poker. He's not okay."

"Fuck." Oskar hung up.

Jimmy pushed an empty oatmeal bowl away and pulled the next one to him.

"You can take a nap, if you want," I told him, like having slept with Phil one night made me hostess here. "I'm going to shower."

I turned the water on, but I didn't have clean clothes, and the thought of Phil's bathrobe made me sob. I sat down on the tub edge.

I didn't know what to do.

I thought about calling Oskar back; he'd tell me what to do. But it was more important that he stop Phil from going all Lady Macbeth at The Palms. Besides, two kinds of people have the courage to make someone else's decisions: the hero, who comes to your rescue when you can't even cry out for help, and the tyrant. The only difference between them is the hero listens. As soon as you can talk, he'll put you down if you say so. I wasn't sure Oskar even had ears.

I knew for certain Celeste didn't.

And they were both very busy right now making decisions.

I turned the water off.

Jimmy hadn't moved from his middle stool. There was no oatmeal left. "Too hot, too cold, and just right?" I asked him.

He laughed without smiling. "I never realized what an Aristotelian Goldilocks was."

"With a name like that, are you kidding?" I said. "Her parents were hippies. It's Buddha's Middle Path all the way."

He just stared at me.

"Let's go," I said.

"Why?"

"Three reasons: because I saw what you did with my bosses last night and that wasn't evil, because I'm the reason Celeste can still stroll the Garden, and because I'm in love with Phil."

Jimmy looked hard at me. "What I did with your bosses won't make a difference beyond a few hundred people. If you're the reason Celeste has autonomy, our wisest action would be to kill you and retire the stub, so you should think before you broadcast that. And you might love Phil; he might even still love you, but if you and Celeste are that entangled—and I can't see how you wouldn't be—it will be more than Phil can handle. Game over, Renee."

"Can I take your car, then?"

"No," Jimmy said, standing slowly. "I'll drive."

Phil

It was Wednesday afternoon, so The Palms poker room wasn't very busy. There were some limit games, and a short-handed one-three no limit, but no two-five.

Greg said, "Hey, Phil. Want the one-three?"

I was about to say yes when I felt a hand on my shoulder.

I turned around and was staring up into Oskar's too-blue eyes. "Let me buy you a cup of coffee," he said.

I didn't want to. I wanted to be where everything vanished except information and odds, and where the only options were raise, pass, or call, and where if you made a mistake you could put a magnitude to it and know exactly how expensive a mistake it was. I didn't want to be in that world where you had to make everything up as you went along, and the consequences of mistakes were fuzzy, and might wear you down, or vanish entirely to reappear in years or lifetimes later. If I was going to find love, I didn't want it to be a fraud. If there must be pain, I didn't want it to be meaningless. I wanted there to be a God, even if he did play dice with the universe.

Oskar was still holding my eyes. "Quit whining to yourself," he said. "We have things to deal with."

I glanced at the one-three. It really did look like a crappy game.

"All right," I said. "But buy me a cup of coffee at the bar." I didn't want to go to the café just then.

We found seats at the bar in the wide open middle of the casino, and even now there was the fake sound of fake coins hitting fake trays as the losers got enough of their money back to keep them playing. He got me coffee. I added cream to it. I usually drink my coffee black except in the evening, but I wanted to watch the cream hit the coffee, permeate, gradually turn it from black to brown. I drank some.

"What?" I said. "What do you need?"

"I need you to graze," said Oskar.

"What can I graze for that Jimmy can't better?"

"It's one of yours. I can't be sure I have it right; facts only tell you so much. But I'm guessing I found the right one. September 18, 1606."

"Christ, Oskar. Is this really important? Now?"

"Yes," he said. "On several levels. Go thou and graze, my son."

The old same place. The smell of cherry blossoms, the taste of chive, the villa, the table filled with scrolls. I focused on finding the right table, the next right table, the right date, and I put my hand on the right scroll. I unrolled it.

A room lit only by a single candle; blank bare walls. A couple of pieces of bad furniture. The stench of rotting vegetables and dung coming in through the window along with a halfhearted breeze that couldn't even blow the candle out.

I was writing, jaw clenched, seeding a message to be read by anyone who wandered by my front gate. I wrote in an artisan's simple but urgent hand, "I may have found a potential recruit for Betsy's *souche*. If some of you want to look it over, the most important details are in the white porcelain mug on the small table in my dining room."

Yes. In those days, the fastest way to speak with each other was to leave messages in the Garden, which we'd check from time to time. That custom, which had been going on since we started scattering, pretty much ended in the late twentieth century when long-distance telephone calls became trivial, and was gone completely with email.

I stopped writing, and I wondered what Oskar was on about. But it was my memory, and so I relived it fully, and so even as the memory trailed off and faded, I was filled, utterly if briefly, with all of my feelings of that moment:

Funny, they were a lot like what I was feeling right now.

I came back. Oskar was watching me. "Was I right?"

"How could I do that?" I said. "How could you guys let me?"

"I wasn't around," he said. "But, the Second of my Primary didn't question you. You were Phil. You'd been around for sixteen hundred years. If you said it—"

"Jesus Christ. Didn't anyone know? I was lonely, I was miserable, a girl smiled at me, and—"

"And you were sloppy. You just barely checked her over, and no one else checked her at all, and we spiked a selfish, unstable personality into the group. Everything we do is based on every one of us. We didn't have email back then, Phil. You didn't wait. You spiked her too quickly because you wanted to."

"But Betsy wasn't my lover!"

"No. And no one else was. We are all alone, Phil. I mean, everyone is alone, but we're more alone than most. And after sixteen hundred years, you weren't handling it very well."

"Someone should have—"

"Who? How? One thousand, six hundred fucking years, Phil. No one else has ever come close to that. Who could know what effect that much loneliness would have on someone? And, you know, self-examination has never been your strong suit."

"So, this is all my fault?"

He smiled. "Yep. No way around that. All you, buddy."

"One thing I admire about you, Oskar. You always manage to keep an even keel in the face of someone else's pain."

"I learn from the best."

"Why are you doing this to me?"

"I should think that would be obvious. This is your problem. You caused it, now it's biting you in the ass. So, okay. Quit hiding behind a poker table. Go fix it."

I came very, very close to taking a swing at him. It would have been stupid, because he's bigger, stronger, and probably faster. But I came close.

Instead, after a moment, I said, "All right. I'm going home. Want to come?"

"I wouldn't bother," he said. "I'm sure everyone will be here soon."

I looked around the bar. "We should find a better place."

He pulled out his phone. "I'll tell them where to meet us. I imagine it won't be long."

Ren

Jimmy's phone rang as we were leaving. "We're already headed that way," he said.

He was quiet for a while, then he looked over at me. "No," he said. "She looks like hell."

"Thanks," I said.

"Okay, Oskar. That's what we'll do." Jimmy stuffed the phone back in his pocket and started the car. "Sorry," he said to me, "but Phil killed someone at The Palms last night. It's bad enough we have him wandering their casino shell-shocked. People have seen the two of you together, and you're not a local. We'll take the garage elevator up."

"Up where?"

"Ops suite. Oskar's taking Phil there now."

We rode through the sunlight to the cavernous parking lot then up the elevator. When the doors closed, I started to shake.

"You wanted this," Jimmy reminded me.

"No, I didn't," I said.

He knocked on a door and Ramon answered it. "Matsu is sleeping. Hello, Ren. Can I get you anything? We have a small kitchenette and room service."

"No," I said. "Thanks."

I'm not sure what the rooms we were in had been intended for, but right now they looked like every Internet startup I'd seen. Sofas shoved into a squashed U-shape in a halfhearted nod to civilized conversation, and all the rest of the space filled with collapsible tables sagging under computers, printers, routers and scanners.

Oskar was sitting at a computer. Phil was on the sofa.

"Hi," I said. "What's happening here?"

"Same old, same old. I was kind of upset before, on account of, you know, being in love with you and thinking maybe you loved me until I found out that you only loved me because you'd been bitchmeddled. Like that term? Bitchmeddled? I just made it up. Anyway, I was upset, but then Oskar showed me that, really, it's all my fault because of a mistake I made four hundred years ago, so now things are fine. How are you?"

"If I love you, does it matter what Celeste did? Does the Why have to matter?"

"The fourth axis?" Ramon asked.

Phil didn't say anything. And he didn't look at me. "How the hell can I answer that?" he said at last. "How can I even look at it to answer it? I mean . . . shit. Obviously it matters, or I wouldn't feel this way. Do you mean should it matter? I don't know. This isn't a situation I've ever been in before." His laugh was all mustache and no dimple. "I remember you asked me once if anything could surprise me." He glanced at me, but didn't hold my eyes. Matsu came into the room, not looking sleepy.

"Well," I said. "Now I know Celeste can."

"Yeah. Well. We need to fix that."

When I was hurting this much, why did Celeste matter more again? Why was it her, not us, that needed fixing? But Matsu's calm, clipped voice called Phil off before I could. "I think it would be best," he said, "if you did not try again at fixing Celeste."

Now Matsu had Phil's complete and furious attention. I wanted it back. "Matt, my dear friend, that woman has controlled and dominated my life for the last four hundred years. Now she threatens to continue doing so indefinitely. And you think I shouldn't try to stop her? What do you suppose the odds of that are?"

"What do you suppose the odds are that you can this time, given your rage and your record to date?"

"Infinitely better than if I don't try."

"Phil," Jimmy said, and something in his voice made me look at him. All the richness was gone from his dark skin. "Phil, I can only begin to guess how upsetting this latest discovery is, but if you imagine that, even if you succeed, it's going to simply fix this problem between you and Ren, you are living in a dreamland."

Phil pulled his eyes from Matsu to Jimmy and shrugged. "It doesn't matter." Which made me want to scream.

"Okay, Phil," I said, trying to keep the rage out of my voice. "Let me ask the question a different way: What does matter?"

I watched the fight seep out of him.

"There's a big piece of me right now trying to say nothing does, but I'm ignoring it," he said. "What matters is that we take whatever time we have, Incrementalist or amnemone, Primary or Second, forty thousand years or two thousand or fifty, and do what we can to make this ugly world we're stuck in a little less ugly. That's what matters."

"Beauty matters?" I said.

"Yes. In the broadest sense of beauty."

These men had seen me poisoned and vomiting. They'd seen me in a bathrobe and morning-after hair. I could have walked over to Phil and wrapped myself around him. It wasn't because of them that I didn't.

"Better matters," I said. I wanted him to look at me. That was all it would take.

"Yes, by any reasonable definition of better."

"So what is going to make this better?" I asked.

"Making sure that the sick, twisted, ugly, evil personality of Celeste is not getting in the way of our work, or my life. I have two thousand years behind me. I will happily trade whatever I have left to see her gone."

Fucking Celeste! I needed Phil, and she had him.

"We're pretty sure we know how to get that done," Oskar said.

"Eh?" said Phil.

Matsu nodded. "We've been working on it for a while, and the three of us agree. We need to bring in two others to consult; and

Phil? This, my old friend, you cannot take part in. You must let go, and let us."

Oh, God. I thought. Oh, no.

Phil sat back on the sofa with his eyes closed. "Wait," he said. "You're saying you can do it?

"Yes," Oskar said. "We can do it. All we need is for you not to meddle with it. Just leave it alone."

Phil looked to Matsu, who nodded. "We believe we can."

I glanced at Jimmy. His eyes were full of tears, and he wouldn't look at me. He had warned me. Their wisest action.

"Good lord. Okay," Phil said. "I need this done. I want this done. I thought you were telling me that . . . shit. Fine. Jesus. My manhood is not tied up in who pulls the fucking trigger! God! Go! Do what you have to! I'll sit on my hands. I'll play poker. I'll stay the fuck out of your way. Fix this thing!"

Oskar looked pleased. Matsu looked. Well, Matsu looked like Matsu.

"Will you tell me?" I asked.

"No," Matsu said. He met my eyes and held them.

"Matsu?" Phil said, wary.

"You are both too close to the problem," Oskar said. "We need a clean field to operate here."

Ramon held Phil's eyes as steadily as he had held mine. "We're flying Felicia and Nick in," he said.

Phil nodded. "Okay."

Jimmy cleared his throat. "We'll send Ren back to Phoenix," he said.

"Is that where you want to be, Ren?" Phil asked.

"I'm not sure what I want is on the list of what matters."

"It matters to me," Phil said. He could look at me now, but I was the one watching the floor.

"I want to know what they're planning," I said. "And I want to stand up for Celeste."

"You want to—which?" Phil almost jumped off the sofa.

"She doesn't have a voice here, and I can give her one," I said. "But most of all, I want to stand up for not having all the fucking answers every goddamn time."

"Beloved," Phil said, and that word in his voice made me want to never stop crying. "Celeste has many voices. She has her voice when she takes over your mouth. She has the voice she used to meddle with me. She has the voice she used to meddle with you. She has the voice she used to meddle with the rest of the goddamned group. She has nothing but voice. I think I'm tired of hearing it. We know goddamned well we don't have the answers, that's why we argue all the time. We do our goddamned best to ask the right questions."

"Okay, Phil," I said. "Here's a good question. What if Celeste wanted to go virtual, to play Ghost in the Garden and meddle with the meddlers instead of screwing around with the nemones? Wouldn't making you love me be the perfect protection for her?"

"I have no reason to believe Celeste meddled with me in that way. And I do love you. And I have no interest in protecting her. So evidently not."

Ramon hadn't moved. "Celeste and Ren are the same stub, Phil."

"I know," Phil said.

Ramon nodded. He was quiet for a moment, watching for something I couldn't see in Phil's face. When he found it, he said, "There's no Ren without Celeste, Phil. And no Celeste without Ren."

"I'm not convinced that is true indefinitely. And, it would seem, neither is Celeste."

"Let us take care of this Phil," Oskar said. "Like you said. Don't meddle. Let us fix it. Go play poker."

Phil nodded. "Ever heard of Gila River?" he asked me.

"Nope," I said.

"It's an Indian casino. Beautiful poker room. Right outside of Phoenix."

"I've wanted to watch you play since the first time I heard you talk about it." That wasn't a lie, but the casual tone I was matching or mocking in Phil was.

"Well, if you're going back to Phoenix, I have no plans," he said. "Although, really, if you're after excitement, watching grass grow is marginally above watching me play poker."

"Don't know as I'm really looking for excitement right now," I said.

"Perfect, then."

Ramon and Oskar exchanged glances. Jimmy was in the kitchenette.

"I have to stay here through tomorrow," I told Phil. "The call with Jorge and Liam that Jimmy set up is too important to risk taking on a cell phone in the desert. But after that, God, I've never wanted to leave anywhere as much."

It might kill me, but I was not going to goddamn cry.

"That works for me. We can fly to Phoenix after that, or if you'd prefer, have you ever driven across the Bould—the Hoover Dam?"

"No," I said.

He talks too much. I told him last night he talks too much. He smiled at me. "You'll like it."

"Okay," I said. "I'm going to go up to my room now."

"Rest well," Phil said.

"Yeah," I said. "See you."

"Yes," Ramon said, but Jimmy and Oskar were both too engrossed in what they were doing to notice I was going.

"Do you want me to tuck you in?" Phil asked.

"No, I'm okay," I said, which might be the biggest lie I've ever told.

"He's not reaching out. He's not reaching out," I whispered in the elevator. "And I can't keep pulling him."

Phil loved me. I knew he loved me. But he was going to let Oskar make decisions for him, and Oskar was no hero. He'd kill me if it took that to silence Celeste for Phil.

I shut the door of my room and pushed the night lock into place. I was afraid, and angry, and hurt, and not at all sure I wasn't crazy to boot. Were there enough drugs to make this stop if I told a nice doctor my story? I knew there weren't.

I'd gone up to that room to advocate for doubt. To look Oskar in the face and ask him how he could be so sure Celeste was evil when she was as certain he was. I went, armed only with questions, to a war of answers. I never had a chance.

I went because I love Phil. And love turns up, even with no answers.

I went because I am an Incrementalist. And beauty fucking matters to me. Even before Phil and Celeste, I believed in Better because I was never any good at Good. Maybe I should have worked harder at learning to appreciate each mountain climbed rather than setting off right away for the next peak. Maybe Good should have been good enough. But if Good is as good as it gets, why get up in the mornings? Just to keep circling in the holding pattern? I don't even think that's possible. Inertia will get you. You can't balance on the mountain's pointy peak. You fall off. So you find the next mountain. You learn to enjoy the climb. You get better at falling. Or maybe that's what I'd always told myself because I could never get peaceful on mountaintops.

Either way, I was tumbling down.

SIXTEEN

Cracks Like Lightning

Phil

I drove back to my house. I tried to think, but thinking has never been my best game. I could feel, but I didn't care for it much. I listened to the voice in my head that said I should maybe spend a little less time feeling sorry for myself and think about Ren. I listened. I agreed.

It didn't change anything.

I knew that I was in the process of creating one of those memories that you'd pay ninety percent of your bankroll to wash out. But it's like full-on tilt; you watch yourself make stupid play after stupid play, and you say, "I should stop this. I should stop doing this now. I should get up and walk away from the table."

One plus zero is, ah, to hell with it.

Fuck.

Two thousand years and I was no better than this?

Forty thousand years, and the human race was no better than this?

Bullshit.

Pain forces your attention on yourself. My pain was making it impossible for me to reach her, and her pain was making it impossible for her to reach me.

What we needed was a way to break the pattern. Neither of us wanted that pattern, but neither of us knew how to break it. And it should be so easy. All it should take is the right—

Yes.

The right trigger.

Or, as we Incrementalists call it, a switch.

Fortunately my car appeared to know how to get home, because I'm not sure how else I arrived there.

I walked into my house and threw myself into my chair. I opened up my laptop and composed an email.

> **From:** Phil@Incrementalists.org
> **To:** Ren@Incrementalists.org
> **Subject:** Gift
> Wednesday, July 6, 2011 1:13 pm GMT - 7
>
> It's all going wrong, and I don't know how to fix it. Maybe if I'd spent some of the last two thousand years meddling with, or at least examining, my own head instead of everything else, I wouldn't be this bad at something this important. I don't know. The idea of doing that is strangely repellent, so perhaps, at some basic level, I'm incapable of it.
>
> I know that you are more precious to me than anyone I've met in the last 2000 years. If there is something I can do that you can put into words, I'd be grateful if you did so.
>
> But meddlework is funny. You can change someone—a bit. You can make a guy less of a prick, or more of a decent human being. You can push him to do something he probably wouldn't have, or get him not to do some-

thing he wasn't one hundred percent convinced was right. But you can't turn night into day. Some things are fundamental, and if those are impenetrable walls between us, then so be it. I am who I am, not who Celeste wanted me to be, nor whoever I might guess you want me to be.

There is something I want you to have. It is the only thing I have that, really, has any value. If it turns out to have no value for you, then I guess that says it all. But of the two hundred and four Primaries, over forty thousand years, this is a first. I hope I get some credit for that, at least.

There is a suitcase under the olive tree behind my villa. I offer it with love.

Yours,

Phil

There. Done.

All right, Phil. But do you have the balls to send it?

That was the real question.

It was by far the most terrifying thing I'd ever considered doing.

Fear is a powerful force.

But—

Suppose you're sitting on top of two pair, $1,200 in the pot, a possible flush on board, and your opponent pushes. You have $300 in front of you, so that's the effective bet. With the way the hand played out, and with what you know of this guy, you figure there's about an eighty percent chance that your hand is no good.

If you call and lose, you've lost $300. $300 times .8 is $240, your expected loss.

If you call and win, you win $1,500. $1,500 times .2 is $300, your expected win.

The net gain is $60. If you make that play a thousand times (and you will), you'll win $60,000.

Okay, so, what's my point?

That sometimes you can believe you're losing, and it can still be the right play to push all of your chips into the middle.

Fear is a powerful force. But math is even more powerful, and however much it hurts, however terrified you are, your job is to make the right play.

I closed my eyes and tasted chive and smelled cherry blossoms. I climbed up the stairway, and down the hall, and up again to what would have been my bedroom if I'd really lived there. Under the bed was a suitcase. Samsonite. Black. I set it on the bed, opened it, and started filling it.

Here was popcorn and beer and mustard and sweat: the smell of the stands at Three Rivers Stadium when Chuck's dad and uncle would take him to games.

Here was the sound of the bat hitting the ball, from the same person and time.

Here was the feel of the seat and the handlebars when Chuck finally got his BMW.

This is the smell of exhaust.

And before that, Reggie Fox, from Cleveland, and here is the feeling of Boland, Reggie's Yellow Lab, licking the inside of Reggie's ear.

Boland smelled like this.

Now we'll put in the taste of collard greens that Reggie's mother learned to cook when she was a girl in Mississippi. They were hard to get in Cleveland, but that just made them more special.

Reggie's mother loved jazz, and here's "Celeste Blues" by Meade Lux Lewis, scratchy on an old 78. His mother used to dance him around the room to that.

Here's how her hair smelled when she did.

And another, and another, and yet more; emptying the metaphorical bag into the virtual suitcase. I took it all the way back to Cal, Calvin White, of Kansas City, Missouri, and when he was four he got his own little chalkboard, with his own chalk, so he could add and subtract all day, because that's what he loved doing. Here's the smell of the chalk.

Here's how it felt in his little hand.

And this is from Cal, too: the taste of an orange slice, with powdered sugar on it.

Any further back and the memories don't have power anymore, so we can stop there.

I closed the suitcase, brought it downstairs and outside, and I set it under the olive tree.

Then I opened my eyes and hit Send.

Ren

He'd packed me a suitcase.

I read Phil's email seven times trying to figure what it meant that he'd left a suitcase for me under a tree. I wasted some time cursing Ramon's damn wobbly alpha, because Who and When and Where were so not the point with the suitcase. I wanted to stick a pin through the flickering body of alpha. I wanted enough light to see Why.

Was he just answering the question I'd asked about what mattered? Was he saying the memories he'd packed in their casing of symbol and put out for me, these memories, or the symbols for them, are what matter to him?

That he wanted me to have them mattered to me.

It was a symbol. Like the little bird in Great-auntie Cece's fairy tale. Few things have as much power. But it's never the symbol—the bird itself, the cross itself, the prophet's name in and of itself that is sacred—it's the welter of emotions, ideas and insights it triggers. If it triggers nothing, its power is nothing.

Or was the suitcase his way of saying good-bye?

I took a shower and wished I had a bathrobe. I didn't want to wear anything I'd packed for the three-day business trip I'd been expecting. Not that I owned the right clothes for today. It was five o'clock in the afternoon. I put on my pajamas and carried my laptop from my desk to the bed.

I found nothing new in my in-box except a forwarded political rant from my uncle, a selection of new sex-and-drug and sex drug spam, and a request for my expense report from Cindi. No changed meetings or new calendar items with Incrementalist fingerprints on them. Nothing else from Phil.

I emailed Brian and cc'd Cindi, introducing them. I suggested Brian take his grocery receipt for the dinner he was going to cook for me by HR. Liam had said he'd reimburse him. Cindi loves Italian food and needs a little syncopation in her life; Brian needs an optimist, so I told Brian Glyphx was on Central and Adams where there's an adorable little coffee shop. Getting them in a room together would be enough, with my flakiness to laugh over together.

Then I read Phil's email again.

This was him reaching out. But Celeste would be in the Garden, and I'd used up my day's worth of courage.

This was Phil saying who he was: a closed case left, not a package delivered; a memory, not a conversation. But he wanted me—or was at least willing for me—to open it, and to know him. Was he symbolically offering to share his memories and himself with me?

I closed my eyes and was blown back against the headboard by the tumble of images, memories and emotion. I breathed through it. I reached out for the quiet mudflats, the saline stretch of goopy, gooey, undifferentiated morass, and realized it scared me a little less now. And the taste of root beer always made me smile. I placed the filters one at a time: Phil's villa, the olive tree, a suitcase; and I found a seedpod. It was black and shiny as fake leather. And almost as big as I was.

I wrapped my arms around it. It was balloon-light, but unwieldy as a mattress, and I dragged it to a clearing where a cypress stump made a crooked seat. I sat down and rested with Phil's gift at my feet.

It looked overfilled, pregnant and impenetrable, and I knew it could hold only what he had once seeded in the Garden. All I could do by opening it was learn. I wouldn't live experiences with him or see them through his eyes. I would only know what had happened to him.

"Just the facts, ma'am," I told the seedpod, and slit it with my thumb.

It pooched open, and I reached into it. I pulled out a slippery green seed and knew what Mississippi collard greens taste like in Cleveland.

I nearly threw the fuzzed and golden sunflower seed back for the ticklish slobbery facts it imparted.

And then a powdery orange seed told me a taste I already knew, and memory tightened the edges of my tongue: the citrus-sweet memory Phil had meticulously constructed as a gift for me. More than a memory. A secret.

"Oh Jesus," I whispered. "Oh, no."

I squeezed the edges of the split-open husk back together, grateful that the halves knit themselves closed. I walked yards and yards away from the pod. This wasn't a symbol. Symbols are inert in the hands of those they don't trigger. This was a trigger. It was all the ammo there ever was against Phil. Every one of his switches.

Sometimes Why flickers like a lightning bug. Sometimes it cracks like lightning. Right between your eyes.

I picked up the seedpod and held it close to my body and let the filters lift. My cypress bench and the little pond where the frogs moaned all began to slip, and when the ground under me was good and runny, when I was starting to sink, I pressed the weightless seedpod which housed the heaviest things I knew away from me. I buried it in the undifferentiated mud of memory where it would grow and bud and flower in intuition and not knowledge. I pushed until I was certain there was nothing left for Celeste to eat. Then I opened my eyes.

From: Ren@Incrementalists.org

To: Phil@Incrementalists.org

Subject: Re: Gift
Wednesday, July 6, 2011 6:41 pm GMT - 7

I've unpacked and put your things away.

Come home.

Phil

I drove slowly, because it isn't safe to drive when you're tearing up, and, by God, I was going to make it there without being pulled over, or hitting anything. Nothing would be wrong on this drive. Too many things could go wrong after it, but nothing on this drive.

I felt my heart beating.

It's only a couple of miles from my house to The Palms. I could have walked; I often do. But that would have taken too long.

I arrived, and I delivered my car to valet and went in the front door—that wouldn't take me past the poker room. There was exactly one person I wanted to see.

The elevator took forever to arrive, and the ride up slightly longer than that.

I made myself walk, not run, down the hall.

"Come home," she had said. Jesus.

Don't be stupid, Phil. Go slow. Don't go touchy and grabby before you know where her head is at. Don't make things worse.

I stopped in front of her room; I knocked and the door opened instantly, like she'd been waiting behind it. She looked up at me and I took her in my arms and crushed her, and she buried her head in my shoulder and I felt wetness there. I kissed the top of her head and squeezed until I was afraid I'd hurt her. Somewhere, miles away, the door snicked closed behind us.

"There are so many problems," I said. "But I—"

"Phil."

I stopped.

"You really do talk too much," she said.

Ren

Sometimes a life pivots in a way you can't fight or deny; the first warning sign is your old self dead at your feet. Sometimes what you need is the opposite of what you want because it makes you reach for it. Sometimes none of the constructs or plans or pivot points matter.

He was all that mattered. The taste of his mouth on mine, the solid unyieldingness of his body that my body wanted to wrap and mold and form itself around. Everything else felt irrelevant and trivial to me, and we almost shredded our clothes trying to get free of them fast enough to fill our hands and mouths with each other again. There was no fear, no pulling away or even holding back, nothing reserved or restrained or considered. His hands hurt me, and I wanted them to. His mouth took from me and I wanted nothing left behind.

Sometimes all you are is want.

"Lie down," he told me, and I climbed, naked, into the center of my big hotel bed, knowing he watched me.

"I'm sorry," he said, eyes refocusing on mine once I was lying, only undressed and wildly awake, exactly as I had when I first opened my eyes after he'd staked me. "I didn't mean to sound so—"

But I held his eyes and opened my legs, and he stopped talking with a noise like the sound of something breaking in his chest.

"Turn over," he said.

I twisted onto my belly, and even though I only wanted to arch my back and raise my ass to him, I couldn't stop it from rocking. I couldn't hold it still.

"Turn back," he said, in a voice I knew would not be able to talk in words again tonight.

I rolled again onto my back, my hips dancing against the coverlet, my breasts heavy with needing his hands on them. He walked from the foot of the bed to the side, beautiful, primitive and naked, looking down at me, and my thighs and breathing. My belly and squeezed-tight breasts shook with wanting to be where his eyes touched.

He sat on the edge of the bed, leaned over me and took one breast in his open mouth. I think I screamed. Or I whispered something stupid. My fingers were in his hair, untwisting the band that held it, pulling my body deeper against his insistent tongue and unforgiving teeth.

Then he was on top of me. In a single uncoiled spring, he went from sitting by me to pinning me. My arms wrapped his back. My legs wound his. He pushed into me.

And it was enough.

My body gasped around him, and suddenly, it was enough. Enough to have his back under my hands, his body and mine occupying the same space.

And just as suddenly it wasn't. Wasn't enough, would never be enough, couldn't ever hold everything I felt. He reached a hand down my back and lifted my ass up hard against him. He caught his other hand in my hair. And this time, I know I screamed.

But he kissed me. He held me pinioned, inside me, on top of me, and under me. He held me, gripped and mastered. Held me slave and savior. Held me still, and kissed me. I twisted under him.

My tongue and hips and breasts ground in hungry circles. He took his mouth away and tightened his grip on my hair and ass, and pressed his temple against mine. And I saw through the Gardens.

All of them.

The patterns overlapped, and I saw the symbol for symbolic things. I felt the name for things that name things. I was—we were—the metaphor that tells how metaphor communicates. As he reached, and reached again into me, all the symbols dissolved. They ran in layers of meaning over my skin, and spun impossibly down into bottomless oceans of time, and past, and hunger, into a blackness that closed with a zip. Not Samsonite, but Eagle Creek for our summer house on Eagle Lake. And for a moment, I remembered everything. But I was pummeled by his wanting, and by my want reaching back, and it didn't matter.

If fear pulls away, love pushes in. For every withdrawal, a deeper penetration, and if I ever felt afraid again I would reach, not for Fibonacci, but for the simple truth that I was loved. And I would have told Phil that—I wanted to, panting under him—but words were gone with the symbols we swam in, were diving hard down into. I reached with my temple, touched it to his, and came in tiny vast compressions no smaller than forty thousand years of shared symbols, and no bigger than a pivot.

SEVENTEEN

What We Can Do

Phil

"Have you ever noticed," I said, "that there's something erotic about hotel rooms? I mean, just being in a hotel room. Any hotel room."

"No," she said. "Never noticed that. And especially not a Vegas hotel room. Nope, never noticed that at all."

She nuzzled her head onto my shoulder.

A little later she said, "So, I take it you don't mind that I was meddled with?"

"I mind a lot," I said. "I hate it."

"No, I mean—"

"I know what you mean." I slid down a little so I could kiss her, then slid back up. "I still mind that, but I've decided that will in no way prevent me from taking advantage of it."

She laughed, and her hair tickled my chest.

"How about you?" I said.

She was quiet for a little while, then said, "I don't know. I'm still working it out."

"Is it 'leave me alone to think' working it out, or 'talk to me about it' working it out?"

"It's let me think, I think."

"All right."

"We need to go to Phoenix today." Her voice had a sort of scary stillness.

"I know."

"I should get up and shower."

"Want me to scrub your back?"

She raised her head and looked at me. "Yes," she said.

Ren

Phil left to pack, his hair still wet from our shower, and I seriously considered paying too much for a bathrobe from the hotel gift shop. Instead, I called Elise. She and her boyfriend were both out, like I was hoping they'd be, but she gave me her apartment address and told me where to find the spare door key. I put on the clothes I'd packed for the flight home and took a cab.

Elise's place was exactly what I needed: quiet, pretty, and nowhere an Incrementalist would find me without some work. I changed the message on my phone in case Phil called before our appointed pickup time back at The Palms, and then I got comfy on Elise's little, red-and-gold tapestry-draped sofa. Across from me, a TV perched on a large and rambling crimson bookcase, reflecting the gold-framed mirror on the wall behind me which, in turn, reflected the compact TV and the exuberant sprawl of books. I would have liked to have read the spines, but I was already short on time. I closed my eyes.

Salt air and root beer, the undifferentiated mud of my memory. No wonder Phil had trouble saying who he was when he has had so much more time to survey, and his Garden is full and fruitful.

My Garden, such as it was, stretched in front of me, still and peaceful, under a pale summer moon. At the very least, maybe I could roll it up like a dung beetle, into a doughy ball bigger than I was. I unzipped the Eagle Creek duffel.

Celeste had made and hidden a secret backup of her stub; I was here to see if I could do the same. *If you're the reason Celeste has autonomy, our wisest action would be to kill you and retire the stub.* Sorry, Jimmy, I'm not a martyr. I know that.

I know it because Celeste taught me to study myself. And that moonlit strand of habit, from the journals I kept, through the philosophy books I read, to the psychology/design double major I took in college, that whole thread of deliberate self-discovery ran through my life like a strain of music. Its tune began with sheets stiff from the clothesline, softened by the humid bodies of my sleeping cousins, and wove dozens of instruments' worth of people and places, with each of their hundreds of notes of separate clear memories, into a music—crunchy and damp—that sailed into my canvas bag. I was introspective, to a fault sometimes, but immutably. Packed into my duffel.

It was not what I had expected. Where were my tidy seeds like the ones Phil packed when he gave me his switches? I'd swept them up in my song of introspection. It had been not just select, specific, symbolic memories that packed meaning into history, and came with the taste of trust or the texture of curiosity, but a whole symphony of who I was. A singing twig of a stub.

And the one beside it was the other half of my double major. I'd studied psychology and not philosophy. And despite my life-long love of beauty, I took design instead of art. Because I was practical. Percussively. The drumbeat of worries my mom never shared but couldn't hide about our rent and clothes joined the rattle of the fun we had at thrift shops shaken free by relief as much as creativity, and the ringing timpani of drugs I didn't take, and the foreign exchange I did, rolled into a rich, dense ensemble, not of privation, but choice. Martyrdom is indulgence and wouldn't have survived under this barrage of sound, even if it'd been innate. And the practical drum line marched thundering into the bag.

Nana's minced bird matzo ball soup, my switch for trust, played tuba in the courage band (I am brave, in part, because I trust people will help me when I ask), but it sang coloratura for sex. I could have watched that opera for hours, but a priest with a basso profundo started singing flat, so I went backstage.

It was dark and vast, and every puppet, hanging by its strings on the back wall, had two faces. I picked up Practical and found Frivolous. I turned over my Strength and saw I was Broken too. And even though Know Thyself was already in the bag, I surprised myself with whispers I couldn't quite hear. So okay, Oskar, it looks like I'm a dialectic too. And goddamn it, Celeste, fine; I am unfathomable. And yes, Phil; it's a jumble.

The Eagle Creek duffel was not a harmonious symphony of interwoven songs of myself—fuck, I contradict myself—but a roar of static, like a house on fire. But I was going to go out singing. Over the noise of all the signals, despite not knowing what the hell I was doing, I'd make up something loud. Not a memory from the Garden of all memory, but a dream from the fields of the uncreated of work and love. I thought about the RMMD which I now knew must record more than memories and information linked to auditory cues, but songs and stories as well. And I thought about Phil, with his dimple and eyebrows and his curiosity and conviction. And I sang, "Our memories aren't all we are," to the tune of "Camptown Races," and I zipped it all up before the final *"da."*

I left Elise a note and twenty bucks for all the Cap'n Crunch I ate, and I put the key back under the ceramic frog.

Phil

It was about four hours later that I got back to pick up Ren. I paid for her late checkout because I felt like I owed it to her boss, and after Jimmy's lecture about evil, I couldn't bring myself to do even a light meddle on the clerk.

The valet retrieved my car, we loaded up Ren's suitcase and her laptop, and hit the road.

"How do you like to road-trip?" I said.

"Not as a verb," she said.

"Correction noted. Are you of the Stop Everywhere school, or the Just Get There school?"

"Very much of the Just Get There school. You?"

"I'm adaptable, but Just Get There is my preference."

"Good, then."

"Except you have to see the Hoover Dam."

"I'm fine with that."

She put her hand on my leg and I felt a smile grow. A little later, she said, "Do Incrementalists ever see the future? Get premonitions? That sort of thing?"

"No. What are you feeling?"

"Nervous. About Oskar and Ramon and Matsu fixing what should be our problem. Like something is doomed to go wrong."

I was quiet for a while, then I said. "I don't believe in premonitions. In forty thousand years, I haven't seen anything remotely like evidence, in us or in anyone."

"All right."

"So the feeling is coming from something else. Something you know or suspect or noticed but aren't consciously aware of."

"That isn't much better," she said.

"I know."

"Are you looking forward to being home?"

"Yes. No. I think so."

"You like Phoenix?"

"I'd prefer Tucson. Hey, do you think we could do anything about that obnoxious new law?"

"The immigration thing? Maybe. We sometimes do things on that level. Kevin did pretty good with the gay marriage thing in New York."

"That was us?"

"Well, it's never that clear. We pushed here and there, and helped. Kevin was handling it. How much difference he made, I don't know."

"We need to fire our people in California, then."

I chuckled.

"What about the Green Revolution thing in Iran?"

"Not us. Long, ugly arguments on that one, but in the end we stayed out. I think we were right to."

"Why?"

"The heart of Mousavi's program was cutting social services for the poor."

"Oh."

"Celeste wanted to support Mousavi, and lord, you should have heard Oskar."

"I can imagine."

I nodded. "But in the end, Goli had the last word. She lives there."

"Must be tough for her."

"She likes it. Says she's doing good. And she's crazy into the music. Don't get her started on the first new creative music in two hundred years. Seriously. Don't get her started."

Ren laughed and my heart flip-flopped.

I parked the car and we got out and walked around and looked at millions of tons of water held back by concrete and steel.

Ren said, "By *we* do you mean humanity, or the Incrementalists?"

"What?"

"You just said, 'Look what we can do.'"

"Oh. Did I? I meant humanity. It always hits me like that."

She put her hand on my arm and I grew about half a foot and my cell phone rang.

"Are you going to answer it, or just stare at it," she said after a while.

"I might throw it into Lake Mead," I said, but of course I answered it.

Ren

"That was Ramon," Phil said.

I watched the held-back water and didn't say anything.

"He wanted to know if either of us has checked email."

I shook my head. "I haven't," I said.

"He wants us to." Phil hadn't put his phone back in his pocket, and the way he was holding it—sideways in his hand and weighing it—he looked like he still might just pitch it over the dam.

"I don't want to," I said.

"I know." Phil put his arm over my shoulder and I leaned against his side.

"I don't want the real world to catch us," I said. "I know we're running away, and I know we can't do it forever, but I don't want to stop."

Phil tightened his arm around me. "I know," he said. "But that's how you know it's the real world you're running from. It keeps being there, even when you leave it."

I dropped my head against him and tasted something cold, like graphite or shale, wrapped in a rag that had once been an apron, which had been a flour sack before that. I ran my tongue over my lips, but it wasn't in the water-sprayed air. I closed my eyes and felt along the edge of buried memory. A fierce union man on a visit to someplace green and hilly. Phil would remember his name. I just stroked the profile of his Stand-and-Fight switch, and wondered if I had one too. My mom, maybe? The way she'd managed no matter what.

"Do you know why I have only the memories of my life to draw from when I'm trying to see my own switches?" I asked him.

He shook his head, still resting on the top of mine. "Something to do with Celeste, I'd guess," he said.

"Yeah," I said, enjoying hearing him say her name like you'd say, "Something to do with the weather."

"I guess, at least for now, she's able to hang on to most of that stub."

"Oskar and Ramon are right, you know," I said.

"Fuck them."

"It's the perfect answer."

"Fuck perfect."

"I don't know, Phil." I rolled from under his arm to against his chest, my arms tucked in, and he put his around me. "I don't know what's right to do. I'm all conflicted and confused, and a thousand other modern and inconvenient things. And Oskar and Celeste are so decisive. Ramon too. If he has concluded that the best way to keep Celeste from hurting you is to get rid of me, there's a part of me that wants to be noble enough to accept that."

Phil's body was rigid against mine. "Acceptance isn't what we do," he said.

I shrugged. "And anyway, Celeste was right, I'm no martyr."

"Martyrdom isn't what we do either," Phil said. "We do better. Not perfection, not redemption. Just better."

I grinned against his chest. "Perfection is overrated," I said.

"Yeah. And all the perfectionists are just too good to be true."

I laughed. "We should be The Betterists."

"Sounds like pederasts."

"We shouldn't be that," I said, looking up at him. "That's not better."

"No," he agreed, matching my serious tone. "This is better," he said, and kissed me. I stood in his arms and closed my eyes and in the same way all the meanings and implications and contexts of a massive idea can concentrate in a single symbol, all the sensations and emotions and nerves of my body concentrated in my mouth, and his kissing me was conversation and love and sex, tasting and biting, as demanding as it was responsive, as profound, and as subtle. I wound my hands over his shoulders. He still had his phone in one hand and I felt it vibrate against my back even before I heard it.

He stepped away from me and looked at his phone like he wasn't sure what it was. I took it out of his hand and stuck it in the back pocket of my jeans.

"Maybe," I said, "it would be better if we checked our email."

"Better than what?" he said, narrowing his eyes. "Better than standing here kissing you? Unlikely. Better than checking into a hotel somewhere between here and Phoenix and getting lost in each other for a couple more hours? Decidedly not."

"Better than having your phone ring every half hour, no matter where we are or what we're doing, until Ramon shows up at our door and starts reading aloud to us?"

Phil shuddered. "Ray doesn't always notice if a man's dressed or not," he said.

I pulled his phone out of my pocket and handed it to him. He took it with a dimple-cracking grin. "You know, it's not like its prior location would have dissuaded me from going after it," he said. "Quite the contrary. In fact, perhaps in the interest of improved communication, you should start carrying it for me, and I'll just reach for it whenever I feel the need to be connected."

But I'd already taken out my own phone and was pulling up email. "Oh, fuck," I said.

I tucked my back against him so he could read over my shoulder. I didn't know the sender's name.

From: Kate@Incrementalists.org
To: Incrementalists@Incrementalists.org
Subject: Disturbance in the Garden?
Thursday, July 7, 2011 7:36 am GMT-5

Hi All,

So a weird thing happened to me. Anybody else? I've been getting together switches for some meddlework I want to do on a teacher at my kids' school. She's a nice lady, but a little overinvolved in the children's home lives, if you know what I mean. She's always asking my kids what they ate for breakfast, and how many hours of TV or video games they play. Like that's any of her business! Details, if anyone cares, are the yellow Matchbox tow truck on top of the TV in the living room.

So anyway, I was keeping her switches in this adorable red-and-white sock yarn in the center row of cubbies in my wall of cotton blends. I went in today to wind in the plaid shirt she was wearing on the day in seventh grade when no one in the cafeteria would let her sit with them, and there weren't any empty tables. Poor thing, she'd just walked around and around the whole period with her food on her tray.

So I went to add this to the skein and it wasn't there! I found it later in the NYLON BLEND wall. I'd never make a mistake like that. I'd love to know if any one (Hello, any Salt reading?!?) has any idea how something in my own Garden could have gotten that out of place. I mean, I put it back, but sheesh.

Thanks!

Kate

Phil's phone rang in his pocket, against my ass.

"Tell him we're coming back," I said. "It was Celeste in Kate's Garden. I remember it."

Phil

"I need to learn that expression," she said as we came over the rise and Lake Mead dropped out of sight in the rearview mirror. "I'm guessing it has to do with frustration management."

"A bad job of," I agreed.

She put her hand on my leg and I covered it with my own.

"I'd have thought you'd have a sports car. Or at least something with manual transmission."

"Last year I went through a brief spell of being environmentally conscious. I'm over it now. But I like the car. I hit a hot streak and paid cash for it. Used, but still. It was a good feeling."

"A hot streak?"

"Yeah, you know. When everything is going right, and every laydown is correct, every call is correct, and all of your good hands hold up."

"But . . ." she broke off.

"What?" I said.

"Do you need hot streaks? I mean, with what you can do."

I stared at her, then pulled my eyes back to the road. "Honey," I said. "I don't meddle when I'm playing poker. That would be, uh, no, I don't do that."

"Oh," she said.

"You mean, you thought I was cheating all this time?"

"I didn't think of it as cheating. Have I offended you, Phil?"

I considered. "I don't think so. Startled me, is more. It isn't that I have such a high regard for meddlework, it's that I have a high regard for poker."

"You love the game."

I nodded.

We were starting to get Las Vegas traffic now, and it was rush hour. Yes, Virginia, Las Vegas has a rush hour.

The Prius was nice, but too small to hold an elephant. I finally said, "So, you can sense when Celeste is in the Garden."

She nodded.

A pickup truck cut in front me; I braked and said, "Can you tell what she's doing there?"

"No."

"Have you tried?"

"I don't know how I'd go about that." She sounded like her voice was even and steady only because she was putting a lot of effort into making it so.

"You know Celeste's sense images," I said. "Use them. See if you can track her, look over her shoulder."

"Now?" she said, as if I'd asked her if she had any last requests.

"No. Let's wait till we get to The Palms and see what they think of the idea."

"All right," she said, her voice telling me how pleased she was with the Governor's reprieve. She said, "How can someone be loose in the Garden? It's a metaphorical construct. It doesn't have an objective existence, does it?"

"It has all sorts of objective existences, scattered everywhere one of us is. But that doesn't mean you're wrong."

"It is infuriating that I have to ask these questions. I know, I know, that this is the sort of thing that ought to just be flooding back to me; all of the answers about what we can and cannot do, and how we meddle, and where to search for switches. She's taken that from me."

"Just delayed it," I said, wishing I were sure of that.

We finally reached the 15, only a few minutes away from The Palms and, I hoped, some answers.

"You can fight her, you know."

I felt her glancing at me. "What do you mean?"

"Do you remember our first meeting at The Palms?"

"I'll withhold the sarcasm, and just say yes."

"Two things struck me about that meeting. The first was that it was harder to convince you to let me sit down than I had expected it to be. The other was that, when you asked me how old I was, I got angry, upset, even though that's an obvious question that we always expect."

"Go on," she said. "What does it mean?"

"The first means you were fighting her, and the second means I was."

We drove in thoughtful silence up to valet parking at The Palms.

EIGHTEEN

Unpleasant Personality Traits

Ren

We stopped in front of Jimmy's door to listen to the shouting on the other side, and Phil's face split in a wide grin.

"What?" I asked.

"That sounds great," he said. "All the quiet, serious conversation was starting to worry me."

"Ah," I said, like I understood. He raised a hand to knock, but I slipped between him and the door and kissed him. "For luck," I said.

"You don't need it," he said, but he kissed me again anyway, one arm braced us against the wood veneer, the other around my waist. If the door had opened suddenly we would have fallen, him onto me, into the room. But it didn't, and we didn't, and when I opened one eye just a little, his eyebrows were drawn together like I'd only seen them when he was furious. But it didn't feel like the time he'd kissed Celeste.

He must have felt me looking, because his face softened and he opened his eyes. "Are you worried?" he asked.

"Nah," I said.

He smiled at me and tugged his shirt straight where it had ridden up between our bodies.

"More like terrified right out of my socks," I said.

"Well, that's okay then." He squeezed my hand and knocked.

The shouting stopped abruptly, and Matsu opened the door.

Jimmy's suite somehow managed to look expensive without being elegant or beautiful, but the living room was spacious and all the furniture was new. Ramon stood with his back to the balcony, radiating beneficent calm. Oskar clutched the back of an upholstered armchair, and two people I didn't know sat on an overstuffed settee.

Matsu pushed two more chairs in from the bedroom while Ramon introduced me to Felicia and Nick. Felicia was striking—the kind of beautiful that makes everyone nervous, and I felt suddenly grubby in my jeans and anxiety.

If Oskar had any sense he'd stop glaring at her and try smiling. He had a nice one, and they'd make a handsome couple. Instead, he prowled the space between the bedroom and living room, and got in everybody's way as the chairs were arranged and drinks doled out and quick updates given.

Nick's voice was liquor-scorched and accented, the least attractive Incrementalist I'd met yet. Not that physical beauty meant anything, I reminded myself. But it made a peculiar contrast, Felicia's sleek to Nick's mangy, her poise to his slouch. I shook hands with them both, and smiled as openly as I could manage under their scrutiny.

Phil kissed Felicia on the cheek, shook hands with Nick, and sat in the chair Oskar had been abusing. He leaned back and grinned. "So," he said. "Why the hell are you two here?"

Felicia widened her lash-fringed, green eyes. "Ramon called me and said to come."

"Did he say why?"

Her cheeks pinked. "Yes."

"Want to tell me?"

Felicia looked at her hands.

"What'd Ramon tell you, Nick?" Phil asked.

"That you were in trouble."

"Ah," Phil said. "That's true. Did he offer you a place in the Salt?"

"He knows I don't want one."

"Did he suggest one might be opening up?" Phil kept his tone conversational, but he had a grip on the arms of his chair like he thought they might fly off.

"Jesus, Phil," Oskar cut in. "We told you we were bringing them in. You didn't have an issue with it."

"I'm asking why," Phil said.

"For our expertise and experience," Felicia said, with just enough English on "experience" to imply seniority without saying so.

"Why they are here is not important," Ramon said.

"It is to me," Phil said. "And Ren."

"They are here at my invitation," Ramon said.

"Not good enough."

"They are here to help," Jimmy said. "And we need all the help we can get. Have you seen Kate's email?"

Phil nodded.

"It was Celeste," I said.

Matsu nodded. "That's what Phil said."

"There is no way that's possible!" Oskar exploded. "The Garden isn't a real place people can go. It's a metaphor. It's a way of thinking about an abstraction that's too . . ." He gestured wildly out the window, into the bedroom. "Abstract," he said. "Ren can't know Celeste was in Kate's Garden any more than I can."

"Have you been in Kate's Garden?" Phil asked.

"No," Oskar snapped. "It sounds insipid."

Phil smiled without dimpling. "So tell me how it's not a contradiction for you to have been in her Garden or mine or Jimmy's, and that makes sense, but Ren knowing Celeste was in Kate's doesn't."

"Same way it makes sense for me to have been in your house, but Ren wouldn't know whether Felicia had ever been in it."

"I know Celeste hasn't," I said.

They all looked at me.

"I also know Celeste never visited Phil's house," I said. "Not the one here."

"Because you now have Celeste's memories," Ramon said slowly.

I shrugged. "I don't know why," I said. "I just know."

"I want to talk to Celeste," Oskar said.

I felt Phil go taut in the chair beside me.

"No way," I said.

Oskar started to say something else, but Felicia interrupted. "Have you tried grazing for her?" she asked me.

"You've been to her Garden," Jimmy added. "Maybe you could go back there?"

I shook my head. "I could try that," I said, "but I don't think it'd work."

"Ren," there was something like urgency in Ramon's voice. "We need to know what Celeste is meddling in now."

"Goddamn it!" Oskar said. "How can Celeste meddle at all? How can we even talk about Celeste like she exists somewhere? Celeste is dead. Has been for a while now. Irina too. There is no Celeste. There is no ghost of Celeste in the Garden."

"Oskar," Phil said very quietly. "Sit down."

"There are our memories of Celeste," Nick said.

"And there are Celeste's memories," I said. "I don't have them all."

"What *do* you have, Ren?" Ramon asked.

I closed my eyes to keep from looking at Phil. I didn't know the answer to Ramon's question. All I knew was of the infinite possible answers I might find, maybe six wouldn't hurt Phil. Of those, I wasn't sure even one would give whatever love we were creating enough air to thrive or fail on its own merits. If what I had of Celeste was too much of her, or even too much like her, how could Phil stand to love me?

I still wasn't going to eat the fucking birdseed. I kept my eyes stubbornly closed.

"I knew Celeste was in Kate's Garden," I said, "because I recognized the pattern. It's like what Matsu said in Phil's Garden with the olives. From just two stones, you can know a diagonal. It's the diagonal-ness I recognize. The Celeste-ness. And trying to explain that is like trying to explain anything without either an example or a metaphor."

I opened my eyes.

Matsu nodded. "You recognized the Celeste pattern. A Celeste way of ordering information. The data points didn't change, you just saw the lines Celeste would have drawn between them."

Oskar grunted.

"Yeah," I said. "I guess so."

"Can you just go find it, see what it's doing?" Nick asked.

I shook my head. "You aren't going to like this," I told Phil. "Her pattern isn't in the Garden now. I don't know where Celeste is."

Phil

There are at least three things that it is impossible to avoid when you talk about yourself as much as I've been doing here: lies, errors, and revealing nasty, unpleasant personality traits. Now it's time for the one of the latter: I was taking great pleasure in how discomfited Oskar was by the whole thing. With everything else that was going on, I hope I can be permitted a bit of pleasure at Oskar's pain, but permitted or not, there it was.

There was nothing else I was enjoying.

"All right," I told Ren. Then to the others: "What were you trying?"

They all looked like they weren't sure they should tell me, except Ray, who said, "We were trying to use your and Ren's alpha-axes to triangulate Celeste's x-axis." I had an inordinate amount of trouble translating that into English, until Ren said, "You were trying to pin down enough of a Why for Celeste's actions towards me and Phil that it would lead you to Who she is now?"

Ray got a look that said his way of saying it was more precise, but he nodded.

Jimmy said, "It occurred to us that Celeste is fundamentally a new Who now."

"Not a bad thought," I said. "Didn't work?"

"We weren't done trying," said Ray.

"Must be rough on you, Oskar, looking for something that you know doesn't exist."

"I didn't say Celeste doesn't exist," he said, looking irritated.

"My apologies. You said she can't exist. That's entirely different. But if she does exist, she can't, and what's more, she exists in a place that doesn't exist. So simultaneous existence and nonexistence. Very dialectical."

For just an instant, he looked positively furious, then he stopped and his mouth fell open. "Yes," he said slowly. "Yes, it is."

Now he had everyone's attention, and for a moment I forgot that I'd been trying to needle him.

He stood up and started pacing. I do that, too, when I think, so I really wish he wouldn't. He said, "If I had a license as a practicing materialist, it would be revoked. The Garden is externalized thought."

Ray said, "Well, yes, of course—"

Oskar rolled over him. "Thought is matter in its most highly developed, highly organized form. Consciousness is one property of brains, not of thoughts. I was so hung up on the impossibility of the Garden having consciousness, or anything in the Garden having consciousness, that I completely missed that consciousness is an attribute of the brain, of an organism, not of thoughts produced by that organism. Consciousness is a description of certain kinds of thoughts produced by a material organism, it can't have an independent existence."

He fell silent and looked at us.

"Well," I said after a moment. "That solves everything then."

He shook his head impatiently. "We've been looking for Celeste. We keep saying that. We're looking for Celeste. And so, we get this image in our heads of Celeste; Celeste as we knew her, as a person, as a being. But that person is dead. That person no longer exists. What exists is a set of memories, and responses, and reactions in the form of thoughts, trapped in the Garden. Personality, but no consciousness."

He stopped and looked at Ren. "You should go get your memories back."

Ren

I shook my head. Oskar's confidence in his own doggedly achieved conclusions, and his willingness to direct others to act on them, was really starting to irritate me. It probably would have rankled less if he hadn't also been right. "The memories don't matter," I said.

Six people opened their mouths to argue.

"Okay," I said. "Celeste's memories matter. I do want them. I know they're part of what I was supposed to get when I joined this thing of ours, and I do want the full meal deal, but right now, they're dessert. Extraneous. Celeste's memories can't tell us what she'll do next."

"Celeste is personality without consciousness," Oskar said. "She can't do anything."

"No," Ramon spoke very deliberately.

Oskar, pacing between bedroom and living room, seized the door frame with enough force that a watercolor illustration from a children's Bible I've never seen jumped into my mind. Samson at the temple, his arms braced against carved marble columns, head bowed, shoulder muscles mounded in furious protest. "We agreed on this, Ramon," he ground out.

"I think 'personality' is imprecise."

Oskar almost howled.

"What then, Ray?" Phil asked.

"Ramon," Ramon said. "It's Ramon."

I saw the dimple before he said it. "Celeste is Ramon without consciousness?"

Oskar actually roared.

It startled Felicia, but Nick opened his goat teeth and laughed. Ramon waited.

Once we all settled down, he tried again. "I think it is not Celeste's personality, but a selection of her personality's attributes that remain active in the Garden. Her fearfulness, for example."

"Attributes don't have agency," Oskar snapped. "Celeste's fears can't do anything. They can't misfile fucking yarn balls."

"It seems they can," Ramon said. "To cling to belief in light of countervailing evidence is dogma, Oskar."

Oskar was mute, and so were the rest of us. "All right," he said at last. "Then what's the mechanism?"

Ramon frowned. "Yes. That's the question."

"It still doesn't matter," I said.

"How can you say that?" Felicia asked.

"Jimmy," I said.

Jimmy didn't look at me.

"Jimmy?" Phil's voice carried a danger even Matsu could not have protected Jimmy from.

"Oskar says personality," Jimmy whispered. "Ramon says attribute. I would say essence."

Oskar let out an exasperated sigh, but Jimmy had everyone else's complete attention.

"When we spike a new recruit, we introduce not just memories, but the way memory knits up experience into learning, how learning patterns behavior. We introduce a disembodied person into an existing person and we watch and wait until one of them dominates the other. If the essence of the dead Incrementalist wins, the person the recruit was effectively dies, and we continue to call him by the dead Incrementalist's name." He looked at me. "You would have become Celeste. It's terrible.

"Don't you remember, Phil?" Jimmy was almost pleading. "Do you remember Chuck's mother? What did she say? What do they all say? 'It's like I don't know you anymore.' 'You aren't the boy I raised.' And then, finally, 'You're dead to me.'"

"A self dies," I said. "Same as it does when a heart breaks."

"Or when a man is made a father," Nick said. "He becomes a new thing. Pivots destroy and re-create us."

I was still looking at Jimmy. He was still not looking at me. "When you say essence . . ." I said.

Jimmy nodded. "Yes, I mean *rûh*. Soul."

"Essence," said Oskar slowly, "is movement. Call it soul, call it spirit, but matter is always in motion, and when we speak of essence, we speak of the most basic, most primal movement."

"And so?" said Ramon, gripping Oskar's face with his eyes.

"Matter moves according to different laws. The laws of motion for planetary bodies are not the laws of motion for subatomic particles. The laws of motion for the spread of ideas are not the laws of motion for evolutionary biology. You study, and you learn, and you test, and you verify. Deducing the laws of motion from the facts is science; imposing laws of motion on the facts is schematism. What we're doing now is a new thing. These are the laws of motion that determine personality maintained in an exobrain."

Ramon nodded. "So we can't, yet, know how it will work, or what it will do, or how to confront it." He nodded to Jimmy. "Call it a soul if you want; that's as good a name as any."

I wanted to hug Jimmy for having been so afraid for my soul, even though I wasn't certain I had one. And I was relieved, although maybe stupidly, to know Oskar and Matsu were never going to kill me. Because I don't think I would have done well against either of them, but I would have tried. They had only been risking in me what I had already agreed to gamble: the sublimation of my personality to Celeste's, if she should become dominant in me. And I felt a little silly for the hours I spent in Elise's red-and-gold apartment hoping there was enough of my corrupt great-aunt in me to double her stub-doubling. But most of all, it pleased me that they knew Phil would have fought it too—fought it and them—and he might have stood a chance in that battle. Even against Matsu. It was me he wanted, curled like a princess into the body of a little bird. Even then he had wanted me and not Celeste.

I stood up. "I'm going to go graze," I said.

"Why?" Felicia asked.

"Because we know Who—some shade or essence of Celeste, the pattern of Celeste. And that's just confusing and not helpful. But she's tipped her hand on Where. She's wherever Kate lives."

"Western Pennsylvania," Ramon said.

"Okay," I said. "Someone ought to keep an eye on that from the outside. In the real world, or whatever you call it. I'm going to see if I can find a What in the Garden."

"No," Felicia said. "I meant why are you leaving to graze?"

I shrugged. "It feels like a private thing to me."

I found no comprehension on anyone's face. "Want me to come with you?" Phil asked.

"I'm just going in here," I said, looking into the bedroom. "That's okay, right, Oskar?"

Oskar was sitting on the corner of the bed, looking abstracted. He nodded.

"We'll wait for you," Matsu said.

"Hey, Oskar," Nick called from the living room. "I need a drink. Can you show me where the bar is in this madhouse?"

"Take the fucking elevator to the lobby." Oskar stood up. "Jesus Christ, Nick."

"I'm helpless as a baby," Nick called.

Oskar picked up a meticulously folded suit coat draped over the television. "It'll cost you," he told Nick.

"I was counting on that."

Oskar's eyes caught mine, flicked to the enormous bed behind us, and back to me. The old wolf's smile glinted for just a second. "Have fun," he told me.

"You too," I said.

"I'm drinking the good stuff tonight." Oskar stalked out.

I left the door open and climbed up into the center of the ridiculous bed. I took a deep breath and wondered if it was a mistake to go

Celeste-hunting without Phil. I closed my eyes and saw the mudflats and reached out for the taste of blood.

Phil

I stood up and saw Matt looking at me. Ray was staring off into the distance, and Jimmy had his eyes closed. I shrugged to Matt. He continued watching me as I walked into the bedroom and shut the door behind me.

Ren had positioned herself on her back in the middle of the bed. I got in next to her, and touched her temple with mine.

You can speak of battles of will, if you want, and there may be truth in the concept. But when I think of a battle of will, I remember when I was Reggie and decided to quit smoking. White-knuckle time, you know? Something all happening inside.

So even if this came down to a fight between Ren's will and Celeste's, it wouldn't be the same. It was external, and so it would take the form of something else; it would feel tangible and material and real, even inside the Garden.

I had a flash, then, of someone who was me, still called Carter, who was taking a ship to the New World sometime in the mid-seventeenth century. I was at the bow, watching the ocean, which was perilously wild, and I was thinking, *This would be a stupid time to die.*

I hadn't died, though. I had made landfall, and I'd been part of something that felt big, and I'd liked the feeling. The loneliness that had defined me for the last few hundred years was sublimated in the day-to-day work of building, hunting, farming. The more you're determined to do something, the less attention you have to focus on self-pity.

From the vantage of now, I realized how sad it was that I hadn't decided that fifty years sooner. I would never have recruited Celeste and things would have been better for everyone.

Or maybe not. Maybe we needed a Celeste from time to time, just to keep us awake and aware and paying attention to consequences.

No. Bullshit. We are always aware of consequences. It's that awareness that keeps everyone from agreeing with Oskar. Fear of consequences was the best ally Celeste had during their long battles. None of us could forget Cambodia.

The old familiar taste, the old familiar smell, and I looked around my Garden. A shame that I couldn't physically move in there with Ren. I'd like that. Just for twenty or thirty years, or maybe fifty. Just for a while. Take a break from it all and live a life.

But I'd go nuts and so would she. She was as full of the need to do as I was, or more.

And that, I realized, was the heart of the conflict: Ren's need to do versus Celeste's need to keep from doing. The irresistible platitude versus the immovable cliché.

They were going to have to fight it out, one way or another.

I found Ren, and she looked up at me with no expression of surprise.

"Come on," I said. "Let's end this."

Ren

"Lay on, Macduff," I said, raising my imaginary sword and looking around Celeste's storeroom.

"Right, I know," Phil said. "We have to find her first."

"Hard to fight someone you can't see," I said. "Any ideas?"

"Not a one." He bounced on the balls of his feet, impatient to get going. "Why are we at Celeste's?"

"She had a key on her belt," I said.

"So we're looking for locks," Phil said, which made me want to kiss him. "Let's go."

We scanned the room we were standing in. The same soft, yellow light filtered in from the high windows, the same jumble of tools and ingredients lay scattered on the workbench and stood collected in the jars and canisters lining the walls.

"How do you organize your memories, Phil?" I asked. "How do you keep everything you've done, or wish you'd done, or are sorry that you did in separate places?"

"Christ. I never told you about that. As a titan, I'm a putz. Okay. Long conversation pending, but not now."

I watched the dust dance in the sun. Phil sneezed. "Let's go back to the wine cellar," I said. "It wasn't as dusty there."

"Stands to reason," Phil said, eyebrows threatening. "Celeste liked her wine."

We walked through the back door and down the stairs. Phil pulled up the trapdoor set into the floor and we navigated the awkward twisting and climbing required by its poor design. "Celeste liked wine, but not apples," I guessed. The baskets inset in the root cellar's walls were empty and barred with cobwebs.

Phil and I turned the corner into the cool, whitewashed domed room where I'd watched Celeste back Phil into a corner. "Look," he whispered. Against the far wall a wooden ladder disappeared into a hole in the low, arched ceiling. The rungs were worn thin in the middle and the rails almost gleamed. "Told you."

"Let's go," I said.

We followed the absence of dust and the wear of wood up from the ceiling of the tidy wine cellar through the floor of a muggy greenhouse. The ladder kept going through its glass ceiling, but we both saw the swept paving stones and stepped into Celeste's Garden's garden. We moved through the bombastic flowers to a low stone trough with a crimson hand pump worn to silver at the grip, and pushed our way out through heavy gold velvet curtains. We followed worn places in rugs and dustless trails across parquet, and I remembered a UI story about a college campus that sodded all the space between buildings and waited to see where students wore the grass away, and paved only there. The sidewalks weren't straight, but all the remaining grass grew untrampled.

In a room that looked like an alchemist's apartment, the trail of Celeste's habitual paths ran dry. Every surface and edge of the workspace—cabinets, shelves, cases, and containers—were polished with use and gleaming with age. Every path was worn. And not one thing was locked. Phil flung himself onto the canopied bed with a groan, and I sank into a high-backed armchair that was the only other piece of furniture in the room. I felt a little weird about lying down beside him in her bed, no matter how much I wanted to. He sat up looking puzzled.

"This is just wrong," he said.

"What?"

"Celeste loved comfort," he said. "Demanded it. But her bed's harder than mine."

He pushed the brocade coverlet aside and we both laughed. The bed was a massive chest, secured with a single, recessed lock.

"You know," I said to Phil, "I'd very much like to know what she kept close at hand and locked up."

"I'm on it," he said.

It took him maybe ten minutes. He found a scalpel in a Saltine tin and unscrewed the hinges from the sides of the doors. Together we lifted the massive things and set them aside. Arrayed before us, in various degrees of polish and wear, were rows of differently shaped, colored and sized cookie jars. Phil and I looked down warily.

"I feel like Pandora," I said.

I took the top off a bright yellow ceramic smiley face. Phil reached in and felt around. Finally he pulled his hand back holding only a tiny wad of paper. When he unfolded it, we found "selfish," written in a looping, elegant hand.

I opened another jar and found only tiny paper balls inside it too. I unwadded one, and read "smarter."

Phil held up another he'd opened. "Not pretty enough," he read out loud.

I shrugged and, since it had come out of a cookie jar, I popped the paper I was holding into my mouth. It dissolved into a warm, smug glow filling my chest. "Felicia's beautiful," I said, putting the lid back on the jar. "But I'm smarter than she is, and that's why she doesn't like me."

Phil swallowed hard around his slip of paper. His eyes were wide and almost overflowing. "Felicia never took Celeste seriously," he said, "because she wasn't pretty enough."

I stared at him. He blinked, and a tear slipped down his cheek.

"Phil!" I said. "What the hell?"

He rubbed both eyes with the heels of his hands. "I have no idea," he said. "Holy shit."

"Is Felicia maybe trying to reach us, talking to us through these?" I asked him.

"Yeah. Maybe," Phil shook his head, distracted. "But holy shit."

"What?" I said, no longer feeling smart at all.

"Jesus," Phil said. "The number of times I heard Celeste say both those things. And 'everyone's selfish,' and I'll bet every other damn reason and excuse and explanation in here." Phil looked ready to kick the whole chest in. "Celeste's been baking alpha cookies," he said. "She's found a way to feed us her Whys, to give other Incrementalists a taste of her victimization and innocence and force her perspective on the rest of us. What I believed about her motivations, I didn't understand, I ingested. I swallowed her explanations whole. Oskar too. We gotta tell Ray."

Phil

"Why?" she said. "Is there something he can do about it from there that we can't from here?"

"He has to know," I said. "In case."

"Right," she said. "Seed it, then. In case we don't make it back."

I said, "You're anxious to get on with this."

"Yes. I hate designing when I don't have the specs."

"Mike Caro says people make a lot of bad decisions just to get it over with."

"Who?"

"Poker theorist."

"Great. You're giving me poker wisdom now?"

"It's all I've got. But I have a lot of it. Your job as a good player isn't—"

"Don't."

I exhaled. "All right. One sec."

I made a piece of paper and a pen appear in my hand, put the paper against the wall, and wrote down our latest discovery. Then I stuck my arm through Celeste's wall, into my own, and turned the paper into an African Violet hanging in a small planter next to Raggedy Ann. "Done," I said.

"Good. Now what?"

"Now," I said, "I think we should maybe destroy all these cookies before Celeste gets to hand any more of them around."

"How? I thought you couldn't damage someone else's Garden."

"You can't when someone brings you into theirs," I said. "But it seems to work differently when we break in. I saw the bruises your scuffle with Ramon left on him."

"Oh, crap, I didn't mean to hurt him. I wanted to reach you."

"That's why he showed me. He was making a point, back when I needed it, about you not being much like Celeste."

"Great," Ren said. "So I hurt him while he was helping me and he used the bruises to help me more? Guess I owe him."

"We all owe each other," I said.

"Speaking of," Ren gestured at the cookie jars. "I owe Celeste some wanton destruction. What do you suggest?"

"We alpha-lock her whole box of Whys."

"Can we do that?"

"I don't know."

"No, dear Houdini, you cannot."

I turned around.

Oskar's opinions to the contrary, she sure seemed real. And

Celeste. But Oskar's dialectics were certainly right about one thing: love can turn into its opposite.

"You can't," she continued, "because in order to alpha-lock something, you have to truly not care about the damage you do. And I don't believe you're capable of that, Phil. And I know our little bird here isn't."

I looked over at Ren. Her eyes were fixed on Celeste, and she had the same expression Doyle Brunson had when shoving with 10-2—that is to say, none at all.

"This," said Celeste, "is my existence now. It isn't much, it isn't the same as when we swam in the Pacific, Phil, or when we spent all day making love in that hotel in Montana and I gave you ten orgasms and you swore no one had ever loved you the way I did. It isn't like that, but it's what I have instead, and you know that I can and will alpha-lock the whole Garden if you try to take it from me. I shall do it just by seeding these Whys in strategic places. You know I'm capable. You know there is nothing you can do to me that will more than inconvenience me, and you know that inconveniences annoy me. Do you remember in London, once, when I was annoyed—"

"Celeste," I said, "I don't think you're real. I suspect you aren't real even in terms of this mentally constructed world we're in. But one thing I know for sure, you aren't Mike Matusow. You are not putting me on tilt. Ren already knows the worst of me, so she isn't going to tilt either. Let's get down to business."

"What business would that be, dear Thumper?"

A good question, that. I wished to hell I knew the answer.

Ren

"The business at hand," I said, "is saying good-bye. Good-bye, dear Hoho."

Celeste's head whipped around fast enough to fling a hairpin free. "What did you call me?" she demanded, but she recovered quickly.

"You never called me that. All the other grandbratties did, but not you."

"And now I'll never call you anything else." I smiled at her. "If I think of you at all, which I may not. Shame to be forgotten by all your living relatives."

Celeste came across the polished wood towards me. "No, you'll remember me. Every time you close your eyes," she said. "Both of you will. Not because I will find you whenever you come to your Gardens, but because you'll always know I can. And sometimes I will."

"I'm not going to let that happen," Phil said, and if the dismantled bed-chest hadn't been between us, and too wide to reach across, I think he would have strangled her, even if she didn't have a body to wake up bruised or choking.

"Every time you close your eyes, lover," she said, and puckered her lips into a kiss.

"I'm going," I told her.

"Yes, open your eyes now, but you can't leave me, we're a part of each other." Celeste turned away from me and moved toward the workbench, speaking only to Phil, as though I'd already left. "As long as you believe you love this little bird, you'll never be rid of me, my dear." She walked along the edge of her lab table, fondly touching various bits of equipment. "Me and my dear little great-niece are a package deal. Until she dies. Then she'll be gone, and I'll still be in the stub."

"My great-niece and I," Phil corrected her, but he looked pale. Celeste wasn't the first person who'd told him this. It was what Jimmy had warned me against.

Celeste looked at me. She lifted her arms to display the long sleeves of her gown and made a slow, fashion model turn. "Do you like it?" she asked me.

"It's still the most beautiful robe I've ever seen," I said, watching the pale pink satin billow and puddle around her. Embroidered with velvet and tiny ocean pearls, in the moonlight, it would have looked white.

"Thank you," she said. "Phil gave it to me."

"He has exquisite taste," I said evenly. "But I like his blue-and-white one better."

She laughed and walked over to a shelf the pale green of my Nana's after-dinner mints, which held a framed, black-and-white picture of Celeste at the age she'd been our summer at the lake, and a small crimson box. She took the lid off the box to reveal a single mounded chocolate. "Here," she said, holding it out to me. "Taste this."

"Ren," Phil cautioned, but I started toward her, or the shelf behind her, anyway.

"Do you remember our Montana candy?" Celeste asked him, lifting the chocolate out for me. "Go on, Renee. It would do you good to know how Phil could fuck when he was a young man."

I looked at the treat held on her pale, pink palm. "No, thank you," I said. "I'm done being your little bird."

I was close enough now to be certain the picture of Celeste wasn't a photo, but until I touched it, I couldn't be sure if it was seed, hedge or stub.

"Oh, so you've grown up have you?" Celeste mocked me. "And do you now know thyself, dear Socrates? You think you've found the true princess packed into our drab little Wren? You're no better than Oskar with his neurochemical determinism. 'Bump up the testosterone and any man will grow violent.' Ha! As though, if we gelded Matsu, he'd no longer care to fight."

"I am loved," I told her, but she gave me a patient smile, and I turned the golden picture frame into thin, gilt-edged, shamrock-painted porcelain.

"Do you really expect to keep moving from growth to growth, getting better and better? That's not how pivots work. You will fall over the edge again one day, and when you do, Phil won't be there. Phil leaves."

I took a deep breath. "I'm glad you feel safe here, Hoho. It must be nice being somewhere where nothing can surprise you," I said. "But I'm not afraid of what I don't know. I'm okay with uncertainty."

My throat was so tight with fear it distorted my voice, but I made Celeste's ink-penned face brown into tea, liquid and flat in its frame, and I kept her from looking back at it. I hoped Phil would think the wobble in my voice was anger, and I hoped Celeste's self-portrait was as toxic to her as it had been to me.

"I know finding my own path is slower than following yours, especially here, and it puts me at a disadvantage in speed and confidence, but I'll wager my uncertainty against your fear any day. Doubt is hard, but fear is harder. And doubt comes with something I can make, in spite of it. I can make a decision. You can't make safety. Not even here." I made the green-and-white frame into a cup and the tea filled it. "Life isn't safe," I told Celeste.

Celeste smiled at me, stroking the velvet lapel of her beautiful bathrobe, fingering a pearl button. "Life isn't. But I'm not really alive, am I? I'm just here. Nonmaterial. All the power, none of the risk."

"It's always been about power for you, hasn't it?" Phil said, his voice rough with hatred. "It was what you always fought Oskar over."

I needed Phil to stay where he was, too far to reach me quickly. "Oskar's having all kinds of no fun with your present nonpresence," I said.

Celeste ignored me; she'd rather needle Phil. There's more power in him. "Oskar was always trying to push power into the hands of the nemones," she spat at Phil. "Neither of you could ever see they don't want it. They're constantly throwing their power away. Handing it to gurus and trends, advertisers and addictions. I dragged a tidy fortune, just picking up their discards."

There was only one step left to my plan, if I'd figured things correctly. Two steps, really, if you counted the one I couldn't take, the one where I tell it to Phil, and convince him to do what I need him to do. I took the teacup from the shelf and almost smiled.

"No, the nemones don't even want what little power modernity has left them, with all their rituals debunked and all the great rites commoditized." Celeste's voice was rising, she and Phil picking up the notes of their old song.

But my plan really had three steps, and only time for one. He was tilting. I was going to have to jump it.

"How much of your power did you give me, Phil?" Celeste demanded. "And in the one week you've known her, how much have you already handed over to Ren?"

"I don't want power over him," I interrupted. If this was going to work, I needed Phil rational for me, not out of his head angry with Celeste. The tea smelled like only one I've ever tasted: the one Irina, or Celeste, had made for me. It was Celeste, and it was poison.

"I have his faith," I said. "I don't want more."

She rounded on me. "A failure of ambition." She sneered, saw the teacup, and laughed. "Still playing my games, dearie? I have no body to die anymore. Nothing can hurt me here." She held her hand out, imperious. "Give it to me, Birdie. I'll drink it."

I drained it.

"Ren?" Phil said, his voice gone gentle.

I touched a finger to my ear hoping he'd read the gesture as more than symbolic—or less than, I guess. "Listen," I mouthed to him, but I couldn't hear it myself. Only the porcelain, and Celeste's shattering laugh.

"Ren!" Phil was very close, but I couldn't see him. "Ren, are you waking up?"

No, I'm singing at the tower in the zipped-shut dark.

"Phil," Celeste's voice was sugar cube sweet, "Renee said the business was bye-byes."

"Don't call her that," Phil said, and something else, but I lost his voice under Matsu's, low and insistent from the next room, and Felicia's, marginally hysterical, talking about Kate, her kid's teacher, and Celeste.

The taste of Celeste, poisoned tea on my numb tongue; I opened my eyes in the hotel bed and was not breathing.

NINETEEN

One Equals Zero

Phil

This is where I prove that one equals zero. Ready?

Matt says the thing about fighting is not to hesitate; to instantly make a productive, even if not perfect, response. If you have to think about it, it's too late. That's funny, because I started becoming a real poker player back in the 1880s, when I started learning to hesitate, to wait, to take a moment to think.

I was almost—almost—hit with a wave of, "What is it about the women I love that makes them kill themselves?" but my brain was working too fast to accept it. I hesitated and took a moment to think.

I'm not a martyr.

That was Ren, not Celeste.

Twice, she'd said it. She'd drunk the tea, knowing it was poison, knowing it would kill her, but—

I'm not a martyr.

But then, why?

Listen, she'd said. To what? I listened, and heard nothing. I had to think. I *was* thinking.

Was that the point? Was that what "listen" meant? Just a way to get my frontal cortex engaged? But, if it was, that meant there had to be something to think about. That meant she had a plan.

She drank poisoned tea as part of a plan?

Well, yes, of course she would do that. If she saw a way to win, and if that's what it required, then, certainly. But if it also required me thinking, then it meant it required me to do—something.

What? What could I do? What could she expect, anticipate, that I could do, when she'd just poisoned her mind, which would poison her brain, which would poison her? What had the poisoning accomplished?

Until she dies.

Happening here, in the Garden, it had separated Ren from Celeste. They were no longer linked to each other, bound to each other, because Celeste had to separate herself or be poisoned too. Only there was nothing to keep her from returning if the poison wasn't fatal, so that wouldn't solve the problem unless . . . what?

What?

What is not an axis; there is no "What" in the Garden, because we create and destroy all the "Whats" at will, except for hedges, and seeds, and—

And Celeste had made a seed of all her memories. And Ren knew she had done so.

Not the solution, but the opportunity for the solution. The chance to settle it.

You take what you know, you eliminate as many unknowns as you can, calculate the odds as well as possible, and you make the play. And sometimes, that play looks like a wild-ass gamble that came out of nowhere, but you have the pieces, and the options narrow and narrow until only one is left, which, by definition, is not an option.

One option is the same as no options. One equals zero.

And thinking it through took much, much less time than it has taken to describe the process, because sometimes the symbol is clumsier than the symbolized.

"Your little bird," said Celeste, "made a gallant effort, but her next Second will be my next Second. If she is gone, she is gone, but I'll still be here."

"I think you missed the point," I told her.

"Oh?"

"She isn't going for your life; she's going for your comfort."

That was total bullshit, but I needed something that would grab her attention.

"What the fuck do you mean, my comfort?"

Where was it? What would it be?

Listen, she had said.

I listened, then, and I heard music: Concerto for Drum and Self-Knowledge; Symphony in Suitcase Minor.

I set my mouth on automatic while my brain raced.

"Comfort is the enemy, Celeste, don't you know that? Remember all the antiwar protesters in the '60s, and how, by the time of Desert Storm, they had their jobs and their lives and their houses in the suburbs, and so they decided Desert Storm was different, that it was a justified war, because now they had something to lose? Remember that? That something was comfort. Well, we're going to destroy your comfort, Celeste."

What I was hearing was the moment Ren had understood me. The thing that symbolized understanding. Understanding that comes through pain. Yes. I was so sure I was right, I almost smiled.

I walked over to the wall and put my arm through it, reaching for the reflection of Ren's Garden in mine, where the seed had to be. I reached my hand out for the sound of singing, and I took hold of the handle, and dragged it back: a black, Eagle Creek duffel. Not the suitcase I'd given her; a bag she'd planted because she hoped I'd look for it. A sack full of what I needed, what she needed me to have.

I looked at Celeste and I did smile.

"The end of your comfort," I told her.

She looked skeptical.

"Come take a look then," I said. I opened it, but didn't turn it towards her.

She took a step forward, and then another, and I willed the transformation of the duffel; it was hard and it was on fire and it was in my hand.

She looked at me, and her eyes widened.

"Five plus three is eight," I told her, and drove Ren's stub, as a burning spike, into Celeste's forehead.

Celeste screamed, and her Garden fell apart around me, and I opened my eyes.

Ren

Ritual is symbol in motion. Ritual mixes meaning into time where each delineates the other, and we roll it out like so much razor wire at the perimeters of power. Sex, money, death—all bordered with ritual like police tape. We cordon the sites of pivots and make taboo the words that name them.

A ritual deployed around anything but a true pivot has no power. A pivot unringed in ritual is an uninsulated wire. Phil and I were holding bare metal when the lines went live. And I still wasn't breathing.

Celeste had made a copy of her stub, a memory of all her memories, and alpha-locked it by seeding it with the memory of her death. Almost a week ago now, when Phil drove Celeste's stub between my eyes, I'd gotten her memories. But her symbol for herself, her essence—Jimmy, bless him, would say her soul—had stayed in the Garden in the other, secret, alpha-hidden stub. It had shared a body with Irina in order to access the material world, and Irina had been willing to poison me just to be rid of her. Then, Phil had saved my life, and he'd killed Irina out of rage or despair. Then, I'd saved him.

But saving and safety were Celeste's concerns, and not who Phil and I wanted to be.

I poisoned myself in Celeste's Garden on the wild gamble that Phil, unlike Celeste's pattern of him, would reach out for my mind before my brain ran out of air. And, in a single searing flame, I knew he had.

Celeste pushed into me.

Phil had driven my essence, my stub, between Celeste's eyes, gambling that I, unlike her image of me, was strong enough to keep my great-auntie's pattern subordinate to mine.

But Celeste opened my mouth and stuffed it with negative space. I gasped around her, her mind and mine occupying the same skull. I wasn't enough. I could never hold everything I remembered. I could not breathe.

But it was never a princess who hid in the little bird you made of me, dear Hoho. It was a dragon, and its song is made of fire.

Phil and I gambled each other, and were electrified. We grounded each other, and we won.

I opened my mouth, and breathed her flaming stake to ash.

TWENTY

Spiked

Phil

"Ren? Ren. Come back, Ren. Keep breathing, Ren. It's not a win if you can't drag the pot. I need you, Ren. Please stay with me. Ray says the antidote won't help, because it's not your body you poisoned, but you can still be fine. Please. Please be fine.

"I get it now, Ren. I understand why you wanted to speak for her. It's because you hate arrogance, and you don't trust final answers. It's because you think we're getting cocky in our conviction of what Better means. But don't you see? That just makes you one of us. It means you have to argue with us, and that means you have to be here, and all Oskar will say is that you're strong.

"If you don't come back, Ren, I won't either. I don't mean that as a threat. I won't do anything. But I know that, after all this, without you, there won't be enough of me to go on. I have to keep moving, Ren, and I can't keep moving alone, and there isn't anyone else who can move with me. Don't you see that? I want you to argue with me, Ren. I want you to convince me that sometimes what we see as Better is just more of the same. I want you to show me where doubt lives, so I can embrace it. But Jimmy says you have to save your own soul.

"Oskar is wrong, Ren. And so was Celeste. And they were both right, as well. We are at the time when the amnemones can get what they need, or destroy themselves. That much is true. But there was a piece I didn't get before. Jimmy explained it days ago, I just couldn't listen. I thought it was about whether we should help them, like Oskar wants, or let them stew, like Celeste wants, but I'm listening now. They are us, and we are them, and we're in this together, and we need to make it work that way or it'll never work.

"I understand that now, Ren. And I want a piece of making it work. But I can't do that without you, because you're the one who showed it to me.

"Ren? Please come back, Ren. Please."

Ren

Phil wanted me there. His voice was strong and urgent, offering me belonging and arguments. But I was breathing fire and it hurt.

I flew over the mudflats and saw the grooves cut in my Garden, like state lines on a map, following natural contours sometimes, and sometimes not and arbitrarily straight. Celeste's pattern in overlay on mine. Not Celeste, the dragon had incinerated her, but the patterning force of Celeste, that impulse that makes you want to sing the final *"dahm"* if someone starts Beethoven's Fifth, and stops at *"dah-dah-dah."* That was there under me, inside me, Celeste's pattern of fear, and raking power up.

I had something to tell Phil about that, so I opened my eyes and saw his eyebrows do the strangest things. Then he pulled me up close against him.

"We looped the loop," I said. "Or unlooped it."

"Yes."

"Have you checked your Garden yet for the *kithara*?" I asked him.

"I don't care about the Garden," he said.

"Yes, you do."

"Yeah, I do, but I care about things outside of it more."

"Yeah," I said.

We lay together in the middle of the big suite's big bed, and I missed his awful curtains. "Let's go home," I said.

"We should eat something first." Phil tightened his grip on my body. "And Jimmy and Oskar will want to know what happened. I made them leave." He kissed the top of my head. "And it sounds like something has run off the rails with Kate in Pennsylvania."

I laughed. "Good," I said.

"Yeah?"

"Yeah."

So we lay still, enjoying our bodies soaking into each other's calm, and the overflow sounds of passionate discussion from the next room. I thought I could live like this.

"Celeste's still around, you know," I said, and felt Phil's body tense.

"How?"

"Not her personality or her essence or whatever," I explained. "She'll never talk out of my mouth again, or share a body like she did with Irina, but her pattern is still there, aggregating power."

Phil's shoulder shrugged under my head. "So we'll be the de-aggregators. We'll keep walking into elevators where every decision is filtered through how to keep Mom not-angry, and we'll take some of the power away from her temper. We'll make it better."

"A little?" I said.

"A little."

"Sometimes it'll get worse," I said.

"Then we'll never be out of work."

I laughed and kissed him. "I can live with that," I said. "But I'm not sure Oskar can."

Phil

The problem was not the chair.

I was on the couch with Ren, and so much of me was wrapped up with so much of her that we were damn near fucking right there; so if Oskar wanted to sit in my chair, that was fine, I wasn't using it anyway.

The problem was he was in my house.

"Oskar, why are you in my house?"

"I said—"

"Excuse me," said Ren sweetly. "I think you misunderstood. Phil didn't ask that wanting you to answer, he asked that wanting you to leave."

Oskar glared at her.

"Just so we're clear," she added.

"We need to do something," he said.

"Do it, then," I said. "And please, get together with Jimmy and Ray and Matt, all of whom know better than to be in my house right now, and figure out what. And when you've figured out what, drop me an email. I'll read it tomorrow."

"This won't wait."

"Oskar, I have no idea how the Pirates have done in the last five days, and I don't even care that much, but I care about it a great deal more than I care about Celeste's pattern in the Garden."

"Look, Phil, dammit. The Garden is a mental construct, right? It's a shared imagining that's comprised of, but larger than, the individual minds and imaginations that make it up. But it's not just ours. It never has been. By rights, it belongs to every nemone with a diary. It's the original commons. Time to tear down the fence! If we don't, Celeste's pattern will slowly brick the whole Garden away. She's—"

"I don't care," I explained. "Maybe I'll care tomorrow, or the next day. More likely next week. But right now—"

"Phil. I have nothing against animal passion. I'm a big fan of

animal passion. But can you please delay the animal passion for half an hour so we can figure this out? Half an hour. That's all."

I looked at Ren. She looked at me. We shook our heads. We looked back at Oskar and shook our heads again.

Damn, but I wish there'd been a camera.

Oskar looked exasperated. "We can't do it without the nemones anymore," he said. "They need to know the exobrain is real. They're rooted in it."

"We'll find a way to tell them," I said.

"Next week," agreed Ren. "It was good to see you. Thanks for dropping by." She smiled. "Bye."

He growled, glared, stood, and walked out of my house.

I turned my attention to more important matters.

Ren

I took the RMMD conference call with Phil's head in my lap, drawing slow circles with my fingertips against the unbroken space between his eyes. Sometimes I ran my fingers over his eyebrows and smoothed the wild, irregular hairs. Sometimes I stroked them the wrong way and swept them up like dragon lashes. His face stayed peaceful and vacant; he was grazing.

As the call wound down, with Jorge congratulating me on the PowerPoint deck Liam had demo'd and thanking us both for being so open to his new approach and priorities, Phil opened his eyes. He reached up and traced the line of my breast from the armpit down, then pressed his open palm against it. He stayed that way, feeling my heart beat, or my nipple harden, or both, or neither, listening.

"Do you know what I want?" he asked when I'd said good-bye to my bosses.

"Coffee?"

He turned his face into me and kissed my belly. "Yeah, actually," he said.

"I think," I said, "I shall have tea."

He sat up and studied me. "Good," he said.

He put on his bathrobe, so I grabbed boxers from the floor and followed him out to the kitchen. I didn't need more clothes, as all Incrementalists had been banned from the house by direct email decree. Let them get along without him for a little while. It'd do them good.

I sat on the barstool while Phil put water on for me and started the coffeepot. He got out a mug for each of us and opened the fridge for milk.

"You know," he said turning to me, fridge handle in hand. "This is better."

"Not for falling into," I said.

"No, but for getting milk, and for discovering cold pizza."

"Hooray!" I said. "Will you heat me up a slice?"

He pulled the box out and set in on the counter, which really would have been difficult with the door hinged the old way.

"It's better cold," he said, handing me my tea.

"Your better is not my better," I pronounced gravely.

"Right," he said. "I did promise to embrace doubt, didn't I?"

"Just nuke the pizza."

He put it in the brand-new toaster oven.

"It's better toasted than microwaved," he said. "Trust me."

I sipped my tea, which tasted like tea and not corpses. "We need to get a dog," I said.

"I know."

"Do you think there's any chance Celeste planned it this way?"

"For us to end up in love and happy?" Phil smiled without dimpling. "Not a chance."

"For her to end up in the Garden," I said. "Maybe she was trying to get rid of her body so she could stay safe in the Garden and not have to deal with humanity. Just meddle with the meddlers."

"Celeste was always afraid of the Internet, but maybe she imagined the next step in human evolution was something to do with the whole virtual world. I don't know." The toaster binged and Phil slid my pizza onto a plate and put it by my tea. "I know she thought humanity was at a pivot, a place where universal sufficiency was achievable, if we could find the right fulcrum."

"Either way, I think she meant for this to break you," I said. "Not because you were at a pivot, but because you are the pivot. You're the point the Incrementalists turn on. That's why she kept asking who you were, and liking that you didn't know. She wanted to define you."

"And her pattern's still there," he said. He came around the kitchen bar and sat down beside me. "Oskar's right. We have to tell the amnemones something. At least some of them. We need their help."

I bit into the pizza and let him think. He was right about the toaster.

He finally took a drink from the coffee he'd been staring into. "But how do we tell them, 'Hi, we're this secret group that houses human memories, coded in symbol, reaching back to the birth of symbol itself? We've been screwing with your heads for millennia, shaping the way you think, but oops, sorry! One of our number has gone crazy, so now we're uncloaking?' They'd stub us all."

"Except the ones who would pretend to be us, and start selling Incrementalist services and insights to the highest bidder," I said.

Phil drained his coffee cup. "We mass meddle."

"With everyone?"

"We use switches that will only work on people like us. We arm the ones we love against us."

"We recruit them?"

"Incrementally." His dimple twitched. "Knowing it's called the 'impulse rack' makes you less likely to buy something from the display stand by the cash register."

"But how do we reach them?" I asked.

"Right. How do we become signal, not just more of the noise?" he said. "They can't all be spiked."

I stood up and carried my plate and Phil's coffee cup into the kitchen. "Maybe we can."

"How?"

"Same way we've always done." I put my plate in the sink and filled his coffee cup. "We do it in symbol. That's what makes a memory into a switch, right? The overlay of symbol on it. The sugar-covered oranges *mean* something. They're reference points in meaning, tiny triggers of precise emotion. When you gave me your switches, you gave me the power to make you feel things." I put milk and sugar in Phil's coffee and stirred it, because I remembered he liked it that way in the evening, even though I'd never seen him take it like that or then. "We do the same for them." I put his mug down in front of him.

He put his hands around my waist instead of his mug. "But from a distance, and with our own symbols, not theirs." His hands weren't holding still; I was losing my interest in talking.

"We meddle with who we are," I said, and kissed him. "But Phil, you know what that means."

Phil

"No," I said. "I don't. I'm working on not knowing things, remember? Just for a while. You tell me."

She smiled with all of her, and I drank it in. Yes, I could deal with this. Contentment is fine, if you don't let it get out of hand. I picked up my coffee and sipped, and it hit me that there was milk and sugar in it. She was remembering. She was getting it back.

"It means," she said, running a hand across my forehead, "that it has to be you."

"Uh, not following."

"Think symbol."

"You're enjoying making me guess, aren't you?"

She grinned and nodded and another frozen thing inside of me melted. I wondered how long that would continue.

"Art?" I said. "Rich with symbol, like the Pre-Raphs? I could tell you things about Rossetti, by the way. One time he—"

"I remember, and there's a whole 'nother side to that, and no, that isn't what I meant. Words as symbol."

"Story?"

"Story," Ren said.

"So, we write a story about it? I'm not—"

"We don't write *it*. We write the pivot Celeste wanted to define. We write *you*."

I considered. "And open it up to a hundred different definitions? That could work."

"Oskar said we needed their help."

"We'd have to write it and find someone with no scruples to put his name on it."

"Or find a writer with scruples and meddle with him," Ren said. "Or we put Irina's stub into a writer and have her do it. Irina'd like that."

"It's not a bad idea," I said. "I kind of like it. I used to have a T-shirt with the Ford logo, in the script they use, only it said 'Fuck.' Those who'd be offended by it thought it said Ford, those who actually saw it thought it was funny."

"Yes," she said. "Like that. Let them determine what's there, instead of Celeste."

"You're brilliant."

"It was a user interface problem."

"You're still brilliant."

"Tell me more," she said, so I did.

Ren

Phil has a way of saying things without words that's persuasive, and by the time I'd climbed back off the breakfast bar, he'd convinced me. Who Phil was *was* a story. A tale told by an idiot—or a couple of them—our metaphor for symbol.

Phil went out to the bakery for bread, so I wrote the email—my first to the group. I had the memories of Celeste's Primary, but not of her life. I was the first incremental Incrementalist, but we hoped not the last.

From: Ren@Incrementalists.org
To: Incrementalists@Incrementalists.org
Subject: The Incrementalists
Thursday, July 7, 2011 1:35 pm GMT-7

Phil and I have found a potential defense against Celeste's pattern. If some of you want to look it over, we've put it close at hand.